STORM BRIDE

J.S. BANGS

SF-F

RED ADEPT PUBLISHING
Unlocking New Worlds

Storm Bride

Copyright © 2014 by J.S. Bangs. All rights reserved.
First Print Edition: December 2014

ISBN-10: 1940215358
ISBN-13: 978-1-940215-35-8

Red Adept Publishing, LLC
104 Bugenfield Court
Garner, NC 27529
RedAdeptPublishing.com/

Cover and Formatting: Streetlight Graphics

CHAPTER 1

UYA

THREE ORCAS RAISED THEIR HEADS above the green surf at the foot of Six Pine Rock. Uya crouched behind a drift log so her mother couldn't see her and scold her, and she watched them. One of them carried something on its nose, a sea lion carcass or a fish, and the orcas' fins flashed as they pushed it toward the foot of the stone, with its crown of ferns and evergreens. A surge of seawater hid them from her view, and when it subsided, Uya saw their prize clinging to the rough spire like a ragged piece of kelp.

It was not a sea lion. It was a woman.

She must be dead, Uya thought. The orcas splashed for a moment at the foot of the stone then dove back into the deeper water. The foam surged over the rock.

Then the woman moved.

Uya stood up straight and shaded her eyes to be sure that she saw right. The woman wrapped her arms around the stone to keep from slipping back into the water, then she raised her hand and groped for a higher hold.

"Uya!" shouted Uya's mother from a short distance up the beach. "What are you doing? You're supposed to be gathering mussels."

"The orcas brought a woman to Six Pine Rock!" Uya said.

Her mother guffawed. "Get back to the mussels."

Aunt Mariku pointed across the water, to the narrow spire of stone that the woman clung to, and called to Uya's mother, "Oire, I think I see something."

Uya's mother looked at the base of the stone, then gasped and breathed an oath. "Oarsa help her." Then she ran down the pebbled beach and called to the men.

Uya scrambled around the rock and ran after. *She* had seen the woman first, and it would be fair for her to be the first to tell. But she couldn't match her mother's stride, and by the time she reached the men at the canoes, they had already pushed two of them into the surf and were paddling furiously against the waves toward Six Pine Rock.

"I saw her first!" she shouted to Grandfather Asa as soon as she caught her breath. "It was me."

Asa put his gnarled hand on her head. "So Oire said. You did well." But his eyes were watching the brown-clad woman clinging to the rock and the canoes spearing through the waves toward her.

The lead canoe was past the breakers, halfway to the spire, its red-and-black painted head charging through the waves. A small crowd surrounded Uya on the shore, and everyone watched the canoe nose into the foamy surf around the rock's feet. The men beat their oars wildly at the water and pushed off stones as they tried to keep the canoe upright.

They were soon alongside the rock where the woman waited. Someone from the boat stretched out his hand. The woman seemed to shudder and turn away. Uya could see the lips of the people in the canoe moving, mouths wide open to shout, but she could only hear the roar of the ocean and the shrieks of gulls. A swell washed over the woman on the rock and shoved the canoe aside. With a flurry of oar strokes, the men brought their craft back, and the hand was proffered again. The woman shifted, then like a crow

IV

picking up a minnow, one of the men snatched her off the rock and tumbled with her into the bottom of the canoe.

Grandmother Nei and all the aunts and uncles of the *enna* crowded together when the canoe's prow ground against the black stones of the shore, but Uya slithered past the adults and rested her chin on the lip of the canoe. The woman in the bottom looked to be dead. Her skin was white as a trout's belly, tinted with chilly blue from the cold. A woven cloak had once covered her, though it was now little more than briny rags. Her hands were bloody from scratches, one of her fingernails had torn away, and blood trickled down her face from a cut across her forehead. But most of all Uya marked her hair: orange as a robin's breast, beautiful and strange, matted with salt and seaweed.

With a grunt, two men lifted the woman out of the bottom of the canoe. Only then did Uya realize how *tall* the woman was. Curiosity seized her, and Uya reached out and touched the woman's face.

The woman gasped. She opened her eyes, and Uya cried out and stepped back.

The woman's eyes were large and beautiful, as blue as a jay's feather, but her pupils were white with cataracts and twitched sightlessly. The woman's lips moved without sound. Then she passed into the arms of the men waiting outside the canoe and out of Uya's sight. They carried her swiftly up the beach, where they laid her next to the fire and swaddled her in linen blankets. Women moved forward, bearing pots and poultices. Uya tried to follow to see that extraordinary face again, but she was elbowed wordlessly aside.

Finally she gave up and retreated to the driftwood log on the high tide line. Her *enna* cared for the stranger until dark.

The *enna* lit two fires that night—the larger one around which most of them ate, and a smaller one where the strange woman lay on a pallet of blankets, cared for by the Eldest, Nei, and a rotating group of aunts. Uya quickly ate her fill of steamed clams and salty half-dried seaweed then slipped away from the larger fire to where her mother was tending the stranger. Her mother gave her only a moment's glance as she walked up.

"See if any of the *rugei* traders lost someone at sea." Nei's voice was as gravelly as the high tide line.

"Have any trading ships from the *rugei* come down the coast recently?" Uya's mother asked.

"No. Maybe Deika will have heard something at Suroei."

"And if not?"

Nei shrugged. "Oarsa blesses those who entertain strangers. If we don't find the vessel that lost her in a few days, we'll have to bring her with us when we return to Prasa. We could be caring for her for a long time after that—we only see their ships on our coast every few summers."

Uya crept around the perimeter of the fire, approaching closer. The woman turned her head suddenly, and Uya drew a breath and froze. She hadn't supposed that the woman was awake.

For a moment she remained perfectly still, then she decided that if the woman hadn't been angry this morning, she was unlikely to be angry now. So she crawled forward until she could see the strange pale skin and blue eyes in the mellow firelight. The woman was very young, almost as young as Uya, with smooth skin and bright hair. "What is your name?"

The woman made no response. She cocked her ear toward Uya's voice, but her eyes darted aimlessly from the sky to Uya's face, and she remained as mute as a stone.

"Why were you with the orcas?" Uya continued. "Did you know they would leave you on Six Pine Rock? How far did they carry you?"

"Uya," her mother called out, "don't bother the swift woman."

"I want to know her name," Uya said.

"She cannot understand you. She doesn't speak our language."

"What if she's not a swift woman?"

"Of course she's a swift woman. Only the swift people have hair that color. Now leave her alone until Deika comes back."

So that was why Nei had mentioned Uya's father. Deika could speak to the woman in the trade tongue, which the women did not know. Now Uya, too, was anxious for her father to return from Suroei. She had heard that the *rugei*, the swift people, grew old very quickly, so she studied the woman's face intently to see if she could perceive her skin growing wrinkled or her hair turning white.

"Mama," she said after a moment, "she's not getting any older. Are you *sure* she's a swift woman?"

Oire laughed. "The *rugei* don't get old *that* quickly, silly. It will take her fifty years to get old, which for swift people and little girls seems like a long time, even if it's not so long for us."

The woman remained still under her blankets, her head cocked as she listened to Uya and her mother speak. The *enna* was going back to Prasa in a few days, and the woman would probably still be young then, which meant that Uya could befriend her.

She took the woman's hand and touched it to her own chest. "Uya."

The woman started for a moment at Uya's touch then smiled. "Uya," she repeated.

Uya put her finger on the woman's lips. "And what is your name?"

The woman said something like *Salde*, but the latter half of that name was an unpronounceable twist of the tongue. Uya shook her head. The woman said the name again, slowly.

Uya imitated it as best she could: "*Saotse.*"

The stranger sighed and waited for a moment, then she repeated, "Saotse."

"Oh good, Saotse," Uya said. "Since I was the one who saw you in the water and who learned your name, we will be sisters. And we will love each other until we are very old—well, at least until you are very old—since that is what sisters do."

The woman blinked. Uya took this as a sign of comprehension, for language was no barrier between sisters brought together by the Powers of the sea.

Uya's mother put a hand on Uya's mouth. "Speak carefully," she said. "The Powers hear all things. The swift woman should return to her people as soon as we find them."

"You speak carefully, too, Oire," Nei said from the other side of the fire. She looked ghastly and uncanny through the dance of flames. "Oarsa doesn't send orcas bearing a woman to our beach every day. Let the Powers work as they will."

CHAPTER 2

SAOTSE

THE POWER CHAOARE SPOKE IN the wind that rustled the tops of the trees, and Saotse listened but comprehended nothing. A flight of starlings answered the wind, voices chattering on the gusts that carried them away, while a crow complained from the shelter of the gently creaking pine. The whispers moved across the tops of the trees as the Power passed by, away from the city, up toward the mountains, out of Saotse's hearing. Saotse felt the air still in Chaoare's wake like a fire growing cold in the night. She cocked her head to the west, listening for the ripple of Chaoare's return, but heard nothing.

She didn't call out. She had worn her voice hoarse with entreaties to the Powers in the last fifty years. She had soaked her shirt with tears. She had never been answered.

Her toes tickled the tips of the grass then found the hard-packed clay of the path. She walked quickly, sweeping a pinecone and a flat stone from her path with quick swipes of her walking stick, until she came to the place where the clay under her feet turned into smooth stones tumbling toward the sound of water. The smell of saltwater grew strong with the warm, murky stench of the swampy shoreline and bruised kelp, and the damselflies buzzed over the lapping of waves on the stone.

Saotse stepped quickly, her feet finding the shape of every stone in turn, until the muttering of women's voices rose above the rhythm of the waves. The whisper and crackle of reeds being cut wove into their words, and the slurp of mud over bare feet provided the cadence of conversation. Saotse felt the slab of the quartz cleft that meant the path would soon end, and her steps slowed. The stone paving underfoot gave way to clay, then to mud, and Saotse emerged through a curtain of reeds to where the women worked in ankle-deep water.

"Get yourself to the shore," Oire was saying, perhaps four strides away. "Any woman as round as you should be lying in a hammock—"

"Lying in a hammock in the lodge!" Uya shouted, from a pace farther to the right. "Eating honey cakes and getting fat! Hiding from the sun! Sucking the fat off the fish skins! If you tell me this one more time—"

"Because I'm your mother, and this is how—"

"Oh, to hear Nei tell it, you were twice as incorrigible as me when you bore your first."

"So you want me to call Nei here? If you won't listen to your mother, maybe you'll listen to your Eldest."

"Bah." Three footsteps splashed through the muddy shallows, and Uya's hand touched Saotse's forearm. "Saotse, sister, why are you here?"

Saotse clutched Uya's hand: soft, smooth, nimble. Youthful. Her own fingers were skinny and knobby and ached with age. For a moment her voice escaped her, then she said, "Rada sent me, but I got lost. I'm sorry. I heard something. There was a wind..."

"Oh!" Saotse could hear Uya's smile. "Did Chaoare pass by?"

Uya was so happy, so blithe and cheerful in her exploitation of Saotse's curse, that Saotse could almost bring herself to forgive her. Almost. If she weren't also a model of youth, perhaps. "Yes. She passed by."

"A good omen, then, for the baby." Uya laughed and squeezed

10

Saotse's hand. "Chaoare, bless my child! Oh, Saotse, can you tell me what Oarsa says, too?"

Even hearing Uya ask the question, Saotse could not keep herself from opening up a little, just enough to hear the voices of the shore Powers, the grandchildren of Oarsa, who rose from the waters and hummed in the currents that reached to the depths of the sea, sublime and incomprehensible—but no. Oarsa had fallen silent decades ago, and all her cries had not roused him. But all Saotse said was, "No. But Rada wants you back at the lodge."

"Where you belong!" Oire added. "Not out pretending to gather reeds like a girl."

"Yes, mother," Uya said. "Shall I lead you back to the lodge, Saotse?"

I can get back by myself, just as I came by myself. If it had been Oire or her insufferable sisters or any of the thoughtless men, Saotse would have voiced the thought. But alas, it was Uya, still young and beautiful Uya, and as bitter as Saotse was, she still felt the duty to spare her little sister from her hatred. It was not Uya's fault that Saotse dwelt among the long-lived slow people. It was not Uya who had called Saotse from the piny fjord where the mountains met the sea, had her carried on the backs of whales, and then abandoned her. She could still spare some patience for Uya.

So she let the young woman take her hand and lead her back through the reeds to where the path turned to clay and then smooth stone. They took the right fork where the cleft stone was, up a brief incline that made Uya huff and clutch at Saotse's hand. She muttered something about having to walk these terrible paths with her enormous belly blocking the view of her feet. Then she asked, "Did Rada say what he wanted?"

"No."

Uya made a groan of annoyance. Saotse guessed that Rada was simply inventing excuses to see Uya and the child once more before the caravans left. If Uya had any sense, she would have listened to

11

her mother's advice and stayed in the lodge, if not for the sake of the baby, for the sake of her anxious husband. Saotse had neither husband nor child, and she could understand as much.

Then the sound of many voices reached them, mingled with the murmuring of cedars, the nickering of horses, and the creak of harnesses. Saotse clasped Uya's hand tighter. The area in front of the lodge had become a warren of crates, bales, and wagons that crowded under the lodge's eaves, as happened every spring when the first caravan prepared to leave. Uya touched Saotse's elbow and guided her among the half-packed wagons, nudging her to the side when she almost knocked her ankle against a wheel. The mess was an annoyance, but Saotse endured it in expectation of the day when the caravans would return and the barter with merchants would begin. Nei needed her for the barter, depending on her keen ear to know when the other traders had truly reached their final price. Until then, she was at the mercy of the caravan's chaos.

Men's voices volleyed orders out of the lodge and back and forth across the yard. A pair of boys sprinted past them, singing caravan songs. Uya scolded them with an inarticulate yowl then tugged Saotse across the threshold into the lodge. The packed dirt of the courtyard gave way to foot-worn wood and a closed, warm, and musty smell. Saotse shivered in relief.

"Uya!" Rada shouted as soon as they crossed the threshold.

Uya dropped Saotse's hand. From here Saotse could find her own way to the wooden bench that sat near the door, so long as none of the men had moved it. Two cautious paces from the open doorway, she found the bench and let herself slide onto its planks.

"—Morning," Rada said.

Uya gasped. "So soon?"

"The scouts came back an hour ago. The high roads are clear of snow, all the way to Azatsi's Fingers. Asa's already got half of the carts loaded—he wanted to leave a week ago—and even if the Guza outposts weren't manned, he figures that they'll be ready by the time we get there."

The Guza outposts were unmanned? That had never happened before. A tremor of worry passed through Saotse's stomach.

"But why?" Uya pressed. "By the time you get back—"

"I know. I'll see the child then. It'll be barely born. I won't have missed much."

Uya sighed. "Well, if you must. But I have something for you."

Her footsteps receded behind the curtain setting off the women's alcove, and there was a creak of leather hinges as she opened one of the chests. The floorboards groaned as Rada shifted his weight from one side to another. His affection for Uya was genuine, though Saotse judged that Uya's reluctance for him to leave was mostly feigned. Uya had never seemed to care that much for Rada, though it had been a profitable match for both families. She seemed primarily glad for the rank that her pregnancy afforded her among the aunts.

Uya returned a moment later. Rada let out a little shout of surprise as she approached him.

"I made this," she said. "Carved it myself from bone and set the abalone in its mouth. Do you like it?"

"Of—of course," he stammered.

Saotse's attention was broken by the sound of soft steps crossing the lodge toward her. Not Uya or Rada. Nei. The bench creaked as the Eldest lowered herself onto the end next to Saotse, and her hand clutched Saotse's.

"The gift is a carved orca," Nei whispered. "Very fine. Did you know she was making it?"

"I had heard her working on it," Saotse said. "For Rada, though? I'm a little surprised."

Nei chuckled.

Uya had begun whining again. "I'm sick of being pregnant, and I'm sick of eating honey cake all day. And when you're gone, who will distract my mother long enough for me to be able to go down to the bay?"

Rada laughed. "You seem to do pretty well at it without me.

And once the baby comes, you won't be able to leave the lodge for a while anyway, so you might as well get used to it."

"Oh, don't remind me. You make me feel as old and useless as Saotse."

Saotse stiffened. She turned to Uya, hoping the girl would notice how she had stung Saotse. But no, Uya continued talking, her girlish voice rattling all the corners of the lodge. In a bluster of frustration, Saotse rose from the bench and stumbled out the door alone.

She got four strides from the lodge before her shins struck a basket and she tumbled to the ground. *Curse the filthy caravan and its goods. I can't even find my way out for air.* She rose to her feet, beat the dust from her skirt, then began to feel her way through the haphazard stacks of gourds and sacks.

A soft, gentle hand grabbed hers as she groped for the edge of a line of baskets. "Let me show you," Nei said.

The urge to throw off Nei's hand was nearly irresistible. Saotse's fingers tightened over the Eldest's for a moment, then she sighed and let the old woman lead her. A handful of steps out, her dusty feet felt the cool prickles of the bluejoint grass. Their strides swished through the grasses until Nei stopped and tugged at Saotse's hand for her to sit.

"Here?" Saotse asked. "In the grass, like girls?"

"Sit." Nei's voice was firm but playful.

Saotse sat.

"You *are* a girl to us, or nearly so," Nei said. "It will do you good to remember that."

Saotse laughed. Hollowly. Bitterly. She held up her hand with its narrow, knobby fingers, creaking with arthritis, and its creased and flabby knuckles. "Do these look like a girl's hands to you?"

"No. No, they do not." Nei sighed. "It's unnatural for a swift person to live with us slow people. And you are the one who pays the price for it."

14

The burl of resentment twisted inside Saotse's chest. "Is that why you brought me here? To shame me for growing old?"

"Not at all. I was hoping to offer you solace. You are close to Uya in age—a mere sixty-five years, a youth—but in body you have passed me up. I was hoping that since you cannot relate to Uya as a young woman, you might relate to me as an old one."

Saotse broke a supple stalk of grass in her hand and worried at the stem. "I thought you were an old woman when I first met you. I guessed you were sixty or seventy."

Nei laughed. "I *was* an old woman. Two hundred and eighty! I had already passed the age of childbearing."

"But decades have passed, and you've gotten scarcely older. You told me yourself you might live another fifty years. In fifty years, I'll certainly be dead. I'll probably be dead in fifteen."

"This is why I was trying to comfort you."

"You're not the one who vexed me."

"No, but I'm the one who can understand you. I have grown old as well. I, too, count the years until I will be likely dead. But forgive Uya. She's still a young woman, with her first child, barely married a decade."

"A decade." A cool wind picked up briefly, coming down from the mountains. Saotse listened for Chaoare's voice and heard nothing.

"Why did you choose to stay with us?" Nei asked.

"I've answered this before."

"I know that Oarsa called you across the sea and summoned the whales to carry you. But when he fell silent—"

"How do you know that?" Saotse had few secrets, but that, at least, she did not speak openly of.

"You forget that I am an old woman, Eldest of the *enna*, and that I watch all my younger charges."

"Does everyone know?" If everyone in the *enna* knew she had been abandoned by Oarsa, she might die of shame immediately.

15

The measure of privilege or pity she got as one chosen by the Powers was the only comfort she had.

But Nei said, "No. They've gotten used to having you around. And even those of us who hear the spirits only faintly can perceive that you are gifted."

"It's not as though I can bring them good omens or command the Powers with my voice. Just today Uya asked me if Chaoare had passed by with a blessing for her child, and I can't even tell her if the answer is yes or no. Oarsa is gone. I feel the other Powers, but they don't speak to me. And they aren't mine. I had to learn their names from you because they aren't the Powers that we knew in my home, except for Oarsa. And he has vanished."

"Nonetheless," Nei said, "we want you here. You are immensely useful to us during negotiations. I adopted you as my granddaughter and have not regretted it for even a single day. No one considers you a burden."

"Good, because I have nowhere else to go." Her chance to return home had long since passed. When first she had tried to return with the swift traders, the superstitious sailors had refused to take a woman aboard. And now, even if she found a ship to take her, she feared her aching bones would not survive the journey.

Nei groaned, and the swish of grasses signaled that she had risen. "I seem to have failed at my goal of comforting you. Let me offer you this, at least: Uya won't vex you while Rada is gone. I'll ensure that she is kept busy, and any careless word that she speaks to your hurt, I'll repair. I can promise you that."

She helped Saotse regain her feet and guided her back to the lodge. But when Saotse's foot struck the bare ground near the lodge, she stopped. Something was wrong.

"Come on," Nei said. "Just a little—"

"No," Saotse said.

The ground trembled. It groaned. It wept. *Alone.* It felt for a moment like the beginning of an earthquake, though the dust that lay on her feet was undisturbed. Saotse's toenails scratched at the ground. A gust of wind stirred the tops of the trees.

"What do you hear?" Nei asked.

"I don't know. I don't understand." She took two unsteady steps forward. The soft sound of wings passed overhead, and Saotse turned toward the top of the lodge.

Nei drew a breath.

"What do you see?" Saotse begged.

"A white owl."

The owl mourned *hoo hoo* twice from its perch on the peak of the lodge. An owl was an evil omen in the best of times. An owl in the day even more so.

Nei's hand closed over Saotse's and pulled her forward. The cheer in the Eldest's voice sounded forced. "Let's find our hammocks in the women's alcove. Let the omens worry about themselves."

CHAPTER 3

KESHLIK

THE TRADERS' ROAD WAS LITTLE more than a horse path that wound up the bottom of a ravine toward a low point in the bluffs, guarded by sage and horsebrush and shaded by blood-colored rocks. The little creek that ran beside the path wormed through a narrow defile at both ends of a green-floored gully, creating a convenient choke point for ambush. Yet there were no sentries apparent in the caravan's train, no spears or bows ready beside the drivers of the front and rear carts, and no nervous glances upward to the crevices in the stone.

"Perhaps they're just reckless," Juyut said. "Or very greedy."

"Reckless, maybe, but not because of greed," Keshlik said. "Greedy ones carry double sentries to ensure that their goods aren't stolen."

"Do you think they're just stupid?"

"They're reckless with *peace*. Like the Guza."

Juyut grinned. "Then they'll fall easily."

Keshlik did not raise his eyes from the line of the caravan below. The traders gave every indication of being as indolent and incautious as the Guza, who had been poorly defended and quickly slaughtered. The Guza had fallen to Keshlik and the Yakhat war bands just before the first snows, in time for the Yakhat to take shelter in their homes straddling the Gap. The raiding party that Keshlik led today was the first to descend to the plains on the far side of the mountains since the spring thaw. Judging by appearances, the land on this side of the Gap hadn't seen war for so long that the people had nearly forgotten how to wage it.

But he would assume nothing. *The leopard's soft paw hides its claws.*

Half of the carts had entered the defile and continued on the narrow shore of the creek. Their ponies were fat and slow. The traders might carry knives at their waists, but he saw no bigger blades.

"So shall I set out with my half of the band?" Juyut asked.

"Go. Save your boasting for when the battle is over."

"Ha!" Juyut smiled viciously. "A single caravan plundered barely gives reason to boast. I'm going." He pushed away from the edge of the ravine and ran crouching to where his horse waited, quietly grazing. He leapt onto her back and spurred her forward with a tap of his heels. Juyut and his mount were swift but silent, Keshlik noted with pride. Juyut had learned well.

Keshlik crawled back from the cliff's edge, dusted off his pants, and walked slowly to Lashkat, his horse. She was nibbling on the spring growth that was greening even here on the higher grasslands, and she gave him a look that suggested he not disturb her just yet. There was good, sweet grass here. It reminded Keshlik of the summer grasses between the Bans, and he hoped that the Yakhat women would find it acceptable for the cattle. The herds had thinned in the last winter, and neither the Guza nor these lowland folk seemed to have any stock that might replace them.

He rested his hand on his mare's flank. She whinnied and wagged her ears at him, then lifted her head and gave him a doleful stare. She shook her head, the yellow cords of her mane dancing like lightning bolts around her head, then stepped forward and touched her nose to his face.

"Are you ready?" he asked.

19

Lashkat chuffed. She seemed to smell the battle on him, in the lines of rouged and blackened grease drawn on his face, in the incense of sweat and blood that rose from his skin. Battle was an old friend to them. Keshlik would trust her to carry him alone into battle with a thousand foes, and she would drag his dead and broken body back to the yurts rather than flee without him. Only Juyut was a better companion in battle, though he spoiled it by being proud and wrathful and too quick with his tongue. The horse at least knew when to keep quiet.

Keshlik climbed onto her back, and she loped forward with her head low without any nudge from him. A short ways to the south, in the shade of an outcropping of rock, waited the other three of Keshlik's party. At the sound of his approach, they scrambled to their feet and grabbed the spears that rested beside them.

Bhaalit, the eldest of the band, stepped forward. "Are we going?"

Keshlik grunted. The three mounted their horses and fell in behind him.

There was no path along the top of the ravine, but they did not require one. The plain was a sea of grass, yellow billows undulating like waves across the surface, with outcrops of sandy stone peeking above the surf like the fins of monsters. Green showed at the roots of the waves, where the wind bent the heads of the winter grass to show the upsurge of spring, and here and there an early flower made itself known as a stripe of purple or yellow. A gentler plain for the horses to tread Keshlik could hardly imagine.

He couldn't figure why the traders kept to the ravine. On a plain like that one, you could see your enemy approaching when he was still on the horizon, and you could give your horses rein to gallop at wind speed, to flank and circle back with all the martial skill that a well-trained mount should learn.

The ravine, on the other hand, was an invitation to be ambushed. It saved them a few hours of walking, but why would that matter to these people? Their languid pace suggested they were in no hurry. The horses moseyed down the gentle incline that led to the entrance to the ravine. The rutted trail that the caravan followed grew clear in the broad plain below, and the last of the wagons' dust drifted to the ground. Keshlik pointed forward, tapping his mare's ribs with his boots. She broke into a run, tossing her mane and stretching her legs, and the other mounts followed. With a brief skip, their horses leapt the wagon ruts and turned to the left, following the trail into the entrance of the ravine. Dust stung Keshlik's eyes. The stone rose above their heads, hiding the sun. Ahead he could see nothing but the dust following the wagons, but he heard the distant clattering wheels and shouting voices that echoed off the canyon walls. Keshlik slowed his mare to a trot, then a halt. Behind him, the other three drew up and stopped.

"What now?" Bhaalit asked. "We wait?"

"We wait," Keshlik said. "Juyut has his company at the canyon exit. They'll attack the head of the caravan and drive them toward us. We just make sure no one gets away."

Bhaalit nodded. He prodded his horse to the far side of the canyon floor and leaned forward to watch the approach. The other two, Rushyak and Danut, were young warriors, not even a hundred years old. They would fight like a whirlwind once the time to draw spears came, but they shared Juyut's impulsiveness and fervor. Bhaalit was older than Keshlik, the only one so old who still carried a spear, who still remembered Khaat Ban.

The dust fell and the sounds of the caravan receded. Crows cawed overhead. Rushyak and Danut began to fidget, but Bhaalit, with more than a century of practice with patience, was as still as stone. The sun rose higher in the sky and began to tickle the lip of the canyon.

Quickly now. Keshlik could fight in the shade and he could fight in the sun, but he didn't welcome the prospect of a battle with men weaving in and out of the canyon's shadow.

Someone was running toward them on the road ahead. As soon

as he heard it, he snapped to attention. A young man, on foot, his pace wild with terror.

To his left, the two young warriors tensed and glanced at him. Keshlik nodded and pointed forward. Rushyak cantered his mare forward, his spear held ready. He aligned the runner with the spear, crouched forward, and tensed. The lad at first didn't seem to see them, then he began to shout and wave his arms as if seeking their aid.

Keshlik saw the moment the boy spotted the stripes on their faces, the speed with which the mounted warrior approached, and the glint of the spearhead. He froze in mid-stride, fell to a knee in the dirt, then attempted to scramble to the right.

It was far too late. With a flick of his knees, Rushyak angled the horse to intercept then split the lad's back with a spear-strike. He pulled his spear loose from the victim's back as his horse thundered over the boy, and he circled back and planted three more holes between his victim's ribs.

A rumble sounded off the canyon's walls as the main body of the retreat approached. Two men on foot running toward them, with a wagon driver frantically beating his draft ponies not far behind them. Keshlik nodded at Danut, the other young man, then trotted his own mare forward. Bhaalit moved of his own accord. Keshlik's mare trotted, her ears back, ready to charge, waiting for the cry.

It was time to fight.

Keshlik raised his spear and screamed, and his horse bolted forward. He leaned forward into his horse's neck, one hand in her striped mane, the other clutching his spear. A man retreating on foot had peeled off to the right, and Danut chased after him into the dimness of the dust. The wagon driver, his face white with panic, saw Keshlik approaching and veered to the creek bank, but Keshlik's spear found his throat anyway, driving him from his saddle. The riderless horse fled, and Keshlik wheeled back toward the center of the melee.

Rushyak and Danut flanked the overturned cart, stabbing at the others who came fleeing down the ravine. Bhaalit had already felled two runners and was advancing on another.

Keshlik charged past them and impaled two panicked men with one spear, then trampled a third under his mare's hooves. Further up the canyon, a man was screaming at his frothing ponies to budge an overturned load. Keshlik relieved the man of his concerns by driving a spear into the man's eye.

The battle-glad war cries of his brother's band suddenly surrounded him. He had reached Juyut's band advancing from the other side, and when he turned to the center of the road, he found himself riding into a reef of bleeding men and crushed wagons. Some fighting still remained, as a few of the caravan drivers had armed themselves with clubs or knives. Keshlik crossed the battlefield twice, stabbing the windpipes of those he saw still moaning on the ground, then found Bhaalit at ease atop his horse.

"Heya!" he shouted and smacked the shaft of his spear. "Did you fight well?"

"Golgoyat himself fought among us," Bhaalit said, with a laconic gesture at the carnage of blood and dust around them.

"Did any get past you?"

"None. Where's Juyut?"

"Up ahead. You stay and organize the plunder while I track him down."

Warriors saluted Keshlik with cries of "Heya!" as he passed, waving bloodied spears over their heads. He picked his way through the path of ruined carts, wagons, and bodies. At the end, he spotted Juyut on horseback in a circle of three others, a bound but living man lying on the ground between them.

"Heya!" Juyut shouted when he saw Keshlik approaching. "We've crushed our enemies!"

"Enemies who fled like rabbits." Keshlik grunted. In truth, Juyut had done well, but it wouldn't do to praise him too much. "What is this thing on the ground here?"

"A captive," Juyut said.

"And when did you find the time to take captives?"

"As you said, they fled like rabbits. This one was in the middle of the pack and fell back, then threw himself down and started to weep and beg. I kept him for my amusement."

Keshlik reined his horse and dismounted. Juyut's new slave was smeared with dust, and he appeared to have soiled himself. Beneath the dirt, he was paler than the Yakhat, his skin the color of dried yellow clay, coarse black hair cropped close to his head, and his eyes a cloudy green. Keshlik nudged him with his toe. A gush of incomprehensible gibberish spilled from the man's mouth, combined with several fervent bows and a sob that rattled his shoulders.

"He doesn't speak any language we know," Juyut said. "We plan on taking him to the Guza slaves and seeing if one of them can talk to him."

Keshlik grunted. "Why?"

"The Guza said that a city lies to the south, and he probably came from there. He can tell us how it's defended, and whether its men will flee like rabbits the way this pack of cowards did."

Juyut's reasoning was exactly what Keshlik had hoped to hear. He himself had considered taking a captive for that purpose, but the raid had been Juyut's. Taking a captive for reconnaissance was more foresight than he had expected of his brother.

But proprieties had to be observed. "Do you take him for your personal slave?"

Juyut shrugged.

Keshlik spat. "Don't shrug. Only slaves and women shrug. You know that the value of a living slave exceeds whatever lots you were likely to draw in the division of spoils. You'd forfeit all that."

"Fine, then he's not mine." Juyut grunted. "I take him for the commonwealth of the tribes."

"And what will you do with him after he's told you everything he knows?"

"Well, if I'm taking him for the commonwealth, wouldn't that be for the tribal elders to decide?"

Keshlik grinned and nodded. *He slips away like a serpent.* "Bhaalit was overseeing the plundering, and even a laggard like you ought to be able to lead a raid and split the spoils in the same day."

Juyut nodded and tugged his captive toward Bhaalit and the others. Something glinted in the dirt where the captive had knelt, and Keshlik bent to pick it up. Some kind of fish carved from bone, painted mostly black, with white eyes and belly, and a tall, pointed fin on its back. Its mouth was open and held a tiny chip of mother-of-pearl, polished and shining in the light of the setting sun. Tuulo would like it. He slipped it into his pack and hurried to join Juyut.

The division of spoils was quick and orderly. Bhaalit handed out the lot-sticks, and Keshlik let Juyut draw the lot for their tribe. The goods were plenty, more than they could take back to their camp: long strings of hemp threaded through purple shells, dried fish, casks of salt, carved baubles of turquoise and mother-of-pearl, sealskins, polished whalebone, and papery, dark-green sheets that appeared to be made of dried and pressed leaves. The purpose of those last items was initially mysterious, until someone tasted one and declared them to be edible, a dried form of some lowlander plant. Keshlik drew a sheaf of those to bring home and hoped that Tuulo would find something to do with it.

When the lots of plunder had been divided and moved safely out of the canyon, the band piled the remaining carts and packages and all the slain in a wide place in the ravine. The last duty Keshlik and Bhaalit did themselves. It was not a job for young men. Bhaalit brought a burning brand to Keshlik, and Keshlik set the stack aflame and sang the praises of Golgoyat. When the song finished, the flames licked the sky, and heaven was dirty with smoke.

Keshlik spoke the final words: "Until the Sorrow of Khaat Ban is repaid."

They answered him in one voice. "Till the sorrow is repaid."

———————— ❖ ————————

A river trickled out of the mountains to the east like a line of molten silver, throwing off sparks of light from the reddening sun. On either side of its curls stretched yellow-green pasture, its colors as sweet as butter, cradling in its ripples charcoal-black, brown, and amber specks that barely moved against its tides: the cattle and the cow-maidens on their horses.

Juyut let out a whoop and charged forward, leaving a wake in the grass like a rutting bull. Keshlik tugged at the bound slave, leading him down the gentle slope into the midst of the herds. The slave had slowed Keshlik's pace all the way back to the Khaatat encampment at the mouth of the Gap, but Keshlik was ready to forgive him now that they had arrived. The girls ululated and waved their wide-brimmed caps at the warriors passing by, while the cows grunted and moved slowly to the side. Keshlik looked back once and saw that the slave's eyes were wide with terror, staring at the shaggy cows as if they might be monsters.

If the lowlanders were afraid of *cows*, then it was no wonder that the raiding band had torn through them like a knife through cheese.

The semicircle of yurts was on the near side of the river, in the center of the herds. The smoke of cooking fires drifted over the flags on the yurts' crowns, and when Keshlik finally entered the crescent, he found Dhuja crouched over a pot of milk above a fire, slowly stirring it with her spoon. The sight of his wife's midwife awoke a throb of longing in his chest.

Juyut had already tied his horse to the corner of their yurt, and he stood with his feet far apart. "We've come; we've come! Heya, we've come with plunder and a slave! Heya!"

26

"Dhuja may be an old lady, but she isn't deaf," Keshlik said calmly as he dismounted Lashkat in the half-circle. "You don't need to shout just for her."

Juyut looked momentarily abashed, but his embarrassment turned quickly back to pride as faces began to appear at the doors of the yurts. The elders came out, along with most of the women, and Juyut began showing off the portions of turquoise, mother-of-pearl, and the sheaves of pressed leaves that they had brought back. Keshlik untied the slave from his bridle and handed the other end to Juyut, who was recounting the story of the raid with exaggerated emphasis on his own prowess. Lashkat nickered.

"I'm getting there." Keshlik quickly untied the leather straps holding the saddle and bridle in place, then he slipped the tack off her shoulders. She tossed her head and trotted away toward the pasture. Keshlik laid the tack in his yurt then returned and crouched next to Dhuja.

"Is Tuulo well?" he asked.

The old woman picked a fleck of straw from the surface of the milk. "Your wife grows better every day. She complains about having to eat curds all the time, but you've heard that as often as I have. She remains strong; she'd come out and take this spoon from my hands if it weren't for the taboo."

"May I speak to her?"

Dhuja nodded. She called another woman away from the crowd to stir the curds, then led Keshlik into the east horn of the encampment, to a small earth-colored yurt set just outside the semicircle. A ring of grass around the yurt had been pulled up, bound into sheaves, and burnt to create a circle of charcoal on the ground, with green grass on both sides and the yurt in the center. Keshlik stopped just outside the line.

"Tuulo!" Dhuja cried as she crossed into the circle and lifted the flap over the doorway. The door closed behind them and muffled Tuulo's response. A second later, Dhuja reappeared with the pouch of sacred salt and sprinkled it lightly along the path from the door to where Keshlik waited. Then Tuulo finally opened the flap and ran across the salted grass to her husband.

"Finally! You took so long, I thought maybe you had been turned into cattle and had gone grazing instead of raiding."

Her belly seemed to have grown, though it had only been a few days. Her face was ruddy and beautifully fat, and her gait was starting to wobble. She wore silver rings and combs studded with coral and jewels, the prizes of past raids, which Keshlik had given to her for their wedding. Keshlik smiled and felt like a young man coming to his wife's tent for the first time. "Juyut led the raid. You've compared him to a cow more than once."

"Well." She halted just before the line of charcoal, reaching toward him but stopping short of touching. She smiled. "But Golgoyat fought among you."

"He did. None of our men fell, and none of the traders escaped. They didn't even suspect we were coming. And I brought you something." He reached into the pouch at his chest and brought out the carved fish that he had found, the only thing he had claimed for his private use from the plunder. The nacre in the fish's mouth seemed to glow in the evening light.

Tuulo drew in a sharp breath. She reached to take it from Keshlik's hand, but Dhuja appeared as if sprouting from the earth and slapped her hand away.

"Foolish girl," she said. "It's as if Khou's protection means nothing to you." She snatched the bone from Keshlik's hand and dipped her thumb in the pouch of salt hanging around her neck, then she rubbed the whole surface of the sculpture down. "Here."

"Thank you." Tuulo picked up the handspan of bone and lifted it up to the light, turning it over so the shard of mother-of-pearl caught the sun's last rays, examining the colors and the shape. "Do the lowlanders have fish that look like this?"

"I don't know," Keshlik said. "We brought a slave back, hoping that he could speak to the Guza. I'll ask him, if you'd like."

"Well, I wouldn't want to take time away from the important

28

things you have to ask." She continued to turn the sculpture over in her palm. "Whatever those are."

"The Guza say that there is a city to the south, along a great river. Presumably the man came from there and can tell us more."

"A city? An actual city, or a mere settlement, like the flock of Guza villages?"

"A city. That's what they say."

Tuulo frowned. "That's the first I've heard of it."

Dhuja chided Tuulo with a look. "You are in Khou's circle and aren't supposed to concern yourself with what the war bands are doing."

"Even if my husband leads them?" She gave Dhuja a glare that was equal parts affection and scorn.

Keshlik resisted the urge to cross the blessed line and caress Tuulo's face and belly. "You have a wise midwife and a valorous husband. You worry about our son, and I'll worry about the war."

Keshlik lingered too long with Tuulo, and still he left unsatisfied. For the sake of their child, he would not cross into Khou's blessed circle, but he ached to touch his wife's hand again.

When he returned to the center of the encampment, he found that Hetsim, a Guza slave, had already been brought out from Bhaalit's yurt to translate for the new captive. Juyut, Bhaalit, and a few of the elders sat around and listened. Keshlik stood at the edge of their circle and listened.

"—No walls, because they have no enemies," Hetsim said. "The plains north of the river are uninhabited, except for the Guza who lived in the Gap, and the Prasei who live in the forest valleys have no interest in the high plains."

The captive spoke voluminously, his eyes wide and pleading, as if by complying perfectly with his Yakhat captors he might earn his freedom.

29

"What is the occupation of these Prasei, if they have no enemies?" Bhaalit asked.

Hetsim repeated the question to the captive. The answer was long and eager.

"The people of Prasa are fishermen, traders, and craftsmen," the translator said. "They have an alliance with the great king to the south, with whom they trade in great volume, and they trade also with the swift people who come in boats from the north. All of their livelihood is spent in friendship and trade. Why should they have enemies?"

All the gathered Yakhat laughed.

The captive seemed agitated by their laughter. He looked up, saw Keshlik, then glanced through the semicircle of yurts toward Tuulo's secluded circle. He posed a long question to Hetsim.

Hetsim spoke hesitantly. "This man says that he noticed that you spoke to your wife who is pregnant."

Keshlik tensed. "What about it?"

Another brief interchange. "He says that his own wife is also pregnant and that he hopes you will have pity on him for the sake of their shared condition and allow him to return to his people."

Juyut laughed, and the elders smirked. Keshlik fingered the handle of the knife in his belt. He didn't think that the slave's glance would break the circle of Khou's blessing around Tuulo, but the fact that the man had noticed him and had seen his wife raised his ire.

"Ask him," he told Hetsim, "why I should let him return to the city and warn them about the Yakhat horde."

After a moment, the translator responded. "He says he cares only for his wife and his family, and he doesn't need to warn anyone about anything."

"Does he expect me to believe such a blatant lie?"

Hetsim flinched. He mumbled something to the captive, who didn't respond.

"Tell him," Keshlik said, "that when the Yakhat reach Prasa,

30

the whole city will surely perish. So even if we did let him escape, it would only be a matter of time before we killed him anyway."

Hetsim repeated the words, and the man began to blubber. He threw himself on the ground before Keshlik and began to beg. Hetsim hesitated, apparently uncertain how to translate the incoherent babble.

Keshlik waved aside his attempt. "We obviously can't let him return to the city. Bhaalit, when you're done questioning this man, kill him."

"I took this man for the commonwealth of the tribe," Juyut said. "Isn't that a matter for the elders to decide?"

Keshlik glared at the elders. "Do any of you think we should keep a weak and cowardly slave alive, once he's told us everything he knows?"

None of them said a word.

Hetsim began to speak again to the slave, but Keshlik cut him off. "Don't translate that. You're alive because we may still need you, but your use could expire in a moment. Let this fool talk if he thinks he can buy his life with it, and let him find the knife at his throat after that."

CHAPTER 4

UYA

"COME TO THE LODGE," Oire said.

Uya was resting in the hammock on the Earth side of the lodge, and a spiteful refusal came right to the tip of her teeth. But her mother's expression killed the thought, and she followed. Most of her aunts and cousins were already assembled inside, sitting on the floor or on the wooden benches along the walls of the lodge. Nei sat in the Eldest's chair beneath the ancestor totems. She never sat there except when conducting Elder business. Uya's heart skipped a beat. Saotse sat on one side of Nei beneath the ancestors, and a young man she didn't know stood waiting on the other side.

Uya was the last to arrive, and she lowered herself gently onto a bench. Sitting on the floor was too hard with her belly. Nei glanced at her then addressed the stranger. "Jeoa, this is my *enna*. Tell us again what you just told me."

Jeoa cleared his throat. "Yes, Eldest. As I said the first time, my *enna* set out on a trade mission to the Guza three days after your own left. Your *enna* is perpetually the first to leave once the spring snows have cleared off the high roads, since your scouts are the swiftest and your men ready themselves so quickly—"

Nei's lips twitched. "You may omit the flattery. I've heard this once already. This is for their benefit."

"Yes, Eldest." He kept his eyes downcast, and he spoke barely loud enough for Uya to hear him. "We set out three days after your caravan, loaded just as heavily, and we caught no sight of your caravan on the road aside from the bits of refuse that they discarded. Then when we came to the place where the Saoleka River cuts through a ridge—I don't know if you know it—but there is a small ravine, less than a mile long, where the river channel carved its way through. And there we found them. What was left of your caravan."

He took a short, unhappy breath. His clothes rustled as he fidgeted.

Uya's heart began to pound.

"We found parts of a broken wagon, broken wheels, and torn sacks. Then, further into the canyon, we found the pyre. The ground was all charcoaled and muddy, and the air stank. Every wagon from the caravan had been gathered together and lit on fire. And when we poked through the ashes, we found bones. Long bones, horse skulls, human skulls. We fled back to Prasa as quickly as we could. They sent me to tell you as soon as we arrived."

The air in the lodge was still and closed. No one spoke. Uya's hands trembled. Rada was gone. Her father was gone. Were they dead? Would they even know? Her knees weakened, and she grabbed her mother's hand. Silent tears were running down Oire's face.

"Did you count the skulls?" Nei asked.

"We didn't stay long enough to count anything. We were afraid that the murderers of the first caravan would fall on us as well. We didn't even light fires on our return."

"So you don't know if anyone escaped? Or was taken captive?"

"We don't know, Eldest. I'm sorry."

Another long, morbid pause encumbered the air of the lodge.

Nei asked Jeoa, "Why would the Guza do this? We've traded peacefully with them for centuries."

"I don't know," the man said. "If you don't know, Eldest, we have no way of guessing."

Saotse stirred. "It was not the Guza."

"How do you know?" Nei asked.

"On the night before the caravan left, I felt the ground quiver and tremble with a strange voice, as if a Power were speaking. But it was a foreign Power, not Azatsi or Prasyala or any of the other Powers whose names I know. Someone else. Someone from elsewhere."

Uya quivered with the cold fear rising from her belly. The child inside her seemed to have stilled along with the lodge. "So the Power killed them? There is a new Power on the caravan road that devours men with flame?"

"No. The Power that I felt was not angry or hungry. It did not seek to destroy men. It was very lonely and very sad."

"Then why did it destroy the caravan?" she pressed.

"Don't be a superstitious fool," Nei said. "That is not how the Powers work in the world."

Uya's cheeks burned, and she felt the stares of the other aunts on her. They were all content to remain silent. But Uya had questions, and she didn't care if they called her superstitious. "But—"

Nei answered before Saotse could. "Saotse said only that a new Power is present. We need to discover what this means and what it has to do with the caravan." She added in a quiet, creaky voice, "And we need to mourn."

Silence resumed in the lodge.

"I'm sorry, Eldest," Jeoa said again.

Nei tsked. "Bring our report to the Eldest of your *enna*. I will visit her later and convey our thanks."

"Thank you again." He passed the gathered women, avoiding their eyes, and slipped out the door.

A mournful sigh filled the still air of the lodge. Uya bit her lip to keep silent. Nei descended from the Eldest's seat with a rustle of furs and the creak of skin on wood. One of her hands closed over Saotse's.

"My children," she said. "Oh, my children."

A sob broke through the silence from somewhere to the right. Uya tried to stave off the weeping, because once she began, she thought she would never stop. But the baby kicked in her stomach, and the bitter irony of it set a shower of tears loose like dew shaken off a branch. Uya's mother clasped her hands on her shoulders until she regained herself and looked up.

Nei was watching Uya with her head lifted high, trembling slightly, as if she might fall at any moment. "At sunset we will begin to sing the dead into the west. Prepare yourselves."

The sun dropped into the sea. There was silence around the *enna*, save for the lapping of the seawater on the shore.

Nei came to Uya with the beam of burnt ash. She paused, putting her wrinkled hand on Uya's belly, then kissed Uya's cheek. They hesitated for a moment with their faces touching. Then she smudged Uya on the forehead and signed both of her rouged cheeks.

Chrasu was the last one to be marked for mourning. When Nei had finished, she moved to the center of the circle of the *enna* and sat. She took up a small white drum and began to beat a slow, irregular beat.

For a long moment, there was no sound but the pattering of the drum.

I don't want to be here. Uya knew what was coming, had been through many other funerals with the *enna*, but this time it seemed too much to bear. *Rada, my father, my uncles.* One dead was enough

35

to fill the *enna* with mourning for a year, and handling them all felt like drowning.

Nei began with a quiet, throaty ululation. Uya hadn't heard that sound since they buried her uncle twenty years ago. She had forgotten how it sounded—or perhaps it hadn't been quite so doleful then. Nei mourned Asa, her husband, now. Her song was a quavering, wordless wail, rising and falling with drunken imprecision, growing suddenly loud then feebly draining away.

The sun dimmed in the west.

One by one, the other women of the *enna* took up the song. A few of them used words, but most simply wailed with the same wordless agony that Nei had expressed. Chrasu began to sing. Saotse did not, but her lips twitched in silent agreement.

Uya held back. She did not want to join the mourning. Her composure was at the edge of a chasm, and she felt as if a sea's worth of grief were welling up from her stomach and trying to break through her chest. They would sing this song for a year, never letting the drum go silent or the mourning cease all that time. Her child would be born with the sound of sorrow in the lodge. She didn't want it to start. Once she started, it would go on and on, the whole sea of grief breaking through her ribs and drowning all of them in the flood.

She wanted to believe that Rada would come back. She wanted to believe that her uncles and grandfather would come back. She didn't want to believe that they had all died in some ravine—

And it broke out of her like a wave crashing against the shore. Her wail was high and piercing, almost a scream, until it tumbled into the murmuring pool of the *enna's* grief. She had no words. The matrix syllables *heia haoa* fell from her mouth like rocks, and she lost herself.

The sun drowned in the west, and the stars came out. A cold wind blew in off the sea.

At some point during the night, the drum passed into her hands, and she drummed until her fingers were numb. The drum

36

passed to someone else. She drank a little water. She sang more. The fervor of the song waned, then flared up again when someone let forth a fresh wail.

Some of the aunts began to chant the names of their sons and husbands, recounting their names or favored memories. Uya said nothing about Rada. What would she say? Their marriage was young, and she had only a little affection for him. But none of that mattered. He was her husband, and the father of her child, and now he was gone. She wailed again.

The sun began to brighten the east. Chrasu had fallen asleep beside her, but Saotse and the rest of the women were still awake. A few of them had stopped singing, but there were never less than a half-dozen voices trembling with sadness. The drum passed to Nei. The Eldest rose to her feet, beating more slowly now, and began to walk into the lodge. The *enna* followed her, singing.

The wood of the entrance creaked under their feet as the women ducked through the door and drifted to their places. Nei settled in the Eldest's seat and continued to drum. An aunt knelt and began to blow on the banked fire. The sound of mourning echoed in the rafters of the lodge. Uya found a bench that could support her belly and pulled it next to the fire, crooning softly.

Oire's hand touched her shoulder. "Go. Sleep," she said. "Go with Saotse."

"What's wrong with Saotse?"

"Nothing except the weakness of age. The night was hard for her. You should sleep."

Uya looked into the flames beginning to flicker in the fire ring. Having started the mourning, it seemed too soon to stop. She had barely begun to drain the ocean of sadness from her heart. "I want to stay."

Oire shook her head. "This is just the first day of mourning. You will have plenty of time later."

Uya relented. Saotse knelt behind her, and Uya took her hand

and led her to the women's side of the lodge, where they both dropped into beds and slept.

The drum was the lodge's heartbeat. It stuttered all through the night and battered against the sunrise, underlining the daylight with dolor. Uya took it when her turn came and spent her hours by the fire, chanting softly the names of the dead, then lapsing into a murmur of *heia haoa*. Hours creaked by. She played beneath the ancestor totems until someone took the instrument from her hands.

Days dribbled past. She slept too much. She did not measure the time in sunrises but in her rounds with the drum, and she almost forgot how to speak except in chant. The drum was a refuge. Playing and singing the dead into the west, she forgot that her child would be born without father or grandfather, except for when the baby kicked and reminded her that it still lived. When she stopped, sadness enveloped her like a winter fog rising from the sea. Her limbs felt heavy and clumsy, as if she had swam too long in cold water. She could not think.

There came a bright day when Uya rose from her hammock and came to the fire that burned before the ancestors. Her back ached from too many days sitting in the lodge and lying down, and her belly seemed to have gotten larger in the meantime. Were her feet always so swollen? She needed to move.

Saotse pattered on the drum and chanted, and Nei sat next to her with her eyes closed, swaying gently.

"Where is everybody?" Uya whispered.

Nei opened her eyes. "The Prasada called them into town."

"Why?"

"Do you really not know? Haven't you heard a word that's been said these past days?"

"I haven't paid much attention to the rest of the lodge's whispers. Aren't we all supposed to be mourning?"

Nei considered her words for a moment. "Yes, but the sun rises regardless. You've done more than your share of singing away the dead. You should let others take their turns with the drum more often. As for your question, there is an earthworks being built at the north perimeter of the city."

"What are you talking about?"

Nei sighed. "The raiders are coming. The Prasada has ordered all of the *ennas* to help build earthworks around the perimeter of the city to defend it. Yesterday the Eldest of every *enna* assembled to determine the contributions of food and labor for the next ten days."

Uya had overheard fragments of talk about raiders destroying farms and plundering caravans on the high roads, and hadn't Saotse said something about strange Powers? But she had amalgamated these into an image of demons devouring the caravan and tearing apart the unlucky that crossed their paths. It had not occurred to her that they might move with a purpose, that they might threaten the city. She wanted to ask Nei if they were men and not spirits, but Nei would just berate her for being superstitious, the way she always berated Chrasu. Instead she said, "Then I will go see the earthworks."

"Why would you want to see the earthworks?"

"So that when the raiders are driven back, I will know where to stand so I can spit on the bodies of the men who killed my husband."

"That's not a seemly attitude for a woman with child."

"Should I scrub my face with ash and mourn for another month? Oarsa hear me, I'm going into the city, and I am going to see the earthworks."

With a strike like a heron, Nei slapped Uya's cheek. "You be careful with your oaths. One day you're going to wake up and find that your words are a thorn in your heel."

Uya's cheek stung, and her hand drifted up to cover it. "Yes, Eldest." She hesitated a moment before adding, "But may I go?"

"Go. Your mother is at the Prasada's lodge taking inventory for the construction, but she can rouge you. And take Saotse with you."

Saotse stirred. Her song faltered. "Why are you sending me away?"

"I'm not sending you away. You, too, have mourned more than your share. Go. I'll maintain the song." She pulled the drum from Saotse's hands.

Saotse rose to her feet with a groan. "Uya? Give me your hand. You can tell me what it looks like when we arrive, I suppose."

Uya stretched her hand out, Saotse took it, and they set out for the center of Prasa.

The *enna's* lodge hid in a pocket of firs with the sea to their west, part of a district of well-spaced, stately lodges on the south shore of the river. Bands of piny woodland separated each of the lodges in their district, though a footpath ran through the woods and past the doors of their nearest neighbors before joining the south road into the city. Uya walked quickly, but Saotse's hesitant gait held her back. Saotse was so confident on the paths around the lodge itself, but the moment anyone took her past the *enna's* holdings, she became as shy and cautious as a rabbit. Uya nearly scolded her, but seeing the pained look on Saotse's face, she held her tongue.

Half an hour later, they had left the grand, private lodges on the southern fringe of the city and come to the crowded, muddy district that crouched on the south shore of the River Prasa. These were the fishing *ennas*, and they built their lodges close to the river and lined up long rows of unpainted canoes on the shore. Their ancestor totems were grubby and ill painted. Uya usually pinched her nose at the miasma of humans and horses and fish guts that muddled the streets here, though today the paths between the greasy lodges were nearly deserted. "There's no one here," she muttered, just loud enough for Saotse to hear.

"I hear two old women gossiping and a girl addressing her doll," Saotse said. "There are no ponies or men anywhere. They've all gone up to the earthworks."

Uya couldn't hear anything other than their footsteps in the mud, but she could see the lack of animals. "Really?" she said. "All of them, just for a little mound of dirt?"

"From what I hear, the mound of dirt is anything but *little*."

They came to the bridge, the only passage over the River Prasa, built where the main trade road running north from Kendilar met the river. It was practical and unlovely, long cedar slats tied together with bronze, lying across stone piles built up on the river bed. Most of the city proper was on the north side of the river, and Uya much preferred the clean, tidy lodges that ringed the city's core to the grubby south shore. The lodges here were spaced farther apart and left a few spruces between them, and their ancestor totems were tall and painted turquoise, carmine, and white. Nei always told her not to be so judgmental, but she didn't see any excuse for the mess that the fishing *ennas* made of the south shore.

They approached the center of the city where the Prasada's lodge lay. This was the market district, where women traded bales of dried kelp, casks of salted salmon, mother-of-pearl, polished turquoise, whale ivory, vast buffalo hides from beyond the Gap, the hammered silver of Kendilar, and boxes of dried lemons and spices from Tsingris. The streets should have been noisy with travel. But Uya saw only a few women hurrying along with their heads down. The stone pavement before the Prasada's lodge was nearly bare. The Prasada's raccoon and heron totems seemed to look down on the space with menace.

In all her life, Una had never seen the market when it was anything but brimming with buyers and sellers, and the sight of it still and dead portended doom.

A small crowd of women sat in the shadows of the Prasada's lodge. Oire was among them, a plank of cedar balanced on her lap and a reed pen in her hand. Her face was smudged with white ash. Uya called quietly, "Mother!"

Oire looked up. "Uya, what are you doing here? And Saotse with you..."

"I came into the city."

"Why aren't you rouged? You left Nei alone with the drum, and you—"

"Mother! Nei told me to come and for you to mark us. Besides, it's not as if there's any doubt about my condition."

Oire pursed her lips in disapproval and looked at Uya's belly, but Uya thought she saw a shadow of pleasure in it. "Fine." She set the plank of cedar aside with her birch-bark page, then she bent and withdrew two small clay jars from the basket behind her. "And what if I hadn't brought the colors with me?" she muttered.

"I suppose you'll have to take that up with the Eldest."

Oire looked at Saotse. "And you? Why did you come?"

"I have not been to the earthworks," she said in a small voice.

"Well, I suppose if Nei let you." She opened the jar of white ash, dipped her first three fingers in it, and drew matching white stripes down both cheeks on both Uya and Saotse. Then she dipped her thumb in the jar of oily carmine and drew twin red suns on Uya's cheeks.

"There. I hope I don't hear anything about my daughter's disrespect for the dead."

"If I disrespected the dead," Uya said, "then why haven't I left the *enna* for a month?"

Oire wiped her fingers clean on the edge of her skirt. "If you want to see the earthworks, take any of the north paths. The battlements encompass the whole north side of town."

"Thank you," Uya said. She grabbed Saotse's hand and began walking north.

The cold, empty feeling of the city gradually thawed as Uya

and Saotse began to encounter people on the path. There were men carrying shovels and spades and canteens of mare's milk, and clusters of young men holding hands. A young woman led a pair of ponies ahead of them, and she glanced back at Uya's white-and-red cheeks and pumpkin-shaped belly and shook her head in pity. Uya felt a twinge of self-consciousness. The white of mourning and the red of childbearing were not meant to mingle on the same cheek, though she had managed to forget that since she had left the lodge.

"I smell dirt that's been overturned by a spade," Saotse said. "And I hear—"

"Oarsa's foam." Uya finally spotted the earthworks and dropped Saotse's hand in awe.

She had imagined something reasonable, something small, something *else*. Something like the little dike that separated some of the riverside *enna* lodges from the overflow of the river. But this was a *wall*. The construction was incomplete but already impressive: a stack of four earthen terraces, each the height of a man, reinforced with stone and retained by walls of pine logs, with more earth dug out from inside the city to raise the height of the ravine. One could hide an entire lodge in the interior of the mound and pass a river through the ditch that had been dug inside the city. The structure crawled with men, from boys to gray-headed Eldest, with young women scampering along the outside to carry baskets and relay instructions and pack clay into the crevices between logs.

So *this* was why the entire city seemed to be deserted. Nei had said that the Prasada had called up help from the *ennas*, and Uya realized that this meant *every* man from *every* enna, and a good portion of the women, besides. The city felt empty because every hand in it was hard at work.

Saotse squeezed her hand. "What do you see?"

"Something amazing. And terrible, and troubling. I don't

43

understand what's going on. Why didn't anyone tell me? Can you—"

"Uya, tell me what you see."

She described as best she could, in broken sentences pitted with gasps and omissions and forgotten asides, how the ditch was being excavated and the wide earthen wall raised above it. "And it's new," she added. "Somehow—though I suppose it makes sense if every hand in the city has helped—somehow they've gotten this almost done. I can see the completed wall to the north, curving away just past the lodges like a levee, topped already with little huts of thatch like bird nests, and guarded by archers, as if they were frightening back the sea. It's as if they built it overnight. I don't see how…"

"It's been a month, Uya."

"But do we really need something so big? I don't—"

Saotse dropped Uya's hand and knelt on the ground.

"Saotse? Saotse, what's wrong?" Uya lowered herself carefully to her knees.

Saotse pressed her palms against the dirt as if kneading dough. A febrile moan dribbled from her lips. Her forehead bent and brushed the dirt, then she cocked her head as if listening. Her back arched. "Oh, no. Oh, no. I'm sorry. I'm sorry."

"Saotse!"

Saotse's head jerked to the side. She collapsed to the ground and twitched.

"Saotse!" Uya clasped Saotse's hands in her own and blew into her face. Saotse's eyes were closed, but her tongue moved as if mouthing strange words.

Uya pleaded, "Are you awake? Can you hear me? Saotse! Someone help me!"

Saotse screamed. Her eyes opened wide, as though she saw clean through the milk of her cataracts, and she clawed at Uya's face. "No. No! They have ruined us. There's too much. I can't—"

"Saotse, talk to me—"

Saotse screamed again then went limp. A moment later, she convulsed and gasped as if she had nearly drowned. Her fingers clawed at the ground. She grabbed Uya's face with both hands. "Uya? Yes, Uya. Oh, at last."

"Are you well? What happened?"

"The earth weeps! Ruined! I hate all of them. Lonely, so lonely." She curled up into a ball and began to shake.

"Saotse, Saotse!"

Two nearby men came running. One of them bent to grab Saotse's mad hands. The other asked Uya, "What happened here? What's wrong?"

"I don't know. She just started shaking. I don't know. I don't know anything."

The man looked at Uya's belly and cheeks and shook his head. "Are you of the same *enna*?"

"Yes."

"We'll carry her back to the lodge with you. You should not be out."

Her irritation at being scolded melted from her worry. "Hurry," she said. "I'll show you the way."

"So Saotse's affinity with the Powers waxes once more." Nei sat with her legs crossed at the foot of the bed where they had laid Saotse out to sleep. One of her hands rested on Saotse's knee. Oire had returned to the lodge with them and maintained the drum's heartbeat, singing the dead into the west.

"I've never seen such a dramatic reaction in her, Grandmother," Uya said. Fear for Saotse mingled in her gut with the grim knowledge that the raiders waited somewhere beyond the horizon.

"You helped us pull her out of the sea."

"That was nothing like this! She was weak then only because

45

she had been at sea so many days, but she had all her wits about her."

"But she came from the sea, then. This time she touched the earth."

"What? What does that have to do with anything?"

Nei sighed. "I should send you to the Hiksilipsi, you ignorant, superstitious girl. Perhaps you could sit still long enough to learn the lore of the Powers from them. Since you don't seem to have noticed, I must point out to you that Saotse's affinity has always been for Oarsa. She knew him by a different name, but once she learned our language she recognized our description of him, and she knew that it was he who called her across the sea and sent the whales to carry her.

"This only matters because the Power who touched Saotse today is not Oarsa. You said yourself that she pressed her head to the ground and that she spoke of the earth weeping. And a few weeks ago, she mentioned the presence of a new Power in the earth, and of its loneliness."

Uya said slowly, with great fear that Nei was going to scold and laugh at her again, "I've never heard of a new Power appearing or arriving from somewhere. I thought the Powers always *were*."

"So did I," Nei said in a low voice. She cast her eyes downward.

The baby kicked. Uya startled and put her hand on the place where she had felt the flutter of movement.

Nei glanced at Uya and continued in a quieter, more cautious voice. "Saotse told me once that many of the swift people think that the slow races are actually immortal. Because our lives are longer than theirs, they assume that we last forever. I wonder if the same might be true of the Powers, with respect to us. Perhaps we think them to be changeless merely because they change so infrequently. Perhaps they even die."

"I've never heard of a Power that died."

"Neither have I. In any case, this is just speculation." She smoothed the bottom of Saotse's skirt and looked with pity over

46

the swift woman's wrinkled face. "Saotse herself may be able to tell us, but she should sleep for now."

"And what does all of this have to do with the raiders?" Uya asked. "Why was Saotse stricken right when we came to the earthworks?"

"Saotse might know," Nei said. "But we can't do anything about it now. The construction is almost done. May the Powers help us hold it."

CHAPTER 5

KESHLIK

"I T'S ALL BAD NEWS," BHAALIT said. "We let too many get away to warn the city, and we moved too slowly afterward."

The speakers of all eleven Yakhat tribes had gathered at the encampment of the Khaatat for a council. The afternoon had wasted away in drinking, eating, boasting, and telling jokes, but with nightfall, the council had grown serious. A small fire smoked in the center of the ring formed by the seated speakers, with the other attending warriors standing behind them like pines.

Dheijit of the Tanoutut shouted in response to Bhaalit, "None from our raids escaped. We were sure of that." He tossed a blade of grass into the fire to underline his point.

Keshlik grunted. No one had escaped from the raids he led, either, but he didn't need to remind the men of that. He spoke not for the Khaatat, the tribe he shared with Bhaalit, but as leader of the war band for all the Yakhat. "So what?" he asked. "What defenses did they make? What do I care?"

Bhaalit replied, "I saw this myself: They raised a moat and an earth wall all around the northern perimeter of the city. The moat and wall aren't very high, and they were put up in a hurry. A child could shoot an arrow over the top of it. But it would stop a mounted charge, which is all it needs to do."

"We can fight our way over the top on foot if we need to," said Danyak, the speaker for the Chalayit tribe. He jabbed his fingers into his open palm for emphasis. "These people are used to peace and unfit for warfare. We've seen them scattering like field mice in every raid we've done."

"Yes," Bhaalit said, "but they outnumber us. And in the city, at least, they're prepared to defend themselves. Look how quickly they raised their wall."

"Bhaalit is right," Keshlik said with a sigh. Bhaalit's caution was correct, as usual. "In a siege or a melee, we might lose. Golgoyat gave us horses, and as long as we remain on horseback, he fights among us."

"Then how do you propose we continue?" Danyak asked. "We can't ride our horses over a moat."

"We could simply ignore the city and continue raiding along the river," Bhaalit said. "There are more farms and villages that we haven't plundered yet."

"Bah," Keshlik said. "Farms and villages are cheese crumbs. And most of them have been abandoned at the news of our coming."

The circle of warriors muttered in agreement. They had been raiding along the River Prasa for weeks, and they had picked up every scrap of value already. The younger warriors were grumbling that there was no fighting left to do. But all the scouts who had ventured farther west told the same story: the plains rose and crumpled against a range of white, toothy mountains, which forced them to the south, where the city lay on the shores of a great bay. If they were going to continue moving at all, they would have to move south or west, which meant that the city lay in their path.

"Farms are cheese crumbs," Keshlik repeated. "We're going to the city, and we'll plunder it and burn it to the ground. But we'll take it from the south, where there is no wall."

There was a moment of quiet, then Dheijit asked, "And how are we supposed to do that? The river is too wide to shoot an arrow across, much less swim with horses."

Keshlik nodded to his right. "Bhaalit knows. He remembers how we crossed the marshes between the Bans during the rains."

Bhaalit stared back at him in surprise and responded cautiously, "It's been a very long time since anyone reminded me of the Bans."

Keshlik grinned, relishing the rare chance to take Bhaalit off-guard. "But you remember how to bring the zebu from one mound to another."

"I suppose my memory might go back that far. Ah," he said, raising his hand with a smile. "I see."

The other warriors looked at them in incomprehension. None of them were old enough to remember the marshy Bans, to have guided the herds of white zebu with heavy ears and wet noses. They remembered only the high plains furrowed with little creeks and the cattle the Yakhat had captured to replace their old abandoned herds.

"Then call the tribes together—all the tribes, all the warriors— to the bluffs two days west of the city. Do you know the place?"

Most of the men around the circle nodded. Their scouts knew the land above the river well by now.

But Dheijit spat, "What *is* the plan, then? We swim across the river?"

"We float. We will build rafts."

Surprised grumbling flared up around the circle. The Yakhat had never built rafts within the memory of most still living. "Are our warriors reduced to boat-building, now?" called someone at the far side of the ring.

Keshlik watched the objections melt away beneath his glare, feeling Bhaalit's wordless support beside him. Once the warriors' grumbles faded, he cleared his throat. "Are we done, then?"

They nodded.

Dheijit scowled but said, "We'll follow you, Keshlik."

"Then return to your yurts and prepare your warriors. Come to the rendezvous ready for war."

The council broke up into quiet, private conversations. Keshlik rose and strode away from the firelight into the darkness. It was a cold, clear spring night, with a wind that tasted like melting snow and new grass. He stopped a few paces away and stared into the starry darkness, stretching his legs and arms. He ached from sitting on the cold ground. And though he would never say a word of it to the warriors, he felt a little weary and stretched after battle these days. Sometimes he thought it would be good not to have to carry a spear again. Sometimes. But he remembered Khaat Ban and their unfulfilled vow. The only route to rest lay through victory.

Footsteps rustled in the grass behind him. Bhaalit's voice said, "Do you really think that we can bring an army across the river as if they were zebu? Horses and warriors aren't heifers."

"No, they're not. Warriors are quite a bit easier to lead. Or did you have more obedient zebu than me?"

Bhaalit chuckled. "It's been a long time, though. And the bangag trees don't grow here."

"The willows that grow by the rivers will do."

"I hope so."

A gust of wind stirred the grass and died down. "I'm riding out at dawn with Juyut and the rest of the Khaatat," Keshlik said. "I should say goodbye to Tuulo before we go."

"Go, then. I'll see you at the rendezvous."

The night was moonless and perfectly clear, and the yurts rose like black grease smears against the backdrop of stars. Keshlik weaved through them to the edge of Khou's circle and called out, "Tuulo! Tuulo!"

Dhuja stuck her head out of the yurt, letting a blade of lamplight spill out. "What do you want?"

"To see my wife before I go to war."

Tuulo's voice came from inside the yurt, sounding tired

51

and vulnerable. "Let me go, Dhuja. You're my midwife, not my nursemaid. I can stand for a little bit." She emerged a moment later, her hands in the small of her back, leaning away from her steps to balance out her belly. Her gait looked uncomfortable. "So you're off again."

"We're moving against the lowlanders' city. It'll be ten days, maybe twenty before I can come back to camp."

She nodded. "Dhuja tells me that we're going to move the camp, as well."

"Really? I hadn't heard." He had been too involved with the warriors and coordinating the speakers of all the tribes. Fortunately, the women knew how to look after themselves.

"The cow-maidens decided this afternoon," Tuulo said. "We'll probably be going south. So perhaps your return trip won't be so long. After we've pitched camp, we'll send a pathfinder to tell you our new position."

"And you? Can you travel in your state?"

She stuck her tongue out. "They'll make me sit in a travois. I certainly can't ride. Instead I get to bump along with the yurts and the luggage."

"Be careful."

"You and Dhuja! I'll be fine. But tell me, what will you bring me from the city, whatever it's called?"

"Prasa. And you tell me what you want. The Guza said that it was a rich place, a center of trade, so it probably has anything you could imagine. And they say that there are cities beyond the river that are even wealthier, and all lulled into complacency by too many years of peace. I'll make you an empress with all the plunder we gather."

"I'd settle for being a mother with a soft bed."

"Then I'll bring you a soft bed. A blanket of mink and a cushion of silk."

"Oh, Keshlik." She laughed. "Come back victorious, and avenge the Sorrow of Khaat Ban. That will be plenty."

They watched the river from atop the outcrop of yellow stone, looking down on the sandbar that nestled in the riverbed and slumbered beneath a stand of willows.

The willows were what Keshlik needed. The pines provided ample wood, but the supple willow branches would serve in the place of scarce rope. His band encamped among the pines and set a perfunctory watch, though Keshlik expected no counterattack. The only possible threat could come from the city, and every scout reported that it readied only for defense.

Keshlik and Bhaalit descended to the sandbar. The willows were enormous, stretching overhead nearly to the top of the sandstone cliff that formed the bluff's edge, and their leaves filtered the light into a murky green incandescence. Bhaalit stroked a leafy branch. "Like a woman's hair," he said.

"Not quite the same as the bangag," Keshlik said, "but it should work."

"Can we make them big enough to carry a horse, though?"

"If the old rafts could hold a bull zebu, then they can hold a horse and a rider. The hard part will be getting the men to stand on it."

Bhaalit chuckled. "The hard part will be building them. Everything after that is just standing and pulling."

The next morning, Keshlik sent Bhaalit and half of the warriors with axes to fell the lodgepole pines that grew a few miles upstream. The men were warriors, not loggers, so it took excruciatingly long for the first log to appear in the stream, bobbing to an eddy where Juyut and a half-dozen other young warriors plunged into the water and wrestled it to shore. On the shore of the sandbar, they cut it into sections and laboriously tied the pieces together, using the longest willow branches they could find. Keshlik barked orders up and down the line of warriors, trying to teach them the knots he had learned as a boy, trying to get them to remember that the willow branches would not bend infinitely, and listening to their grumbling at being made to tend trees and do slave work.

More warriors arrived from different tribes. As other tribes' warriors arrived, riding single-file across the curves of the landscape, Keshlik set them felling more trees, weaving, scouting, and hunting. The copse of cottonwoods grew full of the bedrolls of the Yakhat.

It took two days to finish the first raft, and once it was completed, a brave, terrified pair of warriors poled the raft across the river, carrying their only length of rope that was long enough to reach all the way across the river. Once across, it was easy enough to affix the rope to trees on opposite sides of the shore and pull the laden raft from one side to the other. Keshlik sent a few scouts across to explore the south side of the river and set the rest of the men making a second raft. The men seemed to think themselves experts by this time, and the second raft was completed only one day later. And with the pair of rafts ready, the ferrying began.

Another full day passed as they did nothing but ferry warriors and their horses from one side to the other, one raft crossing while the other returned. The camp began to take shape on the far bank of the river, though the warriors' behavior was more nervous and circumspect once they passed to the side of the river where the Prasei still roamed. Keshlik made them sleep without fires and posted sentries far from the camp, to give them plenty of warning should someone approach.

The next day dawned on thousands on both shores, an army anxious to be done with river-work and back atop their horses in the fight. The third day of ferrying passed, then Keshlik called for a halt.

Bhaalit remained with a quarter of the gathered tribes on the north shore. He and Keshlik shared a few words before parting. Juyut was waiting for Keshlik when he crossed the river with Lashkat. The two of them were the last to use the raft.

"I hope this means we're done with this ridiculous river-work," Juyut said. "This isn't what Golgoyat called us to."

Keshlik patted him on the shoulder. "Golgoyat gave you a head, too. It doesn't do any of us a lick of good to go charging into the strongest defense."

Juyut grunted. "We could have made it."

"Then next time I'll let you try it alone." He looked ahead to the west. "But for now, we ride straight to the city."

———◦❈◦———

Dawn. The grass was dewy around their horses' ankles, the air heavy with the threat of rain. Ribbons of mist wound around the trunks of trees and slipped through the ravines.

The cool air kept the horses alert. The men atop them were taut with nervous energy, like coils of twisted rope ready to lash out. Keshlik was glad for it. He had wound them up carefully over the past two days, moving them quickly, as quietly as three thousand horsemen could move, through the wooded wild on the south shore of the river. Last night he had not slept. He'd spent the night in contemplation and mental preparation, and he had roused the men before dawn. They streaked their faces with lines of black and red, their energy threatening to boil over. Keshlik rode the perimeter of the camp, keeping quiet. *The war band's fury mustn't peak too soon.* There were still two hours to ride.

The sun had breached the horizon in the east, drawing deep shadows of purple across the stripes of milky mist. Two miles ahead of them lay a cluster of small lodges, as described by their scouts, beyond which rose walls of pine broken up by larger and larger dwellings, until at last the city lay before them entire. A short ride through the woods would bring them from the camp to the city's outskirts, and from there they would strike like a spear into its heart.

Next to Keshlik and Lashkat, Juyut's horse snorted. "What are we waiting for?"

"Bhaalit. He'll send up his signal before he attacks, and we must not precede him."

Juyut grunted in response and gripped the reins tighter than he should. The poor youth. He still had not learned patience.

The dawn drew gradually brighter, and the mists dissolved. Then Keshlik pointed—a line of black smoke trickled into the sky to their north.

Juyut tensed. "Now?"

"Bhaalit's just begun. Wait a bit longer."

While he was still speaking, a drum began to sound in the north, as quiet and urgent as a heartbeat, the sound whispering through the morning air. Someone had raised an alarm in the city. "Draw the men up around me," he said to Juyut. "I will remind them why we fight."

Juyut nodded. He whistled and shouted the order, and the whistles rippled away through the crowd. The men pulled closer, dismounted, and grew quiet. They were a forest of black-and-red-striped faces, with the bronze teeth of their spears above them, a force vast and unstoppable.

Keshlik's heart began to pound. His voice carried clearly through the still morning air. "Warriors of the Yakhat! Warriors of Golgoyat! Let us remember why we are here!"

Grim attention sharpened their faces. Every Yakhat child knew the history he was about to recount, but their hunger to hear it again gleamed in their eyes.

Keshlik pounded the butt of his spear on the ground. "In a moment, we will ride into a great city, which has been built here by a civilized people unknown to us. Most of you do not remember when we ourselves lived in settled villages on the marshes and hills of the Bans. Most of you are too young to recall when the Kourak, who lived in cities such as this one, came and evicted us from our homes, destroying our villages, and casting us away to the edges of the marshes, where we lived like rats and wished to die. You do not remember it, but I do. They came to Khaat Ban during the Wedding of Golgoyat and Khou, when all of the tribes were gathered under the bond of peace, and they broke our peace and shattered the sacred marriage.

"You have heard this story from your fathers and grandfathers, but I was there, and I need no one to tell me about it. I saw Khou's maiden stolen from her bridegroom, and I saw her raped and killed and her body cast naked into the marsh. I saw my brothers and uncles and grandmothers slaughtered. I saw the marsh water run red with the blood of every Yakhat tribe. I stand before you as a witness of the Sorrow of Khaat Ban. Hear and remember, warriors of the Yakhat!"

The men shouted agreement and stamped their feet.

"Yet we survived," Keshlik continued. "We fled to the hills, without the zebu our parents raised, with only the memories of the Bans we had loved. We salted our food with our tears and cried out to the Powers we served, despairing that they would hear us. And there, where the storm clouds rolled off the high plains and poured themselves into the marshes, Golgoyat came to my father Keishul. He blessed him with the strength of the thundercloud, and commanded him to lead the Yakhat to avenge his sorrow."

The army roared. "Avenge the sorrow!" and "Remember Khaat Ban!" tore the air.

"Tell me, warriors of the Yakhat, was our sorrow avenged when we rose up from the place of our despair and seized the herds of the plainsmen?"

"*No!*"

"Truly, we were not avenged! With the herds we merely fed ourselves that we might not starve. But were we avenged when we struck the Kourak who had persecuted us and burned their city to the ground?"

"*No!*"

"Truly, we were not avenged! With their deaths we merely paid back a tenth of the debt of blood they owed us. But were we avenged when we made war against all of the tribes of the plains, wherever they turned their faces against us?"

"*No!*"

"Truly, we were not avenged! For their arrows slew my father Keishul, the chosen of Golgoyat, and added fury upon fury to his anger. But were we avenged when I took up his spear and turned us to the west, and we passed with much labor over the mountains into the land of the Guza?"

"*No!*"

"Truly, we were not avenged! For the wrath of Golgoyat has no end, even as the thunderstorm has no end until it has passed from one horizon to the other, and you can no more stand against it than you can catch a thunderbolt in your hand. We must hold every land guilty of the Sorrow of Khaat Ban until Golgoyat's hunger for vengeance is sated. So tell me, warriors of the Yakhat, does Golgoyat still rage?"

"*Yes!*"

"Does Khou still weep?"

"*Yes!*"

"Then today we fight! Remember Khaat Ban! We run with the strength of the thundercloud! Golgoyat himself fights among us! Go!"

A gale of screams and shouts rose up from the army. Keshlik raised his spear and pointed it toward the city, then spurred his horse into a gallop. Behind him pounded the hooves of the Yakhat, beating the earth with a rumble like thunder. The trees of the forest flew past. The last mile between them and the city passed under Lashkat's legs in what seemed no longer than a heartbeat.

The outermost lodge of the city appeared through the pines. Beneath its eaves, women were waiting. They looked up, their eyes lit up with fear, and they fled like leaves driven before a storm.

Keshlik's heart pounded. His spear was ready. The strength of

Golgoyat was in his blood, and the fury of the thundercloud was on his lips. He screamed, and his spear found its first victim.

CHAPTER 6

SAOTSE

THE VOICES IN THE LODGE whispered like dying men's breaths, and beneath them pounded the ragged heartbeat of the drums, the warning drum on the wall meeting the mourning drum in the lodge. The air shivered with plaintiveness and urgency.

Uya and Saotse huddled on a bench. Uya squeezed Saotse's hand and stroked the back of her palm in nervous inattention. Around them floated the scraps of the rest of the *enna's* conversation, underlaid by the droning of the women who continued the mourning song.

"They all ride horses, they say. Big, vicious horses, bigger than ours—"

"It must hold. There's no way they could breach that wall—"

"The drums, the drums. I wish they'd stop—"

"At least we're far from the fighting."

Through the flux of human voices, the Powers stirred. The little spirits of the rivers, trees, and winds danced in the air, anxious and wordless. Above them, the greater Powers sang, growing more discordant by the minute. Saotse pled silently, hoping to touch one of those whose names she knew, hoping at least to know that they were present, but she met only a vast and angry darkness, before whom all the other Powers churned like a gale. In desperation she sought even the weeping Power, the one whose touch had stricken her so terribly when she went to the wall, but she was too distant to hear.

Uya sighed and pinched Saotse's hand. "I hope this is over soon."

Saotse squeezed Uya's palm again. Something helpful, something hopeful should be said. She tried to think of it, but every word that came to mind was a lie. She was saved by Uya's sudden twitch.

"Om! The baby kicked again. It's been trying to tickle my kidneys all morning."

"At least it's well."

"*I* won't be well until we've finally driven back these raiders."

Saotse drew in her breath. A rumble murmured outside the lodge. "Do you hear that?"

"No. Oh, wait—"

The voices in the lodge petered out as the commotion grew outside. A tough, strangling silence rose, thick with fear.

The sound of rustling furs announced Nei rising to her feet. "Look out the door, Chrasu," she rasped.

The boy's feet pounded against the floorboards. The fear in the lodge stretched as taut as a thread before it snapped. Chrasu gasped.

"There are horses," he said. "Horses, hundreds of them coming up from the south, and men with bloody spears and—"

The lodge erupted into a cacophony of shouting voices. The sound hit Saotse like a fist. The room seemed to spin, words leaping in every direction through the air, giving her nothing to seize for direction or meaning. Uya pulled her to her feet, shouting something incomprehensible.

Nei's voice split the chaos like a knife, hard and sharp with authority. "Stop! Chrasu, they come from the south?"

"Yes, Eldest, and quickly!"

"On horses?"

"Yes!"

"Then bar the door. Don't let them in. Bring the knives from the chest. If anyone tries to come in, we'll fight."

The room shifted into nervous action. The hasty prodding of their aunts shuffled Saotse and Uya toward the center of the room and tucked them onto a bench with Nei. Around them pattered tense footsteps underlined by whispers.

Something pounded at the door.

The lodge was silent. The pounding sounded again, and brutish male voices shouted incomprehensible words. The cedar planks of the door held, and the leather hinges barely budged. The voices outside said a few more words then seemed to fade.

A few moments of audible movement followed, then the sounds of their horses retreated. The sound outside died down, except for the continuing, far-off thunder of hooves. No one moved in the lodge.

"Did they leave?" Uya whispered.

Saotse tasted the air. "Worse."

The others sensed it a moment after her. Smoke.

The *enna* burst into movement. Shouts crossed the lodge as the women searched for the source of the fire. Saotse drew closer to Uya. If the fire could not be smothered, they would need to run, and soon. She wrapped her hand around Uya's.

"Quiet," Nei shouted. The smoke was beginning to choke the air. "Saotse, is there anyone still outside? Lying in wait at the door?"

She rose to her feet and felt forward with her toe.

"Let me help you." Uya laid her hand on Saotse's shoulder and gently steered her through the crowded bodies of the rest of the *enna*.

She smelled the old cedar of the door beneath the smoke, and she pressed her ear against the soft, worn-down grain of the wood.

Silence. Hoofbeats, but far away, and no voices nearby. Her breath hissed out between her teeth. "No. They lit the fire and left."

"Then we flee. To the north, across the bridge. Now listen, children! If you see an unmolested lodge, take refuge in it. Otherwise, we'll try to reach the earthworks. Powers have mercy on us."

"But Eldest," one of the aunts said. "That's where the battle is."

"The battle is also here, it seems. And we would be better off closer to the men with arms. Now drop everything and follow."

Uya pulled Saotse into her chest, her belly bumping against Saotse's hip. "Stay close to me. Hold my hand."

The lodge was like a tumbled basket as Uya pulled Saotse through it. All the aunts and cousins jostled around them, Nei's voice slashing through the chaos. Saotse's feet didn't find any of their familiar places. Wasn't the bench supposed to be three steps further to the left? But her shin knocked against it anyway. The voices of the panicked women bounced off the walls in weird and impossible ways.

How long could it possibly take them to get out? Yet it seemed as if Saotse followed Uya for hours while the *enna* pressed its way through the door, until at last she tripped over the threshold. Someone caught her—she felt Oire's broad, firm hands.

"Thank you, Oire," she said. "Where is Uya?"

"I'm right here, Saotse," Uya said from just to her right, and she seized Saotse's wrists again. "Follow me."

She pulled Saotse over paths that should have been familiar but seemed as twisted and warped as the lodge had been. The Powers all around her were strange, their movements drunken, and they pressed against her as if to suffocate her. She heard the cries of more women from their *enna* ahead and Nei scolding someone else for falling behind.

"Do you see?" Chrasu called out. Screams answered him.

"What is it?" Saotse asked. "What do they see?"

"Horses," Uya said between heavy breaths.

Saotse realized that Uya was tiring quickly. She was close to childbirth, and she was no more ready to flee than Saotse was.

And then she *smelled* them. The aroma of grass and animal sweat and manure, and the tang of blood and smoke.

Their hooves battered the earth, and screams and ululations followed them. They were coming. They were a multitude—could the others actually see how many there were?—but Saotse only heard them, and what she heard was a vast and furious army, implacable and unstoppable. The crackle of fire grated in the distance. Uya had Saotse's hand and nearly stumbled.

"Run!" Nei demanded, a few steps behind them.

"Faster, Uya!" Oire prodded. "Can't you see them coming?"

"I can, Mother, but—" Her breath was coming in fits like gusts of wind, but she kept moving, and Saotse ran to keep from falling behind.

They reached the footpath that led to the bridge and into the heart of the city. The hard-packed dirt of the path slapped against her feet, and she counted paces as the rumble of horses' hooves grew behind them. She ran, though her old bones protested and her heart complained.

Beside her Uya cried. "It's no use."

She felt the trembling of the ground as the horses thundered by, the hollering of their riders blotting out all other sound. Behind them, a scream—two, three—the gurgle of blood-filled throats, and the sound of bodies hitting the ground.

Uya screamed, but not the scream of death. "Nei!" She dropped Saotse's hand. "Nei! No, Nei!"

"Leave her!" Oire shouted, a pace ahead of them. "Get to the trees, Uya!"

Saotse couldn't hear where Uya had gone. The screams and the horses confused all the sounds and distances. "Uya! Please, where are you?"

Uya and Oire's voices clashed and muddled.

"Nei! Nei! I'm right here, Saotse. Just wait—"

"—Leave her, Uya! She's gone, and we have to get to the trees, their horses won't—"

"—Can't leave her!"

"They're coming back. Run!"

The charge that had passed them the first time was returning. The thundering of their hooves grew louder; the cries of their warriors pierced the air like arrows. The ground seemed to roll under her feet. She began to crawl toward the sound of Uya's voice.

Oire's hands seized her by the shoulders and wrenched her around. "The woods are that way, straight ahead. Can you go? Can you keep a straight line? It's only a hundred yards."

"But what are you and Uya doing?"

"We'll be behind you as soon as I pull her off Nei. Go!" She gave her a gentle push.

For a heartbeat, Saotse was paralyzed with fear and doubt, but she would obey Oire, Oarsa help her. She crawled forward and plunged into short, hard grass that scratched her palms. Behind her was a maelstrom of screams and shouts.

Straight ahead. Straight ahead. One hundred yards was how many paces? But she couldn't count paces while she was crawling.

The ground under her palms dropped away into a little depression, a tiny hollow in the earth, and she pitched forward, scraping her forearms against the weeds. Which way was forward now? Her head had turned in the fall. All she could hear were horses and yelling and—

The horses were coming. The pounding of the hooves was close, too close. They'd be on her in moments. She flattened herself against the earth.

The ground around her roared with hoofbeats, and the air was suddenly thick with warriors' wails and the stench of furious mares. For a moment, all was confusion and movement, then she heard their cries receding again on the other side.

They had galloped right over her.

They must have thought she was dead, or maybe they couldn't be bothered to cut down a helpless old woman. But she was alive. Now she had to move.

She wobbled to her feet, crouched low, and charged recklessly ahead, not caring whether she was following Oire's directions. Away from the line of battle, that was all that mattered. Her hands and feet stung with scratches from thorns and burrs. She stumbled into a dip but clung to her balance and continued to run. Her hands stretched in front of her in the desperate hope that she would feel the needles of the pines before she crashed into a trunk.

The Powers must have heard her. The ground grew prickly with fallen needles under her feet. She slowed then felt a spruce bough brush against her hair.

Saotse dropped to her knees and crawled forward, feeling her way over the spruce roots—going deeper into the underbrush, to where the horses wouldn't go, to where she might hide and be safe. Twigs and needles scratched her arms and face.

She pushed ahead until she bumped into the base of a little bush, and she realized she was hemmed in by thicket too dense for her to crawl through. Any growth dense enough to stop her would certainly keep out the horses. The warriors would only find her if they came through on foot, and Oarsa help her, that wouldn't happen. She curled onto her side and waited.

Only then did she have time to wonder, *Where are Oire and Uya?* No one had followed her into the wood. There were no voices near her, no footsteps breaking through the brush. She rose to an elbow and strained to listen. But she heard nothing that might be their approach.

She called anxiously, "Uya? Oire?"

There was no response—but of course there wouldn't be. They wouldn't be foolish enough to shout and draw attention to themselves in the middle of a battle. Hopefully they had done as she had and curled beneath the roots of a spruce to wait for the warriors to recede.

She lowered herself back to the ground. "Oarsa, if you have ever heard me, hear me now," she whispered. "Help us. Help us."

CHAPTER 7

UYA

U YA WOULD NOT BELIEVE THAT Nei was dead. Despite the gouge of the spear that ran from her breast to her belly, despite the pools of blood that stained the dirt of the footpath, despite the old woman's stubborn, inexplicable silence. Her Eldest was immortal and impervious. She cried again and again, "Nei! Nei!"

Others were shouting at her—Oire and Saotse and maybe Oarsa, for all she knew, but she ignored all them. If she could just get Nei to *wake up*, then the wise old woman would tell them how to get to safety.

Her mother pulled at her shoulder and shouted nonsense, insisting that they leave. Couldn't she see that Nei had fallen? Did she seriously think that they should *leave* her? Why didn't her mother go help with someone else? Uya could see plenty of other people who had fallen down, and Oire would spend her time much better waking some of them up. Or at least she could take better care of Saotse, who was crying plaintively just out of Uya's sight.

"They're coming!"

The words tore Uya's attention away from Nei, and she turned her head to see that, indeed, the warriors had reached the end of the meadow and were turning their horses again to Uya and the others who fled. The warriors had such fearsome, frightening faces, smeared with paint of black and red, and splattered with blood and bits of mud. Their spears' tips were all bloody. Even their horses seemed to relish the fight—their mouths foamed and twisted, and they pawed the ground with sharp hooves that appeared able to crush any skull they found.

Alarm began to build in her thoughts. Perhaps they could drag Nei to safety, if she wouldn't wake up yet. Or maybe they could let her rest for a little while longer.

Oire yelled something. Uya saw Saotse crawling away, hidden in the grass, then her mother grabbed her arm and jerked her off the path. She stumbled and fell to the ground. Her mother continued shouting at her, though Uya couldn't imagine what she hoped to accomplish. The sound of horses' hooves was very loud. Warriors began to blur through the edges of her vision.

Then a horse was leaping forward, its rider crouched low and braced against his spear, the spear whose point was planted in Oire's stomach. Without any sound that Uya could perceive, her mother's hand slipped out of hers. The spearhead tore through flesh and emerged in a halo of blood and entrails. Oire spun a half-circle and fell.

Uya couldn't move. Her mother's eyes were open. Her mother's gut was open. And her mother, unlike Nei, was a creature of flesh and blood, a mortal, a person who might be killed by having her torso torn open with a spear. Uya began to tremble—though it was impossible, inconceivable that her Eldest could die, that she could be split open and lie helpless in a field rather than surrounded by her daughters and her sons, with all her *enna*. Nonetheless, she remembered that Nei was also made of flesh.

Uya screamed.

The warrior that had gutted her mother circled back and pointed his spear at Uya. She saw the bloody point rise, but her limbs were cold and stiff as clay. The point of bronze bobbed and weaved as the rider approached her, her doom dripping from it with the blood of her mother and her Eldest, and she merely watched and hoped she would die quickly. But the rider's charge slowed. The point of the spear dropped, and the horses' gallop ebbed to a walk. They stopped just in front of her, the warrior staring down at her as if unable to comprehend why she was there. Uya shivered.

He uttered a short, hard word as if he were spitting out a stone. She backed up a step. She was *not* dead, for some reason she couldn't fathom, and the warrior before her did not seem to want to kill her immediately. She took a few more steps away. The man flung a handful of gravelly syllables at her, then trotted his horse closer. If he expected her to just stand there and listen to him, he was going to be disappointed. She turned and ran with all her might.

Her belly bounced, and the baby kicked in protest. Uya grunted and cradled her belly with her arms. With a swift flurry of hooves, the warrior overtook her and reared to a stop just in front of her. He jumped to the ground with a nimble leap.

Uya ran the other way, but she had barely gone three steps before his arms wrapped around her, closed beneath her breasts and lifted her off the ground as easily as a mother might pick up a fleeing child. She screamed and kicked back at him, but the baby squirmed with every movement of hers, and she stopped after a moment. The warrior was completely nonplussed by her feeble struggles.

Once she was still, he dropped her to the ground, and with a movement as swift as a grass snake, he seized both of her wrists and pinned her arms behind her back. He said something else in his horrible rocky tongue.

"I don't understand you," Uya said. "Shut up."

He stopped and watched her for a moment. Then he clasped both her wrists in one hand and reached for something on his saddle. She squirmed and kicked again, but even one-handed, he was stronger than her. In a moment, the man had retrieved the length of rope looped over the saddle and began twisting the cord around her wrists.

So he meant to take her captive. Captive, when every other member of the *enna* was slaughtered. A strange chill settled over her, a numbness as if she had fallen into the ocean in winter. The field was strewn with bodies. Nei, her Eldest, looked like a corn doll stained with berry juice. Her aunts lay in broken, horrible poses. There was Chrasu, last male of the *enna*, his body intact except for the skull, crushed by a horse's hoof, looking like a broken gourd. Her mother was spitted on the warrior's spear while she watched. But she was alive, and her child lived.

The man had remounted his horse and tugged at the rope binding her wrists. She stumbled forward a step. The tension sent spasms of anguish up her back and made the skin of her belly stretch, and she clenched her teeth against the strain. The other warriors had left them behind by now, so they walked alone through the field, tending slightly toward the south. She counted more bodies. Should she have been sad? She searched her gut for any feeling of sadness or mourning but found nothing. She was beyond sadness. She just kept walking. In the distance moved what looked like little warriors with toy people fleeing from them and painted flames fluttering up from the tops of a few of the lodges.

The man kept glancing back at her nervously, as if he thought she would bolt or attack him. He was older than she expected a warrior to be, gray at the temples, and his rough, short beard was streaked with white. Deep wrinkles folded around his eyes. Were it not for the bloody spear strapped to the side of his horse, she might have taken him for a kind old man, the Eldest of a fishing *enna*.

Their path bent to the south. She saw the peak of a lodge pass on her right. Its roof was busy with crows returned from the feast of the battlefield. They passed the few other lodges that were scattered further south of the city.

Ahead, at the southernmost extremity of the city, a pair of sentries waited in a clearing between the trees. The warrior leading her shouted something and nudged his horse forward, jogging Uya forward and making her cry out in pain. The man stopped, looked at her with an expression of pity, and then let her follow at the slow pace her pregnancy allowed.

The sentries yelled back at them. A hurried dispute ensued between her captor and the two guards, which ended when the warrior finally handed his end of the rope to one of the sentries, then turned and galloped back to the north.

The sentry gave her a suspicious look and spat a word that sounded like a curse. He jerked at her rope, much less gently than her original captor, and dragged her over to a nearby spruce. The bouncing of her belly and strain on her back made her whimper. The other sentry said something, and the two began to argue, pointing at this and that branch up and down the tree. It ended when the first threw his end of the rope over a low bough in disgust, and the other secured it with a sloppy knot. They turned their backs to her and resumed watching the forest.

Maybe if she pulled on the knot, she could get it loose. Then she would merely be a single pregnant woman in the woods at the edge of a city that had been massacred. And then she would die. The thought came as a sort of relief. She would join the *enna* and be free of the aches of her body and the sorrow in her chest.

But the baby kicked. *Oh.* She sagged against the tree and rested her head against the bark. No. She wouldn't die yet. She couldn't. Not yet.

CHAPTER 8

KESHLIK

B Y SUNDOWN, KESHLIK HAD RIDDEN the entire length of the city, north-to-south and east-to-west, four times. The city had been routed by noon, with the militia along the earthworks crushed between Bhaalit's feint and the larger wave of Yakhat that had surged up from the south. Since then it had been a matter of driving scattered groups of women and unarmed men out of houses, finding the ones that were wealthy enough to loot, and burning or trashing the rest. Everyone that could had fled the city, and those that couldn't had already been killed. Here and there little packs of desperate city dwellers still tried to salvage something from their ruined homes or gather the bodies of family, but they hid like rats whenever the Yakhat warriors came into view, and it wasn't worth their trouble to chase them. The ecstasy of the battle had ebbed into tedium.

He rode to the southern cordon to bring in the sentries. A rowdy sort of camp had formed up in the middle of the city, and there was no need to continue guarding the southern border.

The men assigned to the southern cordon were testy and bored at that point, and resentful of being asked to guard his pregnant captive. When Keshlik told them to leave their posts and go claim their portion of the pillage, they charged off with whoops and hollers, leaving him alone with the woman he had taken. They had tied her to a tree and apparently ignored her after that. He rode up and dismounted.

The woman turned toward him. She recognized him from the battle and didn't flinch when he undid the knot binding her to the tree. He glanced at her wrists, still pinched together and chafing against the rope.

"Do you want me to undo that?" he asked. An unbound prisoner was more troublesome to guard, but he would rather not keep her in pain.

She stared at him in incomprehension. At least she didn't seem to be afraid. A cowering, cringing captive was harder to deal with than one who would walk in a straight line. Plus, his obligation to the woman would require a certain amount of cooperation from her. He reached forward for the rope around her wrists. She pulled back, but a moment later, she understood his intention and offered him her hands. He soon had the knot undone and began to wind the rope into loops.

She rubbed her wrists, studied him, then said something. Their language was soft and slippery, the sounds running together like water.

He guessed at what she said and responded, "You're welcome."

She continued to watch him, with an expression that seemed to combine confusion and sadness. He threw the rope loop over his horse's back and pointed to the north. "Follow me. You'll have to walk."

He accepted the risk that she might try to bolt, which would lead to a tedious and pointless chase, but the woman seemed to sense the futility of fleeing. Though her face betrayed a slight disappointment, she began to plod forward in the direction that Keshlik pointed.

The city was already a ruin. Bodies littered the earth like stones, and the air swarmed with crows. The lodges were either burnt or spewing loot and rubbish from their doors. The woman's eyes darted from ruin to ruin, but she neither wept nor recoiled. And when packs of drunken warriors careened by, swearing and singing, she didn't flinch.

He prodded her ahead of them into the center of the city, where they had found the largest and richest building. The open square in front of it was now filled with yurts and loot, warriors lighting up smoky fires, horses coming and going. The chief warriors of the tribes had taken up residence in former shops or warehouses, and they had heaped up piles of plunder and draped them with their tribal standards. The looting continued throughout the city, with men carrying in armfuls of furs, foods, and chests brimming with gold, silver, turquoise, and mother-of-pearl. Great casks of frothy wine had been discovered somewhere and set out in the middle of the square. Drunk fighters slouched around it, singing bawdy songs and shouting slobbery boasts at one another. Keshlik prodded the woman away from them. The younger warriors were weak in their fear of the Powers, and in their post-battle debauchery, even a pregnant woman might tempt them too much.

A lofty lodge on the west side of the square bore the Khaatat banner. Juyut had stuck to the post that Keshlik had given him. He slouched in the doorway with his spear slung across his knees and a canteen of wine next to him, bumbling his way through a chant that recounted the kills he'd made that day. When he saw Keshlik approaching he stood quickly to his feet and shouted, "Hail, brother! Hail captain of the Yakhat war bands! Now what in Golgoyat's nutsack did you bring with you?"

"A woman," Keshlik said.

Juyut ogled the woman's belly. He leaned toward Keshlik and attempted to whisper, "There were prettier girls in the city today, you know. And ones who were less... rotund."

"I brought her *because* she's rotund. A woman this pregnant is under Khou's protection. I couldn't harm her."

"Khou's protection? Does Khou protect the enemies of Golgoyat now, too?"

"This one, she does."

Juyut glanced from Keshlik to the woman and back. "There were other pregnant women in the city today." His expression wobbled between shame and amusement. "My men weren't so protective of all of them."

"Then maybe your men should pray they don't fall under Khou's wrath."

"Khou's wrath! Ha! A woman's wrath! As if the warriors of Golgoyat are afraid of that."

"Don't forget that Khou was Golgoyat's wife."

"Was. *Was*, brother. But there's been no wedding for the two of them since we left the Bans, which means that we warriors"—he shrugged indifferently—"what do we care?"

There was, alas, a certain logic to that. He'd learned the fear of Khou as a boy in the Bans, but those born under Golgoyat's spear had suckled different milk. Keshlik couldn't force them into the old reverence, and he was no fool. Though he had never struck a madman or a pregnant woman, he knew better than to assume that every warrior in his charge respected those taboos. That was half his reason for taking the woman under his care: if he had left her alone, she would probably have been dead by now.

"You'll care if I say you care," he told Juyut. "Now step aside."

"Aye, aye." He ducked his head and stepped aside for Keshlik and the woman to pass. "I'll care, if I have to."

The lodge was gloomy and dull on the inside. Its valuables had been ransacked and redistributed, and sloppy heaps of loot lined the walls. Juyut had cleared a place for his and Keshlik's bedrolls. Keshlik pointed to the ground and told his captive, "You sleep here."

The woman stared at him blankly. He grunted and laid out a bedroll for the woman, then pointed at her, and then the bed. She shrieked and pulled away, backing into a corner in terror. He took her by the shoulders and tried to push her to the ground. She screamed and retreated further. *Khou's tits, why didn't we bring any of the Guza translators with us?*

"I'm not going to hurt you!" Raising his own voice didn't help, of course. She looked like a startled antelope.

"Juyut!" His brother's wine-ruddied face appeared in the doorway. "Stay here and make sure she doesn't get away."

"What exactly are we doing with her?"

"I took her as under Khou's protection, and I'll deliver her into Khou's protection! She'll stay with Tuulo. In the meantime, I have to meet with the other speakers, and she needs to eat. Find her something—there ought to be plenty to choose from."

Juyut looked annoyed, but he nodded. "When will you be back?"

"Before midnight. Once I return, you can go join the revel. But if anything happens to the woman, you'll pay for it with your own skin. Do you understand?"

Juyut bowed and raised the canteen of wine. "As you say, my brother, my chief."

As soon as Keshlik emerged from the storehouse's shadow, he heard Bhaalit.

"Come, Keshlik! There's something you should see." Bhaalit stood with Dheijit of the Tanoutut and Choudhap of the Lougok at the edges of the square, watching the ongoing debauch.

As soon as Keshlik joined them, Dheijit said, "We've found the chief of the city."

"Eh?" Keshlik asked. "I would have thought that he had fled. Or died."

"He fled. A group of our warriors came across a band of four trying to sneak out of a lodge on the south fringe of the city. They followed the band a little ways and found a small encampment just south of the city. He was among them."

"The others?"

"We killed some, scattered the rest. But this one spoke Guza, and he claimed to be the city's chief."

Keshlik grunted. "Take me to him."

Bhaalit pointed to the shadow of the largest lodge. "He's over there."

An old man was sitting on the ground between two listless Yakhat warriors. When Keshlik approached, he struggled to his feet and haughtily looked down his long, narrow nose. His gray hair hung from the top of his head to his waist, bound by a clasp of silver at the neck, and he wore a cloak of otter fur. Mud splattered his face and cloak.

Keshlik walked to within a handsbreadth of him and looked him in the eye. The man did not flinch or look away. "Are you the chief of this city?" he asked in Guza.

"I am." He pointed to the lodge behind them. "This is my family's lodge."

His accent was peculiar, but his speech was intelligible. "This *was* your family's lodge," Keshlik said. "You have no claim to it now."

"You blood-smeared dogs haven't undone my inheritance of this place."

Keshlik smirked. "No one cares that you once belonged to this place." The old man stiffened but didn't respond. "Where were you going?"

"To the south."

Keshlik smacked the man across the mouth. "Don't tell me things I already know. Now *where were you going*?"

The chief raised a hand to his wrinkled cheek. His pride seemed to smolder. "To Kendilar," he said quietly.

"What is Kendilar?"

"A city."

"Give me better answers, or you'll take another fist to the mouth. Are there other chiefs there?"

"The *kenda* is there."

"The *kenda*? Who is that? Use words that I understand."

The old man pulled his cloak around his shoulders and glowered.

"Talk, old man, or I'll cut your eyeballs out."

The chief spat on Keshlik's foot. The warriors around them surged forward, screaming and waving spears.

"Stop," Keshlik said. He wiped the chief's saliva from his boot. "Why did you do that?"

"Nothing I do will save my life, anyway. The only reason I've told you as much as I have is I want you to know that your doom is coming. The *kenda* is chief of a city twenty times larger than this one, where the lodges are made of stone and the ancestor totems are silver. I sent him word of your approach when I first learned of it, and in a few days, the story of Prasa's fall will reach him. We are children of Vanasenar, and our alliance goes back to the Breaking. He has more spears than there are trees in the forest. It will be the end of you. And when your men lie dead in the grass, he will piss on your grave."

Keshlik looked to Bhaalit and the other tribal speakers. They understood the man's speech, though the rest of the warriors standing guard did not. Bhaalit shrugged.

"If it's true," Bhaalit said in Yakhat, "there's nothing we can do about it now."

"And the man did us a favor by telling us." Keshlik turned back to the chief and spoke in Guza. "This was your lodge?"

The chief nodded.

"And these animal totems represent your ancestors?"

Wariness darkened the chief's face. He didn't respond.

Keshlik looked at Bhaalit but spoke in Guza. "Tie this man in the square so he can see the lodge. Have our men fasten ropes around the pole and pull it to the ground, then let every warrior come to shit on these glorious, silver-inlaid totems—though maybe we should scrape the silver out of them first. When you're done, torch the pole and the lodge. Only then is the chief allowed to die."

CHAPTER 9

SAOTSE

SAOTSE AWOKE TO DAMP AND chilly silence. The ground beneath her fingers was cold and wet. The leaves overhead shook ominously. So she had slept, but for how long? The sun must have set; the air was cool with the touch of evening. Obviously no one had found her. That was probably a good thing. But now she was awake, and it was night, and she had to decide what to do and where to go.

Far above her, a breeze whispered in the crown of the trees, and the branches muttered and moaned. Chaoare's voice rippled in the wind, but the Power herself was far away, and the spirits of the trees barely quivered. Water lapped against the shore not too far away, and its slosh carried the faintest echo of the sea's thunder and the terrible roaring of Oarsa. Saotse could feel it even now, and it made her bones ache. "Oarsa, help us," she whispered again, but even as she said it, her hope receded like the tide from the shore. Oarsa had not answered her once in the past fifty years. If the Powers of this place had not intervened to save the city, then her prayers wouldn't rouse them now.

A moan of despair spilled from her mouth. She was alone, entirely alone. Uya and Oire had not come. She knew that Nei had been dead from the moment that the first charge broke through their line. But Uya? Oire? Chrasu? The rest of the *enna*? Were they dead, or had they forgotten her? Had they fled to safety alone?

She heard no human voices. The battle must have been long gone, then. She lay her head against the ground. Pine needles pricked at her forehead, and loamy soil pressed against her temples.

The smell of moss, earthworms, and mushrooms flooded her with loneliness and heartbreak. She whimpered and curled into a ball. The vastness of her abandonment oppressed her. In her solitude, she remembered every footstep from there to her home, across the high plains, the passes and the cold deserts and the steppes, the plains and the marshes. Every step drenched in blood and soaked in strife. She was endlessly longing, endlessly seeking the place of her marriage—

With a gasp, Saotse returned to herself. That was not her memory. *Whose, then?*

As soon as she asked, she knew. She felt the strange Power keening just below the surface of the earth, alone and far from home. Saotse had fallen from her own sadness into the chasm of the Power's. The Power was one of the invaders, but she was *not* one of *them*, not with the warriors. *Their* voices roiled with a different strength, darker and windy and flashing with rage. The loneliness of the earth was not theirs. But the earth one wielded tremendous power, though it was unfocused, scattered, as fine as dust.

She touched her forehead again to the earth, breathing deep the dark earthiness of the soil. She opened herself to the touch of the Power, inviting the spirit to speak. Unlike Chaoare and Oarsa and the others whose names she knew, this one did not shy away, did not hover just beyond the crying of her lonely soul. As if sinking into a pool of mud, Saotse slipped slowly into the Power's sorrow.

The spirit soaked her. Her mouth and her nostrils felt as if they filled with dirt, and her fingers reached into the soil like roots. Down, down, down, burrowing with the blind, fertile things of the earth, a sister to moles and earthworms, a mother to ants. She bore trees on her shoulders and grew mushrooms from her hands. She exhaled grass. Her thighs were hills; her feet, an outcropping of stone.

We are lonely. Saotse spoke for herself, but her voice was of the Power that embraced her. She was crushed with a memory: a husband who flashed like lightning, strong and fierce as the whirlwind, now distant and estranged, still receding from her with the children that they had borne.

Saotse added her own thoughts, of the *enna* that was kind to her but was not her family, of the girl who had been like her sister but who bloomed into womanhood just as Saotse faded into age, of loneliness, of abandonment.

This is not our home. Home was a marsh that stretched from horizon to horizon, soft wet earth covered with reeds, thick with birds, pregnant with fish, garbed in swampy mist. Little dry hillocks rose above the murk, where men lived and tended herds of dirty white cattle, where women wove clothes from reeds and sang songs.

Saotse added her home from the depth of her memories: a line of wooden cottages above the sea, clinging to the walls of a fjord. Blue mountains rising overhead like knives. The sky white and icy in winter. A hearth of stone, yellow flames kindled by wrinkled brown hands, a haven against the screaming winds.

They have destroyed it. Blood watered the earth. The soil turned black, the water red. Men groaned and gurgled as they were hacked to pieces, gutted, torn. Women wept and begged for mercy. The Power was torn from her husband. She was torn from her family. This hour of destruction bestrode time like a mountain over the plains. It did not pass. She was raped every dawn; her husband was killed every evening. The horror and the sorrow bloomed like the grass, renewed every day in perpetual memory.

Saotse added the sound of hooves, the screams of the *enna*, and the smoke of Prasa. Wails of despair went up from both of them.

"Did you hear that?"

Saotse woke as if from a dream. She was a woman again. She was alone, beneath a shrub, hidden in a stand of spruce. The Power had left her. *No, not again. I can't bear it!*—but in the moment that she thought she was alone, she smelled again the humid breath of the broken-hearted earth. Saotse relaxed. The Power, whatever her name, did not seem eager to abandon her.

And now, present in herself, feeling only the dirt beneath her hands, she heard a second voice reply, "Be quiet, or they'll hear you."

There were two of them, both men. They were Prasei, not invaders, judging by their voices and the furtive way they shuffled through the wood. The invaders did not speak Praseo. And if these were Prasei, then they might be able to help her.

Saotse raised her voice just above a whisper. "Hello?"

Their movement stopped. "Who's there?" someone replied, with a suspicious edge to their voice.

"I'm from Prasa," she said. "Of Nei's *enna*. I hid here, but I can't see you—"

"Quiet," he scolded. "There are still riders in the city. Where are you?"

"Beneath a bush of some kind. Here, let me come." She began to crawl toward the sound of their talking.

"Can you see me waving?"

"I'm blind."

"Blind?" The man grunted in annoyance. The other muttered something just below her hearing, but she could guess what it was.

"Don't leave me," she said. "My *enna* is gone. I've been hiding here all day. Please, I'll just—"

"Quiet! I think I can hear you moving." Their steps rustled closer to her. "Can you wave? Are you standing up?"

"I can stand." Her knees creaked with cold stiffness as she bent them to rise. A little gasp of pain escaped her mouth.

"I see her," said the second man, the one who had muttered. "Just behind that spruce."

"Stay there. We'll come to you."

Footsteps crunched through the thicket. A heavy hand touched her shoulder. "Over here, auntie. Quiet."

She turned toward the voice, and the man's hand took hers. His skin was rough and callused, a worker's hand.

"We have a canoe at the water's edge, but we have to stick to the woods. Can you follow?"

"You might need to carry her," the other said.

"No, I can walk," she insisted. "I'm not a cripple."

"Good. What's your name, auntie?"

"Saotse."

"Really? I've never heard that name before."

"I'm not from here." A twinge of shame tightened her belly. "I am a swift woman."

"What?" asked the other man. His voice was rougher, thicker, suggesting he was much older than the one holding her hand. "She's not even Prasei?"

"I've lived here for many years," she said. "In Nei's *enna*, as I said."

"Never mind," said the younger one beside her. "I am Tagoa, and my brother is Bera."

"May the Powers remember your names."

Bera snorted. "Better than they remembered the names of Prasa. Now, let's go."

Tagoa pulled her forward, and she kept up, feeling ahead with her toes to find the roots and the stones that she had to step over, ducking wherever the man warned her of spruce branches. The lapping of the seashore grew closer. The scent of the wood mingled with the cool smell of the water, and the ground under her feet changed from moss and fallen needles into bristly shore grass.

"So what now," Bera said. "Do we leave her here and go back?"

"We can't leave her here," Tagoa replied. "Anyone who rode by the shore would see her, and then they'd find the canoe, and then we'd be done for."

"But we didn't come for an old woman!"

"Well, we've got what we've got."

"We could have her lie down in the canoe and wait."

"I would do that," she said. Hiding in the strangers' canoe was humiliating, but at that moment, she was happy to trade her pride for her life.

Bera growled. "Fine, but we'll have to find what we can quickly. Hurry up and get her in the canoe."

With a sigh, Tagoa tugged on her hand. "You'll have to follow me. We hid the canoe in the brush. If you lie down in the bottom, you should be safe. We'll be back before long."

They hurried along the shore. A thorny shore brush scratched at her legs, then her knee knocked against the wooden side of a canoe.

"Up, now." Tagoa grabbed her elbow and helped her up. The canoe rocked in the mud as Saotse knelt in the bottom. "Just wait a little while. We won't be long."

They sloshed up the shore until their steps padded into the grass and disappeared. Saotse knelt with her head between her knees, trying not to shake and set the canoe splashing in the shallow water. A chill had started in her feet, wet and exposed to the cool night air. But at least someone had found her. If she had stayed in the copse, with the city full of raiders, it might have been days before someone found her, and... She would not think about it.

Her misery descended like a mist. She briefly felt the keening of the earthy Power. But the water touching the canoe stirred. A distant presence, vast and deep, thrummed in her chest with a painful sweetness. It was *him*, and even this attenuated echo nearly overwhelmed her. It brought forth a memory of splashing in the surf as a girl, of the water rising up to kiss her, of the whales ascending to proudly bear their master's maid.

Oarsa. The faint footfall was as close as she had heard him since she had first descended onto the shores of the Prasei, and he was drawing closer. He passed by *now*? Now, when the city was already ruined? Now, when she had wept for him for decades? Anger welled.

The waters around the canoe sang. Her mouth filled with the smell of seawater and sand, and she felt the Power's tug like a current swallowing a canoe. No. Her toes dug into the floor of the canoe, and she braced herself against the sides as if the sea's Power would lift her bodily into the water. *No.*

And like letting out a breath pent up under the water, he passed. The water ceased leaping. The winds moved. She was alone again.

She shook for a moment in the floor of the canoe, then realized that she could hear her rescuers approaching.

"—Most of it," Tagoa said.

"But we found the cask, and that's what's important. Auntie, are you still there?"

Saotse raised herself to her knees. The canoe wobbled beneath her. "I'm here."

"Good, but get back down!" A moment later, they splashed into the shallows and dropped something into the bottom of the boat. The canoe tipped to one side as someone climbed in next to Saotse, then the other began to push the craft free of the sucking mud. A moment later he, too, leapt over the prow and nudged the canoe away from shore with an oar.

"Did you find what you were looking for?" Saotse asked.

Bera laughed from the front of the canoe. "Most of the city is burned already. The raiders have been through most of the lodges. But we got the things we wanted from our lodge."

"And where are we going now?"

"Ruhasu."

Ruhasu was a fishing village on the shores of the bay a few

miles north of Prasa. In the fall, after the salmon run, the Ruhasei would bring the surplus of the fish they had smoked and sell it to the traders. Saotse had spent many an hour assisting Nei in that barter.

"Have many other Prasei fled that way?" she asked. *Maybe Uya, Oire, Chrasu, and others will be waiting for me there.*

"My father's *enna* is in Ruhasu, so we moved most of ours up that way. My brother and I turned back only to see if we could find anything in the city of use to us."

"Ah." So they were from the poor regions just south of the river. And they were cowards and looters. But they were also alive, in the same pitiable state as Saotse.

"I expect you're right, though, auntie. Ruhasu will grow in the next few days," Tagoa said quietly. "We're not the only ones who got away. We'll see who else drifts in."

The water around the raft gurgled with their oar strokes. Saotse heard a muttered word in its movement, and she felt Oarsa's whisper. She put her hands over her ears and hid her head in the bottom of the canoe until the Power's presence abated, and she heard no more save the rippling of their oars.

CHAPTER 10

UYA

UYA HAD LEARNED EXACTLY TWO of their names: Keshlik and Juyut. She practiced turning Keshlik's name into a curse, spitting it violently from her lips ask if she were expelling a fish bone. Their language had just the sound for swearing, too. It was full of short, rough sounds, like stones on the seashore grinding together.

She lay in a storeroom, just long enough for her to stretch out. Her hands were bound in leather thongs and tied to a post. The fibers chafed her wrists, red and raw from her four days of captivity. It would have been worse, except that Keshlik came four times a day to bring her food, unbind her ropes, and massage her wrists. Sometimes this seemed like kindness. Sometimes she stopped hating him. But the muscles of her back ached from the way the child sat inside her, and her feet continued to swell, and she remembered her hatred.

A Yakhat face appeared in the doorway. It was Juyut, the younger one, whom she guessed was Keshlik's brother or nephew. He glanced in at her then left, shouting a response to someone unseen.

Keshlik appeared a moment later. He spoke a few soft words, then knelt and began to undo the ropes binding her hands.

"What's this?" she asked. He had no tray of food, and it was too early to eat.

He grunted. In a moment, her hands were free, and she began rubbing her wrists. Keshlik stood and offered her his hand.

She looked at it and continued massaging her chafed skin. She wasn't about to accompany him anywhere if she could help it.

He bent and grabbed her arm just below the elbow, then pulled her roughly upright. An arrow of pain stabbed through her feet, and her legs folded like reeds, unable to uphold her body. Keshlik caught her under her shoulder before she hit the ground. He propped her up so her feeble legs barely touched the ground, and he helped her limp forward from the storeroom.

Her body had discovered all sorts of new pains in her four days tied up. Her legs shrieked with the effort of holding up her pregnant body, and her spine burned and creaked as Keshlik guided her forward. The baby squirmed in her belly, protesting the movement. Uya winced at the light as the warehouse's shadow slipped behind them, then opened her eyes.

The old market square was full of men on horses, packs brimming with plunder, clouds of yellow dust, carts creaking under their loads. The carts were pulled by stout Prasei ponies, looking dwarfish next to the tall, slender Yakhat breeds. Keshlik pulled her to a cart half-filled with furs and hemp sacks and motioned for her to sit. Were they all leaving, or just her? She heaved herself and her belly up onto the cart and took up a position she hoped she could hold for a few hours. Keshlik tied her hands to the rail of the cart.

He grunted and said something in their abrasive dialect. She spat at him and tugged at the rope. She had plenty of slack to move, but the knots themselves were tight.

She laid back against the hemp sacks of plunder that filled up the rest of the cart. Something sharp and brittle dug into her back. She shifted once or twice, unable to find a comfortable position, and heard the sack's contents scrape together. The bag shifted in a new direction, and something clattered against the boards of the cart.

She glanced over her shoulder. It was a mussel shell, the sort used for jewelry. Her breath stopped.

The savages had no idea how sharp a broken shell could be. She quickly closed her hand over the shell and tucked it into the waist of her skirt. She folded her hands in front of her and shifted so that the shell was hidden between her and the other loot.

Her heart pounded. Keshlik rode back and forth across the square, talking to one group of men and then another, while carts and laden horses began to leave in batches.

No one had seen her grab the shell.

Finally Keshlik's brother came out of the warehouse they'd slept in, carrying the orange and blue banner that had hung above the door, and a group of men converged around him, shouting and chanting. Keshlik said a few words, and the whole group moved out in a line, with Uya's cart in the middle of the train.

The dogs had had their run of the city. Filth, filth everywhere. Perhaps a third of the lodges that Uya saw were burned down, leaving skeletons of charred wood over rotten beds of ash. Others had brutal trails of splintered wood, trampled rags, and broken pottery weeping from their entrances. Ancestor totems had been toppled, their painted faces defaced with mud and urine. Charnel heaps of bones blackened the ground where bodies had been piled and burned.

She chuckled in black mirth as they rode past the useless heap that remained of the earthworks. So much effort to defend the city, and they hadn't saved anyone.

Keshlik and his brother rode in front of her at the head of the procession, a straggling line of horsemen and carts behind them. She sighed and leaned herself into the side rails of the cart. They entered the forest beyond the city, and the scar of the earthworks receded.

Despair tightened her throat. She had never been north of

90

Prasa. She had never been far from her *enna* and their lodge, had never traveled with the men even as far as the little villages on the north shore of the bay. And now she was leaving, tied like an animal to a cart, with the city in ruins.

She fingered the hidden shell, then tugged it from its place and pressed it against the wood of the cart's bed. The wheel hit a rock, the cart lurched, and her weight snapped the shell in half. She ran her finger over the edge, as sharp as a knife, then hid it in her fist.

<hr />

They traveled without pause until after sunset. Keshlik left Uya tied to the cart while he and the warriors around him made camp, with small fires and bedrolls on the ground. The horses wandered into the forest in search of grass. Keshlik came to Uya with an old bedroll under one arm and loosed one end of the tie, leading her to a place a little ways from the main encampment. So he intended to give her privacy. Well, he would regret that.

He did not untie her, nor did he check what she clenched in her fist. He tied the other end of the rope binding her wrists to a nearby pine. A few moments later, he brought food and set it on her woolen bedroll: jerky, dry cheese with a strange smell, and a few leaves of pressed kelp looted from Prasa. He left without a word.

She ate only a few bites, despite her piercing hunger. She had to save something for her flight, regardless of the insistence of her stomach. The warriors gathered around the fire, talking in their gravelly tongue, while she sat atop her bedroll. Keshlik glanced her way every few minutes, but the rest of them ignored her.

Darkness fell. She lay down on the matted wool. She could look down the trade road and see a long line of glittering yellow fires trailing back toward Prasa. She would have to avoid them all.

91

She stayed awake, determination firing her mind, as one by one, the warriors around the closest fire fell asleep.

Finally, only Keshlik and Juyut remained awake. After a last glance into the woods, Keshlik lay down, and his brother stood, stretching. Loosening his belt, he walked into the woods on the far side of the road.

Now. She took the shard of shell and sliced at the leather binding her hands. It bit and cut back a piece as long as a thumbnail. She kept cutting until the leather was ragged. Juyut returned from the shadows and stood over the fire. She tore at the leather with the shell one more time then pulled the ties apart with a snap.

Juyut looked her way. She froze.

For a long moment, the only sound was the beating of her heart. Then the warrior relaxed and resumed watching the heart of the fire.

Uya scooped up the remaining food and folded it into the corner of her blouse. She slipped off the bedroll and into the ferns with only a ghostly rustling, and she padded away into the forest.

The Powers smiled on her. The night was clear, and the moon half full. She could see just well enough to avoid the largest sticks and stones in her path as she scrambled through the ferny undergrowth away from the fire.

There was no commotion behind her. Had Juyut not heard her leave? She dared not believe that the Powers had blessed her as much as that.

The night grew chilly, and wisps of mist rose into the air. Her pace slowed. Her breath came hard, and her feet ached. The moon slipped beneath the peaks of the spruces in the west, and with its passing, the forest floor became as dark as ink. Only the cold, white stars lit her path. She could not stop until she had put enough distance between herself and the warriors.

She went on, feeling with hands and toes for the obstacles in her path, until her foot slipped on a mossy stone. She tumbled to the ground.

She twisted to land on her back rather than her stomach, and the blow knocked the breath from her lungs. She struggled to breathe and watched the stars swim. Her back throbbed, and nausea rose from her stomach. Was the baby okay? Had they heard her? Had she fled far enough?

She tried to rise but collapsed back to the earth with a groan. It would have to be far enough, because she could go no further tonight. A little ways away, some low-hanging spruce boughs offered some shelter. She crawled to them then collapsed into the bed of needles. In an instant, she was asleep.

———— ❦ ————

Uya awoke to rain dripping on her face. She sat up and shook a shower of water loose from a low-hanging pine branch. A quick glance at the sky brought a twist of fear to her stomach.

The sky was swaddled in clouds, and mist hovered over the tops of the spruces. In the murky gray light, she had no idea which way was east, and she was bereft of any landmark. She had only been this far from Prasa once, when her father had taken her with the men to the edge of the valley, to see where the pines grew short and let out onto the great yellow sea of grass. There were few villages near here, and she might wander for days before finding one. She didn't even know which way to flee.

Downhill. The sea was downhill, and her only option was to follow the water to it.

She rose. The pain in her back had subsided, and her feet had grown numb with cold. But the worrying twitches in her stomach from the night before had stopped, and at least she wouldn't feel the sharp twigs underfoot anymore. After checking her feet and finding them bloody and blue, she decided not to look again. She untied the corner of her blouse and ate a strip of jerky and a cube of cheese, then stumbled forward out of her shelter.

The forest sloped down gently to her right. She followed

it, ferns soaking her skirt as she swished past them. Misty rain dripped down from the fog overhead, soaking her clothes in a few minutes and plastering her hair to her head. She began to shiver.

A fire. She would need a fire tonight—except that she had no dry wood, and nothing with which to light it. She didn't even have a blanket. She had to keep walking. The heat of her movement was the only heat she had. She shivered again and fought the urge to weep.

The gray gradually brightened. Somewhere above the clouds, the sun was rising toward noonday, though the drizzle showed no signs of stopping. Hunger began to gnaw at her throat, but she denied it. She needed food, for herself and for the child, but she still needed to wait.

Then she heard the crackle of a footstep behind her.

Uya froze. In the distance, a man, his face the color of red clay, loped swiftly through the forest, looking toward the ground. In the next moment, he raised his eyes and saw her.

His shout splintered the peace of the forest.

Uya tried to run, but even as she turned, she knew it was hopeless. Her feet slipped on the mossy ground, and her belly shortened her stride.

The man was beside her, grabbing at her wrists and shoulders. She squirmed away and slid to the ground. The man jumped to where she had fallen and pinned her shoulders down.

She jerked and swatted at him once, twice, but it was futile. Her escape had lasted less than a day.

CHAPTER 11

KESHLIK

K ESHLIK WOUND THE BANDAGES AROUND the woman's feet as tight as he could make them. "Does that help?"

Her expression was dead, blank. She had been mute since the scouting party carried her back to the caravan, and she'd let them tie her up with no more resistance than a doll. Her determination to escape had surprised him, but her failure seemed to have sapped that energy from her.

"I don't know why you bothered going after her," Juyut said from atop his horse. "You took her under Khou's protection, but once she left…"

"So you let the plunder just get up and run away, now?" Keshlik checked the knots binding the woman to the cart then verified that nothing sharp was within her reach.

"The woman is plunder, now?"

"I'm giving her to Tuulo for a slave."

"That's not what you said before."

Keshlik remounted Lashkat and whistled for the party to move. The cart jerked and moved forward. Lashkat whinnied at the pony pulling the cart then plodded forward next to Juyut and his mount.

"Maybe I changed my mind," Keshlik said. "It amounts to the same thing."

Juyut spat. "Nothing good can come of it. The woman has already been more trouble than she's worth."

———— ❖ ————

Keshlik could not remember the last time that he had brought so many spoils into the Khaatat camp. The whole tribe came to meet the warriors, and their surprise and pleasure resounded off the walls of the yurts. But he already had more treasure than he could use. At the first opportunity he found Dhuja, who was examining a necklace of hammered silver.

"I brought a woman back from Prasa," he told her.

"Is she as pretty as this?" she asked, holding up the looted jewelry.

"She's pregnant. She needs to go into Khou's circle with Tuulo."

Dhuja looked up, her brows pinched into a scowl. "You brought a pregnant city-dweller woman here? Khou's tits, why?"

"She is under Khou's protection. I couldn't kill her."

Dhuja laughed. "I don't think many people remember those old taboos." But her scowl faded.

"So you can bring her into the circle? She will at least be company for Tuulo."

"Does she speak any language that we know?"

"She may know a little Guza. I'll bring the translator to talk to her."

"Good enough." Dhuja folded the necklace and dropped it into her pouch. "My grandsons bring me gifts from the slaughter, and the war leader of the Yakhat brings me another charge. I shouldn't be surprised. Bring her to me."

Keshlik fetched the woman and presented her to Dhuja. The midwife looked her over, pursing her lips and poking at the captive's belly and breasts. "She looks healthy. I'll bless her with the salt and take her to Tuulo. Don't come to the circle until that's done. After I have resealed the line of blessing, you can come speak to your wife."

"I'll be there when you're ready."

The anticipation of seeing Tuulo again warmed his belly and added a tint of mirth to his voice as he traded stories with the other Khaatat warriors. A glance back at the isolated yurt showed that both Dhuja and the woman of Prasa had disappeared inside. He slipped away from the circle of yurts and went to the line of burnt earth calling his wife's name.

Tuulo came out from the yurt smiling, huffing, and heaving her belly around. She had gotten as round and red as a berry.

"Eighteen days since I last saw you," Keshlik said. "How is it that you look almost ready to give birth already?"

She smiled at him and shook her head. "I'd give birth right now, if the baby would only come. I'm sick of it. My back hurts, my breasts feel like overfilled canteens, and Khou's circle has gotten awfully small."

"I'm so sorry. I'd carry the baby for you if I could."

She laughed out loud. "That'd be a sight to see. Would you still go riding into the battle with a baby in your belly?"

"Ah, maybe not. But if I carried the baby, then you'd have to carry the spear."

"Dhuja would slap us if she heard us talking this way. Or at least scold me for half a day." She smirked at Keshlik and glanced slyly back at the yurt. "Were you victorious in Prasa?"

"Golgoyat himself fought among us. But nineteen spears were broken."

"May their smoke rise to Golgoyat." She closed her eyes and cupped her hand over her mouth, then opened it upward to offer her breath to the sky. "Were they Khaatat?"

"No, none of ours. A few of the Chalayit, a few of the Budhut, and some from several of the other tribes. All from Bhaalit's group. The hardest fighting fell to them, as they had to assault the north wall while the rest of us attacked the undefended south. I've rewarded their clans with an extra quarter portion of the spoils. And the spoils of Prasa were rich, Tuulo."

"Well, I saw that you brought me a slave. Did you think that I was lonely in the yurt with just my midwife?"

He laughed. "Well, I didn't bring her for that. I wouldn't slay her, since she's under Khou's protection."

"And you couldn't just leave her there?"

"And let the other men get her?"

Tuulo gave him a skeptical glare. "I can't believe this is the first time you've found a pregnant woman on your raids. And you've never brought one home before."

That question had rattled in the back of his mind ever since Juyut had mentioned it. He hesitated. "I've never had a wife inside Khou's circle before. Perhaps I'm especially afraid to anger her now."

"The leader of the Yakhat war bands fears a woman now?" She smirked.

"I know. Juyut said the same thing."

"Really? That's probably the first time that we've agreed on something. In any case, she's already been cleansed and brought into the circle, so there's no getting rid of her now. Though I have no idea what we're supposed to do with her once she gives birth."

"I'll leave that to you and Dhuja. But what about you? Are you well? Is the baby well?"

"It kicks like a colt, which I hope means it's well. Dhuja says that all of my signs are positive, and that I'll bear before the new moon. And oh, I hope she's right. My back hurts, I can't sleep, and I can barely walk. I'm ready to have a *baby* and not just a *belly*."

Keshlik looked at her with a gush of fatherly pride. He reached across the line toward her, stopping with his fingers a few inches away from her cheek. She blushed and looked away.

"Do you think it's a boy or a girl?" he asked.

"Dhuja says that I have the signs for a boy. But I don't really know."

"We'll find out soon enough."

"Will you be here?"

"I don't know. We've routed the city and plundered most of the homesteads north of the river. As far as the Guza have told us, there is no one else in this country that could challenge us. But there's always *something*." The Praseo chief's warning about Kendilar tickled at the back of his mind, but he wouldn't burden Tuulo with that. He sighed. "I'd like to rest from raiding for a while. I've been riding for so many years, it would be nice to lay down my spear for a while. I'd like to be here when our child comes."

She smiled at him. "It'll be soon."

He glanced back at the circle of Khaatat yurts. "But not yet. I have to go speak to the elders and the warriors. We have to ensure our mastery of Prasa and the plains. And Juyut isn't ready to take up leadership. Soon, though. Soon."

By the time he returned to the center of the encampment, the spoils had been divided. The Khaatat share was generous, and the portion allotted to every yurt was abundant. Almost too much.

A lifetime of plunder had made the Yakhat rich. Their flocks were descendants of those long-haired cattle that they had first seized from the plains tribes, and their yurts were made of leather and wood stolen when Keshlik was still a young man. Every yurt had a chest of silver and gold trinkets. Keshlik had baubles of opal and mother-of-pearl, rubies the size of a crow's eye, and emeralds like pebbles. The furs and casks of wine and carved combs of whale ivory plundered from Prasa were now laid down next to the treasures of the dead Guza. If they warred only for wealth, their battles would have ended long ago. But the Yakhat fought because they knew nothing else to do.

The old men of the clan were sitting in a crooked circle around the central fire of the encampment, with the women and warriors gradually retreating to their homes. Keshlik entered the circle and bowed to each of the men in turn, beginning with Deikhul, the eldest. Once he had finished, Deikhul began the formalities. "What news do you bring of the battle?"

"Golgoyat himself fought among us," Keshlik said. "The city of Prasa is overrun, and our warriors have returned with the plunder that he has given into our hand."

"Has the Sorrow of Khaat Ban been avenged?"

"No. Golgoyat still rages, and Khou still weeps."

Satisfied with the ritual exchange, the elder leaned back and folded his hands. "So what now, Keshlik? Will you let the war bands rest?"

"Have the war bands rested since Golgoyat first roused us?"

The elder grunted. "We haven't ceased from war, but we have occasionally tarried along the way to battle. And this seems like a good place to tarry."

"I agree that this is a good place to tarry. I am as eager as any of you for a rest from war." *More eager, probably.* "But we can't rest yet."

"Why not?"

"Too many escaped from the city, and they might strike back."

Tashnat, one of the retired warriors, spoke up. "Are you really afraid of the ones who fled from the city like rabbits?"

"Alone? Not at all. But if there are enough of them, they might gather their courage. And we barely know what lies further to the south. There is a rumor of a greater city there." He told them about the captured chief of Prasa and the man's tale of Kendilar.

Deikhul seemed nonplussed. "So what do you propose?"

"We should subdue the last of the survivors. Scatter them or slay them, and ensure that none of the city-dwellers will strike against us again. Once all of the land north of the river is ours, we can tarry here until Golgoyat sends us out again into battle."

"So will you lead the bands again?"

He hesitated. "I would like to stay here until Tuulo gives birth."

A low chuckle sounded around the circle.

"You want to stay with the camp?" Deikhul asked. "Maybe you'll send the cow-maidens against the city-dwellers?"

The chuckles thickened into laughter.

Keshlik grinned at them. "If the cow-maidens want to go out with spears in their hands, I wouldn't stop them. But until then, I might send my brother Juyut."

"It's fine if you want to send Juyut," Deikhul said. "But we and the women are more than content to stay here north of the river. The plains are copious and wide, and we're safe for the time being. We could rest well here."

"Once we know that we *are* safe from every side."

Keshlik came up behind Juyut and smacked him on the back of the head, just as Juyut had cracked open another cask of Praseo wine and dipped a bowl into it. "Don't get too drunk now," Keshlik said. "I need you to lead a warrior band."

Juyut spat a mouthful of wine on the ground, and he turned and swung at Keshlik.

Keshlik easily sidestepped. "I hope your fighting is better than that when you go out against the city-dwellers."

"Bah," Juyut said, grinning. "I may not be able to hit the leader of the Yakhat war bands, but that doesn't mean I won't be able to kill the rabbit-men of this place."

"Let's hope so." He settled down next to Juyut and accepted a bowl full of wine. He sipped, carelessly splashing a bit into his beard. "Are you ready to lead a Khaatat band against the remnants of the city?"

"Are you seriously worried about them?"

"I worry about every survivor we leave."

"Bah! They're off hiding on the fringes of what we've already plundered. They're no threat to us."

101

"Just like the Yakhat were no threat when we were hiding on the fringes of the marshland?"

Juyut grunted. He knew those meager, miserable years only from stories. As far as he could remember, the Yakhat had always been warriors. "So you're expecting Golgoyat to call up one of them the way he called up our father?"

"I'm not expecting anything, but I also don't take any chances."

Juyut nodded with a lopsided grin. "I suppose that's why you lead the war bands and I don't. Yet."

"And if you don't learn some caution, you'll never live long enough to take the command from me. Remember that even Keishul, Golgoyat's chosen, fell to the plainsmen when he charged into an ambush with too few men."

"So you're saying you're better than Golgoyat's chosen?"

"Golgoyat spoke to our father, not to me. What I lack in the Power's touch, I make up in caution."

"But not valor?"

Keshlik finished the last of the wine and tossed the bowl onto the grass. "Caution and valor are thunder and lightning. A true warrior, like a true storm, has both of them."

"Listen to you today! So full of pithy sayings."

"Shut up and give me some more wine."

Juyut picked up Keshlik's bowl and dipped it into the cask, then handed it back to Keshlik with a chuckle. "So where do you want me to lead our warriors?"

"West. We've scoured the riverbank to the east all the way to the mountains. Those who escaped from the city must have headed to the west."

"And how many warriors are you giving me?"

"You can take all you want of the Khaatat, but don't ask the other tribes. We can handle this ourselves."

"I'm sure *I* can handle it. But what about you?"

Keshlik grinned. "I'll be staying back here. With Tuulo."

"Ah. Maybe I should get myself a wife so that I can stay out of battles, too."

"Bah. By the time you convince one of the cow-maidens to share her yurt with you, you'll deserve to stay out of battles. You'll be practically an elder."

"Like you, you mean?"

Keshlik laughed. He hadn't gone into Tuulo's yurt until he was into his second century, long past the age when most men sought wives. The callow cow-maidens who had simpered around him, all too eager to open their yurts if only he would proffer his spear, held no interest for him. It was the proud, playful Tuulo who had finally caught his eye. "If you get a wife as good as mine," he said, "then consider yourself lucky to have waited."

"You're probably right." Juyut finished the bowl of wine and wiped the drops out of his beard. "In the meantime, I guess I'll just have to scatter these rabbit-men."

"Yes, chasing rabbits. That sounds appropriate for your skill."

Juyut laughed, refilled his own bowl, and settled onto the grass next to Keshlik. They fell into silence. The sun melted into the horizon in the west, bleeding onto the tips of the western peaks, and dropped into darkness.

CHAPTER 12

SAOTSE

STANDING ON THE BEACH BELOW the lodges of Ruhasu, Saotse heard Chaoare kissing the surface of the waters and stirring them toward the ruins of Prasa. Oarsa turned in his depths, responding with a groan that made the beaches creak. Saotse shivered and wondered at the groaning. For so many years, he had been silent. Now he stirred, though he did not yet speak.

The wind over the bay had come from the south the first day after the attack, and it carried the smell of smoke from the plundered city. The refugees in Ruhasu wept and begged for relief, and since then, Chaoare had blown from the north, tumbling down from the White Teeth above the bay and holding council with Oarsa at the ocean's doorstep. Saotse had listened to them for three days, and she still had no notion of what they were saying.

This bothered her less than it had before, for she still shivered with the touch of the weeping, earthy woman. *That* Power had remained since the day of the attack, though she hadn't smothered Saotse with her loamy breath since the escape. Saotse kept her presence near the surface of her mind, and every step that she took on the ground seemed to well up with tears.

A man's footsteps crushed the gravel of the beach behind Saotse, scattering the chimes of the Powers' conference like flies.

"You should come to eat, Saotse," said Tagoa.

"I'm not hungry." In truth her stomach was muttering at her, but she preferred to fast. Every bite she ate from Tagoa and his brother was a debt owed to an *enna* not her own, and she already owed too many.

"Please come," he said. "You are our honored guest." But the tone of his voice belied his words. It was politeness, false courtesy. The people of Ruhasu were already suffering too many honored guests. There had been a hundred people in the village before the attack, and twice that many had taken refuge from Prasa. Even more had been turned away, or had gone on and sought safety in other, more remote villages further up the coast. Food was already scarce.

"No, I don't want to eat. Thank your Eldest for the offer."

"Fine, then," Tagoa said with an audible note of relief. "But you can come if you want to."

She pitied them, really. The ten *ennas* of Ruhasu had a single *akan* between them, and he had rarely needed to use the powers of his title to keep the peace of such a small and peaceful hamlet. The poor man had no idea what to do with the plague of refugees, most of whom came without *enna* and without Eldest, none who would answer to the *akan* of a fishing village when they were used to speaking to the chief of Prasa. She had crouched at the fringes of their conversations in the last few days, listening to the beleaguered *akan* try to hold on to order in the face of angry and heartbroken survivors. He seemed desperate for them to leave. But they wouldn't, not unless the city of Prasa rose suddenly from its ashes and the Yakhat retreated back across the Gap.

Tagoa crunched back toward the lodges, and Saotse stirred herself from the shore and turned to the east. The Powers were speaking on the water, but not to her, and she had no reason to remain. Her walking stick prodded the ground in front of her and kept her off the water and out of obstacles. Not the familiar footpaths of the *enna's* old lodge, these. Insistence and stubborn refusal to lean on the hand of a guide had earned her this stick, and she had spent several hours beating her ankles against stones and tree stumps until she learned the layout of the village. Cautiously and slowly she moved, and still she tumbled into a low spot on the path every now and then, but the occasional bruise of independence was better than Tagoa's officious hospitality.

Sentries guarded the eastern side of the village, armed with bows and fishing spears hastily converted into weapons of war. The *akan* had wrangled that much out of the fractious survivors, eaten as they were by fear. She had walked out to their position and returned to the stinking, overcrowded village seven times last night, slowly memorizing the way. She headed toward them again, her stick tapping ahead of her. In a few more nights, she might make the circuit without the stick, if only she could be sure that a branch never fell across the path.

The footpath leading out of the village ran through a battalion of vigilant spruces attended to by ferns and salmonberries. She could smell the wet cloak of moss on their trunks. The humid soil on her feet quivered with the distant Power. Saotse hadn't yet learned her name, and there was no one here who could tell her. Here in Ruhasu, she hadn't breathed a word of her affinity for the Powers, but in any case she knew the names of all the Powers that the Prasei honored: Azatsi, who slumbered in the stone of the mountains; Chaoare, the wind that stirred the treetops; Prasyala, the river who came leaping down from Azatsi's Spine to meet his stern and ancient father; Oarsa, of the deep waters. There were others whose names the Hiksilipsi knew, but the Hiksilipsi teachers were few in Prasa, and there were none at all in Ruhasu. In any case, Saotse was sure that her Power was none of these. She was, she admitted to herself, proud and defensive of this fact. The nameless Power that she had met was her own, not something that anyone else could claim to name or understand.

"Hey!" cried one of the sentries. The voice was familiar from the night before.

Had she reached their perimeter already?

"Don't worry about me. I'll turn back," she called back to them.

"Is that the blind woman?" the other sentry called out.

"Yes," the first sentry replied, but the rest of his response got lost among the ferns as Saotse reversed course. They would probably insist she was crazy, talking walks by herself from the edge of the village to the sentries and back. *Well, let them.*

She knew the opposite end of her circuit by the smell of cooking fires and fish guts and the twitter of bickering. The Ruhasu *ennas* wanted her less than the sentries did. She didn't linger there but repeated her lap to the sentries. The movement did her legs good.

She had reached the halfway point with her walking stick when the path under her feet wobbled. She stopped and leaned forward on the stick to regain her balance—but the problem was not with her balance. She felt the keening of the earth and the tremor of horses' hooves, as if their footfalls gouged marks in her own skin. The Power was roused. Something approached.

What does this mean? she asked the Power trembling in the earth. The answer was a howl of confusion and betrayal.

"Danger! Raiders!" shouted sentries, running past her toward the village. One grabbed her hand. "Come! There are horses approaching."

Saotse stood motionless. *Not again.*

She could hear the horses now, a rumble of hooves approaching on the footpath. The sound in her ears and not in the awareness of the earthen Power, but the senses joined. She knew their approach as the pounding of hooves over her head, tearing through ferns and leaping over fallen wood, soil upholding their feet and crying at the injustice, and the thunder of their approach to where she stood, an old woman in the path of the warriors whose cries already keened around her.

No, no, no. The wails and slaughter of Prasa returned to her. She curled her toes into the soil and reached out to the Power, and she met a memory as potent as her own. Again the foreign warriors struck against the innocent and spilled blood like water. *Not again.* Her thought echoed in the heartbeat of the weeping Power. *We will not allow it. We will not lie passive again. We will not wait for the murderers. They will not ravish us again. They will not. They will not. They will—*

She screamed. The earth erupted around her: a roar of soil, a violent belching of the land, and her own wail. Here there were hoofbeats. One of the murderous raiders galloped toward her, shouting and seething.

And as simply as closing her hand over a fly, she reached up and closed her root-veined fist over him.

Power and rage suffused her. She opened her mouth, the earth yawned, and three riders pitched forward into the sudden chasm. She ground them to paste with her rocky teeth. There was confusion now. The attackers hesitated. They were afraid. *They were afraid!*

Yes. Let them fear me.

She twitched, and the earth rolled, snapping the legs of their horses. She pulled stones from her belly and hurled them at their hateful faces. A swipe of her arm blasted apart the flank of their attack, sending men and horses flying into the air. *Let their blood water the roots of my hair.* She roared, and the whole land shook with an earthquake.

Now they were fleeing truly, their horses whinnying in fear, their fierce ululations reduced to whimpers of terror. Snatching after them with fingernails of flint, she gouged two open. Yakhat howls filled the air.

She tried to chase, setting the ground rolling after their mounts, but as they receded, her might waned. The Power could still feel their hooves on her skin, but there was a limit to Saotse's reach. She grasped once, twice, spitting gravel after them, and then they were gone.

The Power drained from her like water from a wrung cloth.

She became aware of a wet, heavy pressure, holding fast her limbs and her chest like a cold hand.

Get up. I should get up. But she couldn't move. Her hands were like stone.

The Power still trembled in her chest. Saotse clasped it with the last tatters of her strength.

And like a mist rising over the water, darkness drowned her mind.

***

Saotse floated in a pool of milk, with a warm and buttery sweetness on her tongue. A voice murmured above her like a mother's cooing. But it was not her mother. Was it Uya? Nei? No, they were all dead. Was her mother dead? Most likely. And even if she lived, her mother certainly wasn't the young woman she heard speaking above her.

But then, it wasn't a woman speaking at all, was it? The calm, maternal hands that cradled her neck were not a woman's. They were not calm, and they were not maternal. Rough hands. A man's hands.

She was not floating, but lying on a bed of straw, and Tagoa spoke with fearful care above her. His voice gradually took on a shape, like a stone emerging from the fleeing tide. Only the last of his words were intelligible to her: "... go, now. She's waking up."

Feet scraped the dirt floor of the hut, retreating. Tagoa breathed deeply and put his hand on Saotse's forehead. "Can you hear me? Are you awake?"

She worked her jaw to bring spittle to her tongue. Her lips pressed together soundlessly like strips of bark.

"Wait," Tagoa said. "Here's some water." He lifted her head and touched the tip of a leather pouch to her lips.

She sipped at its contents. "Thank you."

His care, for once, did not seem like the rehearsal of a

burdensome duty, but neither was there real empathy. What did she hear hiding in his voice?

His voice quivered as he asked, "How do you feel?"

He's afraid of me. How curious. "Where are we?"

"On the women's side of the *akan*'s lodge."

"Where is everyone else?"

"They're waiting outside."

"Are they afraid of me, too?"

He didn't answer for a while. When he spoke again, he sounded even more afraid. "What happened? None of us understand. What did you do?"

"Well, what *did* happen? Do I look like I know more about it than you do?"

"You were... You were there in the middle of it. Don't you know what happened?"

"I don't know that I do. Tell me."

"I don't really know, either."

"Tell me what you know! How can I explain anything if you won't tell me what you need explained?"

"Yes, yes, of course, Grandmother."

Oh bother, now he's starting with the honorifics. Whatever she had done under the Power's influence, it had frightened them all badly.

"Well, to start, two of the sentries found you buried up to your neck in soil in the middle of the forest. The other two were dead."

"So the Yakhat *were* here?" She wasn't sure whether she had imagined that part, or if it were part of the vision that the Power had given her.

Another hesitant pause. "They were here, yes. They killed one of the sentries. The other one was crushed by a tree that fell on him."

"A tree? Who was pushing over trees?"

"Well, we don't know— That is, we thought it was—but of course we shouldn't assume—"

"Oh, come out with it. Why do you think it was me?"

He gave a short, nervous laugh. "Well, you know, the whole ground between the lodges and the perimeter is torn up like a giant's plow went through it. The trees are all uprooted, fallen over and burst into splinters. There are stones that landed in pools of hot mud after flying through the air. Heaps of earth folded over corpses. We've pulled over a dozen dead Yakhat from the mud so far. And one of our sentries. There could be more. We don't know. The two sentries who survived, though, said they saw you in the middle of it, screaming and swinging your arms and making the earth on every side of you ripple like the sea in a storm. So we assumed you were the cause of the... the earthquake. If that's what it was."

Saotse fell silent. *Not a vision after all, then.*

The Power had filled her—or she had taken hold of the Power, she couldn't say which—and they had done *something*. She reached, just to see if she could, and found the Power of the earth. No part of her body touched the soil, but she could feel the Power as hot as a coal, burning through the few inches between herself and the ground. She offered a memory: the earth awake like a sheet torn by the wind, enemies crushed and vanquished. The Power's response was a fierce cry of exultation, the mournful memory of slaughter sweetened by revenge. The earth began to tremble. For a moment, the vastness of the Power's hatred and sorrow threatened to engulf her, shaking the room like a rattle, but Saotse resisted, kissed the Power's hand, and withdrew.

It was all true.

A whimper sounded from the corner of the room. "What did you *do*?"

"I merely sought the Power that had touched me before."

"The earth shook like a drum, and you call it nothing?"

She assumed that tone of weary grace that Nei had used so often when speaking to the *enna*. "It won't happen again. I'm sorry." It was a change to apologize from a pose of superiority, for once.

"You are in communion with the Powers," Tagoa ventured. "Some of the others wanted to kill you for colluding with a demon."

"The demons are merely the Power of our enemies. Or so I've heard the Hiksilipsi teach."

"What are you trying to say?"

"If I've befriended one of the Powers, does it matter who it is? She won't harm us. She is our ally and my friend."

Tagoa's nervous breathing filled the room. "You are Kept."

Saotse recoiled. That title had been dangled in front of her once before, when she was a young woman who had just crossed the ocean on a whale's back. But had Oarsa ever given her the power to raise up the sea like a spear? Had he done anything at all when Prasa was ravaged? No, if any Power had the right to Keep her, it was this newcomer, the earthen mother who shared her heartbreak with everyone in the fallen city.

"I am Kept," she said.

"Blessed woman." His hand clasped hers. His lips pressed against her knuckles. "Will you tell me the name of the Power that Keeps you?"

She had no name for the Power, and of course the Power could not tell her. Names were a mortal convenience, given by men to the eternal forces so they could remember and invoke them. But now Saotse needed a name, and if none already existed, she would have to invent one.

"Sorrow," she said. "Her name is Sorrow."

CHAPTER 13

KESHLIK

"THERE ARE KHAATAT WARRIORS ON the horizon," Bhaalit said. "Juyut's men."

"Sooner than I expected." Keshlik scraped the spearhead across the spinning whetstone and tested its edge. "I hope this means good news."

Bhaalit didn't answer. Keshlik stopped with the whetstone above the bronze and looked up. Bhaalit's face was darkened with concern.

"Tell me," Keshlik said.

"Not all of them are coming. And they approach slowly."

Keshlik stood. "Who saw them?"

"One of the cow-maidens who was grazing her cattle in the west. She relayed the message in with her sisters."

"I'm going to meet them." The spearhead gave a final ring as he stroked the whetstone along its claw, then he set it aside with the others. "Tell one of the young men to put these back in the stockpile. I have to ready my horse."

"They're probably fine," Bhaalit said softly, resting a hand on Keshlik's shoulder. "You don't need to hurry."

Keshlik brushed the hand away. "I want to see them. That's all."

Anger and fear simmered together in his throat. It had been Juyut's first raid entirely alone. It should have been a simple thing. Had he been such an idiot as to split up his band? Had something happened to them?

Maybe *he* was the idiot for letting Juyut go raiding by himself. Juyut was young, hotheaded, impulsive. Why had he let him go?

He found Lashkat grazing with the other mares just outside the circle of yurts, readied her bridle and saddle, and mounted. He slapped her sides and started past the yurts, only to stop when Bhaalit appeared at the edge of the circle, waving his arms.

"Let me come," he shouted.

"Hurry!" Keshlik turned Lashkat in a circle. He didn't want to wait. Fortunately, Bhaalit appeared soon afterward, coming through the yurts. Keshlik simply pointed to the west and kicked Lashkat into a gallop.

The cows did not raise their heads as he and Bhaalit rushed past. The cow-maiden tending the herd waved at them and gestured in the direction where she had spotted the warriors on their approach. At the top of the next rise, he glimpsed a line of slow-moving mounted men creeping forward. His mare's feet whipped through the grass, beating the ground like hailstones. The leader of the formation raised his hand in greeting.

It was not Juyut. It was a red-faced young man named Chuuri, one of Juyut's friends and Juyut's lieutenant for the raid. Keshlik pulled the reins to bring his horse to a stop, then hid his hands in the fabric of the saddle. The warriors should not see his hands trembling with rage and fear.

"Where is Juyut?" he demanded.

"I—He's right here," Chuuri stammered. "He's right behind us, riding in a travois. We had no other way to carry him."

"A travois? A *travois*?" He was alive, at least. The fool, that Keshlik should even have to contemplate whether Juyut was alive. But he *was* alive, so now he had to consider what injury he had suffered, and how he had been idiot enough to get it.

114

Two strides brought him to the travois, a quick lashing of pine branches between two knobby branches, dragged behind one of the other horses. Keshlik didn't even stop to see who had carried it. He pushed past the dismal riders to see a man wrapped in a wool blanket. His face was darkened by congealed blood, his arm encumbered by a sling.

"Juyut," Keshlik said.

The man stirred. One of his eyes was swollen shut, the lid bursting with purple and black. The other stared at him mirthlessly. "Keshlik," he groaned.

Keshlik knelt and took his brother's free hand. "My brother. What are you doing here?"

Juyut turned his face away. "I was injured." Shame stuck in his small, quiet voice.

"Injured? How? And where are the rest of your men?"

"Their spears were broken. This is all that remains of us."

"You fool. You mindless fool. What happened? What are your injuries?"

Juyut moaned and looked away.

"His foot is broken," Chuuri said, "as well as his arm. And, well, you can see his face."

"How?" Even if the city-dwellers had started to fight, the Yakhat could turn a retreat with a single word when necessary. Keshlik had never lost so many men in a raid. Juyut's eyes were closed, his lips drawn taut with pain and shame.

"You fool! What did you do? Did you charge headlong into a defended position? Did you forget everything I ever taught you about tactics? Were you too proud to turn back?" He screamed and spat at the ground. "What happened?"

"I'm sorry." Juyut's voice was raspy and labored. "I'm sorry. I have failed the Khaatat and the Yakhat. The spears that were broken weigh on my soul."

"But *what happened*?"

Juyut hesitated. The other men of the band had gathered

around them and watched with quiet nervousness. Finally, he said weakly, "The earth devoured us."

"What?"

"What else can I say? They have a witch. She made the ground quake and hurl itself at us."

Chuuri grabbed one of Keshlik's hands and pressed it to his chest in a gesture of sincerity. "This is true. The ground split open and swallowed our riders. Stones rose out of the earth and hurled themselves at us. That's what happened to Juyut. A boulder crushed his horse and stones battered him. He was the only one that we could pull out alive."

"A witch," Keshlik said. "You saw this woman?"

"I saw her," Juyut said. "It was an old woman, hunched over and carrying a walking stick. In a village to the west of Prasa. We were going to charge past her, ignore her and plunge into the heart of the village. But then..."

"An old woman," Keshlik muttered. "So she was not in Prasa."

"Eh." Juyut started to say more, but his words evaporated into a gasp of pain.

"If she had been in Prasa, we wouldn't have overrun the city. But if there is a witch among the Prasei, why is she hiding in a village rather than defending their city? No, don't answer, Juyut." He knelt and rested his hand on his brother's chest. Juyut closed his remaining eye, took a deep breath, and let out a gentle moan.

Keshlik turned to Chuuri. "Bring him into our yurt. Get one of the old women. Did you have enough of a mind about you to bind his wounds well?"

"We bound them," Chuuri said. "I won't say whether it's well. We were fleeing, and the witch could have—"

"Shut up. If the answer is *no*, just say so rather than trying to excuse yourself like a wide-eyed girl."

Juyut stirred and croaked. "They did as well as they could."

"Quiet, Juyut." The warriors all had tired, haggard faces, haunted by defeat. The shame of retreat hung off them like a

116

stench. It was disgusting. It was filthy. These were not the warriors of the Yakhat that he knew.

"What are you all afraid of?" he asked.

They answered him with nervous shuffling and sidecast glances.

"Do the Yakhat fear any enemy?"

"We have never faced a witch," Chuuri muttered.

"'We have never faced a witch!' An old woman gives herself to one of the Powers and spits dirt in your faces, and you all turn into rabbits and flee. Is a witch any different than any of the other enemies that the Yakhat have vanquished?"

"No," Chuuri said with a little confidence, and a few of the other warriors joined him.

"Does the warrior of the thundercloud fear a woman flinging mud?"

"No," the warriors said, now in unison.

"Then we fear nothing! Do we fear a witch?"

"No!"

He raked his glare across them. "Then let the hag come. Let her find out that Golgoyat still has teeth. We know that she is there, and we will adapt. We will discover how to defeat her. Golgoyat himself still fights among us."

***

He delivered Juyut into the hands of the old women and chastened the warriors again in front of the elders. It was a necessary humiliation, which kindled the fury of defiance in their eyes. They would fight like wild boars the next time they went into battle, and they would eagerly learn what he could teach them about how to fight such a woman... once he had determined *what* to teach them.

After the warriors left, he crossed his feet and settled on the ground next to Bhaalit, across from the elders of the Khaatat. It was early evening, and the fire in the middle of their circle was young and danced with yellow flame.

Keshlik was silent, letting the fire crackle and hiss, and its smoke twirl up to Golgoyat. At last, he asked, "How do we fight a witch?"

Lochat, one of the elders, sat next to Bhaalit. He was Bhaalit's father-in-law, a grim old man, blind in one eye and missing three fingers—all from wounds gained when he had campaigned with Keshlik's father. He speared Keshlik with the gaze of his good eye. "We hoped that you would tell us."

"How would I tell you? None of us have ever fought a witch before. We never even heard a rumor of a witch when we fought the plains tribes on the far side of the Gap."

"Keishul was sometimes called a warlock," Lochat said.

"But his power was not like this."

Lochat coughed. "That's true enough."

Keshlik made a noise of annoyance. His father, Keishul, had heard Golgoyat's call, and when he spoke to the Yakhat, the thunder of the storm-lord was in his voice. It had been enough to stir the Yakhat from their despair, terrify their enemies, and turn the men who heard him into warriors. But he had never called thunderbolts from the sky or commanded the wind or performed any other feat similar to what this witch had done. And in any case, that gift had died with his father. "Then we'll have to fall back on our own wits," he said. "As we have since Keishul died."

Bhaalit tossed a piece of grass into the fire. "We understand what she does, at least from the report of Juyut's men. She makes the earth shake in waves and hurls rocks from the soil. It's a powerful spell, but she only has one."

An elder on the far side of the circle spat. "So what? We can't ride against that sort of attack."

"Then maybe we don't ride," Bhaalit said with a shrug.

"Bah," Lochat said. "The Yakhat are nothing without their horses."

"Then perhaps there's a different way for us to attack her."

The circle was quiet for a while.

Keshlik's thoughts kept spinning like a poorly balanced spear, and he couldn't find a place to seize them. "We need to know more. What if that isn't her only spell? Do we know anything about the Power that possesses her?"

"Ask the Guza slaves," Lochat said with a dismissive wave of his hand. "They know the Powers of this place."

"A good start. Bhaalit, will you do that for your father-in-law?" Bhaalit nodded. Keshlik continued, "And then I may put together a party of spies. No more charging into villages headfirst. At least not until we know where the witch is and what she does."

"Will you let the other tribes know?" someone called out.

"I'll send riders in the morning." Keshlik stretched his legs and got up. "But now, I want to see my wife. The witch can wait until morning."

His tongue burned with frustration as he left the circle. The elders seemed satisfied, but Keshlik was not. Vague plans for spies and interrogations of the slaves did not sate him. His hands jittered, and he smoldered with unresolved anger. So he was especially irritated when he went to the edge of the blessed circle and called for Tuulo, but Dhuja came out instead.

"What do you want, old woman?" he said.

"I want to talk to you." She was stooped over, but she regarded Keshlik with a haughty, contemptuous gaze.

"I called for my wife, not for her midwife."

"But you'll listen to her midwife, since I hold her life in my hands."

"Are you threatening me?"

Dhuja gave him a wrinkled glare. "Keshlik, a woman like me has no threat to make against the leader of the Yakhat war bands, and I will not barter with the life of a woman in my care. But I want to tell you what the women who tended Juyut said, since no one else has the courage."

That gave him pause. "What?"

"The men today. They were attacked by fists of earth and crushed by stones. Your brother was hurt the worst."

"Did you come to tell me what I already know?"

Dhuja shrugged and peered to Keshlik's right, avoiding the spear point in his glare. "The earth is Khou's flesh, and the stones are her bones. You were attacked by the implements of our mother."

Fury leapt up in his chest at the heresy. "What? Khou is the mother of the Yakhat. She doesn't fight for city-dwellers."

"Can you be sure of that? Your father was called by Golgoyat, but we haven't known anyone who could speak to Khou since we left the Bans."

"You're saying she's taken up with our enemies? You're mad, woman."

"Maybe she merely stopped protecting us. Our warriors fought without Khou's protection, or else the stones wouldn't rise up to kill them."

"Golgoyat fights with our bands. I don't know what Khou does, but don't try to convince me that she's fighting against us. There are Powers enough in this place to possess an old woman without believing it must be Khou. Now let me speak to my wife."

She shook her head, refusing to look Keshlik in the face. "I'll send Tuulo out. But I've warned you."

Tuulo looked like the sun shining in the mist: radiant in the fullness of her pregnancy, but tainted with a film of weariness. She sighed as she stopped a pace away from him. "I'm tired of being pregnant, Keshlik."

"I'm sorry. I have never seen a more glorious mother than you."

She merely grunted. "I'm ready to be done. Dhuja says that I'm so close. *We're* so close. The city woman that you brought will bear at the same time as me, Dhuja says."

"Has she been of any use to you?"

"How are we supposed to talk? We have no translator! And

120

even when the Guza slave comes by, she barely talks to him. She doesn't know their language well."

He had hoped that she would know something about the witch. "Perhaps I'll send the translator by more often."

"Oh, don't bother. I don't want to talk to her anyway. If she weren't as laden as me, I'd say she's the worst slave I've ever heard of." She looked down at her own belly with resignation. "But I understand."

The words leaked off his tongue before he could consider them: "Juyut was almost killed."

Tuulo gave a solemn nod. "Dhuja could not keep from telling me. Will he survive?"

"He's in the care of the wise women. He'll recover. But I... I have to go face the witch. If there is someone that dangerous among the remaining refugees, then I have to strike as soon as possible."

She was staring at him with an intensity that made him uncomfortable. If it were anybody else, he would have slapped them. "You're afraid," Tuulo said quietly.

"I am not afraid."

"Keshlik—"

The anger in his belly burned up through his chest—but when it reached his tongue, he discovered that it wasn't anger. It was grief.

He began to weep. He covered his face with his hands and turned away from the camp, letting a sob score his threat. Tears soaked his beard. "He could have died, Tuulo. My brother, my only brother. He tried to hide it, but he had been so badly hurt, and his men were so afraid. And for such a pointless raid! If he died, I think I would die after him."

"Don't die, my husband. You will have a child soon. And I need you."

Her gaze felt like sparks on his face, and he looked away, blushing from the heat. "I'll be here for you, my wife. You and

121

Juyut are all I have left. My father, my mother, almost every friend I knew in childhood—all are gone. But if either of you—" His words crumbled into a sob.

Tuulo knelt, settling her ponderous belly between her knees, and placed her hand on the ground on her side of the burnt circle, as close as she could bring it to Keshlik's. "I'm here. And I am not afraid. My husband is the greatest warrior of the Yakhat, the leader of the war bands, and the heir to his father's calling. I wouldn't let any lesser man into my yurt to give me a child. And no mere witch will bring him down."

A wind shivered the grass around them. Keshlik wept until the spring of his tears ran dry. He looked up at Tuulo. Her eyes, too, were red and swollen. She smiled.

"Thank you," he said.

"Don't thank me. Instead, bring me one thing."

"What?"

Her grin bore the deadly humor of a coyote. "I've heard that witches have unique eyes, and I'd like to see some. Can you bring me the eyes of the witch? Preferably removed from the head."

He chuckled. "You may need to wait. I need to give Juyut's men time to rest, and I should enlist the aid of a few other tribes. But I'll bring you the witch's eyes."

CHAPTER 14

SAOTSE

D RUMS SOUNDED THROUGH THE VILLAGE. The beating resounded off the walls of the lodges and dove into the mosses on the trees, resting finally in the cedar rafters of the *akan's* lodge, where Saotse sat on a wooden bench next to the Eldest's chair. The voices around her created a mist of expectation. Three days ago, word had reached Ruhasu that the *kenda* was sending emissaries, and the *akan* had invited Saotse to sit next to him when they met their visitors. He was right to do so: she was their prize and their terror.

The women of the *akan's enna* had combed her hair and dressed her in a soft leather gown, talking in hushed tones, calling her grandmother and using their most humble language, no doubt fearing she might strike them down with earthquakes. Their obsequiousness did not displease her. She knew as well as they did that she was the most valuable thing that had ever entered Ruhasu.

The beating of the drums grew louder then stopped with a mighty *daroom* just outside the door. A voice called out, "The speaker Palam of the *enna* of the *kenda* of Kendilar and all the Yivriindi begs permission from the *akan* of Ruhasu to enter."

From beside Saotse, the *akan* said in his mild, hoarse voice, "Come in, Grandchild."

The air of the *akan*'s lodge crackled with attention. A young man's footsteps crossed the threshold into the lodge, followed by a pair of attendants, then a muffled rush as those who had been waiting outside huddled around the door.

"Come and sit, Palam," the *akan* said.

The messenger's feet scraped against the floor as he settled himself on the ground.

"Ruhasu has never had an emissary of the *kenda* before. What brings you to our village now?"

A high, milky voice answered him in a Yivrian accent. "Surely you know, Grandfather. The rumor of your wars has passed Tsingris by now. We received word many weeks ago that the Guza had been overrun and that Prasa was threatened by savages. Not long after that, we heard that the city had fallen. Now the *kenda* comes to repay the insult given to the Prasada, his friend, and to protect his northern border."

"It's unfortunate that he couldn't come *before* the city was plundered." The *akan*'s words were accusing, but the lightness of his tone told Saotse he didn't direct any anger at the emissary.

"We weep for all the city's dead."

You don't know the first thing about weeping.

"We also weep," the *akan* said. "The village is swollen with those whose *ennas* were killed in whole or in part, and even those of us who never lived in the city have given sons to it in marriage. Ruhasu is overfull and deeply taxed. Now what does the *kenda* want with our village?"

"Your aid."

"The *kenda* wants *us* to help *him*?"

"The *kenda* sent me to visit all of the villages near Prasa—those that still stand, at least. He will give spears and bread to any man that will join his ranks. The Yakhat still hold Prasa, but he hopes to draw them out and crush them in open battle. Those of you who were from the city may be able to return to your lodges."

"Interesting that you should speak of crushing. Did you know that we suffered an attack a few days ago?"

"An attack?" For the first time, Palam seemed genuinely surprised. "By the Yakhat?"

"Of course. Who else would attack us?"

"And you drove them back?"

"Well." The amusement grew in the *akan*'s voice. "Do you see the woman on my left?"

"Yes…" the emissary said, sounding confused.

"If anyone can aid you in our campaign against the Yakhat, it is this woman. Her name is Saotse, and she is Kept by the Power named Sorrow. Were it not for her, you would have found Ruhasu a bloody ruin."

"A Kept? Here in a fishing village?" His tone was flat with disbelief.

"Did you see the fallen spruces on the far side of the village?" the *akan* asked.

"No. We came from the west—"

"They were thrown down by Saotse's fury in the Power that Keeps her. The Yakhat attacked us, and Saotse drove them back by rousing the earth and the stones to hurl themselves at our foes."

"Really? And why hasn't any rumor of this ever reached Kendilar? Or even Prasa? I would expect that the Prasada would have told us if he had a Power of the earth at his disposal."

"This was the first time that Saotse roused the Power in that way."

"Ah. The *first* time. Are you certain it was the work of the Powers?"

Saotse perceived challenge in Palam's words and judged that it was time to speak. "Only the first, Grandchild," she said. "Do you think that the work of Sorrow in the battle is easily mistaken?"

"I think nothing, Grandmother. I'm here as a mouthpiece of

the *kenda*, and the *kenda* as of yet knows nothing about you and your Power."

"So you merely intend to put a doubting word in the ear of the *kenda*."

"Saotse," the *akan* broke in, "there's no need to treat the mouthpiece of the *kenda* as an enemy."

"Not as an enemy," Saotse said. "As a friend, I hope. Even I need as many friends as I can get. But a friend does not doubt the word of a friend. *Akan*, this man hasn't even seen the wreckage of the forest where I vanquished the Yakhat force. Perhaps he should witness what was made of the place where the Yakhat fools charged in, and so will believe the story better."

"Of course," Palam said. "I don't intend to bring any word of doubt. But I would bring a better report to the *kenda* if I could report to him that I had seen the Kept's power myself."

The Power's grief was anything but subtle, and once it was stirred up for battle, she might turn the lodge to rubble before she could constrain it. If she admitted that to Palam, he might perceive it as lying or weakness. Instead, she attempted to look haughty. "The Powers do not manifest themselves merely to sate your curiosity. But if you'd like, we could go now to see the place where Sorrow drove off the Yakhat."

Palam chuckled softly. "Perhaps we should do that."

The *akan* made a noise of displeasure. "Fine. We'll go together." His feet scraped on the boards beneath his seat, setting off a flurry of movement around the lodge.

Tagoa was sitting behind Saotse, to her left, and he leaned forward and touched her elbow. "I'll guide you to the place."

She let him nudge her forward and guide her right behind the heavy, slow steps of the *akan* as the lodge was drained of people.

The ruckus of Ruhasu's onlookers and Palam's entourage drowned the sound of the *akan's* footfalls, but she heard Palam fall into step beside her. Tagoa's hand on her arm pulled her back from him a little, as if he were afraid Palam would harm her.

The walk to the edge of the village enclosure took a quarter of an hour. Saotse could hear a large crowd trailing behind them, but when they approached the site of the cordon, the onlookers grew suddenly quiet. Saotse recognized the place by the way the air opened up to the sky, funneling the sound upward, and the smell of wormy, tumbled earth that had not yet regrown its hide of moss and grass.

Palam's footsteps slowed, and he drew a sharp breath.

"So," the *akan* said, his voice heavy with satisfaction. "You see."

Palam breathed heavily. "Remarkable," he whispered. "This was forest before... before what, exactly?"

Saotse answered, "The Power that Keeps me fought against the band of Yakhat. This is the result of her attacks."

"And the men who attacked you?"

"Were swallowed up by the earth."

"Some of them we recovered and buried properly, so they wouldn't be uncovered by landslides or coyotes," the *akan* added. "The ones that we could find."

Palam began to laugh. Saotse heard him kick a stone into the pit. "You need to return with me to the *kenda*. This is a gift too great to put aside."

"So you're not asking for any further demonstration of my power?" Saotse asked.

"I wouldn't dare to impose such a request on one of the Kept."

"And where do you want me to go with you?"

"Back across the bay toward the south shore. Over the water, of course. The city is still taken."

"Perhaps we could free it, instead." Saotse's words came out softly, and she could barely believe that she said them, but she felt a thrilling chill as she did.

"Are you suggesting that we attack the city?" the *akan* asked, incredulity weighing down his words.

"We have an ally among the Powers," Saotse said. "That counts for a thousand men."

"Still, we're only a handful here in Ruhasu. Prasa is still thick with the Yakhat."

"The elder," said Palam, "wishes to demonstrate her prowess. If I don't presume too much by saying so."

"You don't," Saotse said. "Perhaps you're both right. It would be good to let the Yakhat feel our sting, though to purge Prasa of Yakhat might be beyond our abilities. Perhaps a different target."

"With respect, Grandmother, I object," the *akan* said. "Why are we striking at the Yakhat at all? Let's join with the *kenda* and strike against the Yakhat from there."

"No," Palam said. Saotse heard greed in his voice. Though his manner was deferential, he, too, wanted to do more than merely bring announcements from village to village. "The *kenda*'s goal is to drive out the Yakhat, which is better done all at once than piecemeal. If we strike at them now, we'll stagger them, and when we join with the *kenda*'s forces, we can deliver a fatal blow."

"It is just as likely that they'd scatter, and we'd spend ages finding and attacking individual bands," the *akan* said.

"Have the Yakhat been that prone to scatter?" Saotse asked.

No one had an answer to that. They had all heard the stories, but none of them knew much firsthand about the Yakhat's habits in battle. Finally Saotse said, "When does the *kenda* need us?"

"It will be two weeks yet before his main force approaches Prasa. His vast army moves slowly."

"So we have time. A little, at least. Enough to stir up the Yakhat and give them a taste of the defeat to come. Is there a target nearby?"

The *akan* reluctantly suggested, "We heard there were camps scattered to the northeast of here, on the high plains. Within a few days' journey. They don't come into the woods."

"I will survive a few days' journey. I'd rather endure that than be cooped up in the village waiting for rescue or attack. Am I the only one?" There was a quiet, timid murmur of agreement between Palam, the *akan*, and the nearest of those listening. "I say that we strike out to meet our enemies before we return to the *kenda*. Who would come with me?"

"I would go with you," Palam said.

The *akan's* voice was full of resignation. "There are enough men here to equip a force. We have bows and what might serve as spears. If you're determined to go."

"I'm determined," Saotse said. "A blow to draw them into our jaws, and then a blow to crush them. As the Kept of Sorrow, I'll see to that."

CHAPTER 15

KESHLIK

O N THE WESTERN HORIZON MOVED little shapes, like crows picking at the heads of the grass. Keshlik pointed the spot out to Chuuri, his partner in the patrol around the Khaatat camp.

Chuuri stared at them. "It's just prairie grass. We should move on."

"Wait," Keshlik said. "We need to be sure."

Another patrolling pair was still about two miles behind them, visible as a pair of brown silhouettes above the grass, and a third was about two miles ahead. Keshlik had set the Khaatat on this circuit to watch every approach to the camp, lest the witch and her people attempt to strike. He very much doubted that they would, as the Prasei had given little evidence of martial prowess. Still, they had surprised him with their speedy construction of the earthen wall around Prasa. They might surprise him again.

The specks that bobbed along the horizon could have been deer or birds. Or people. The little line of movement dropped into a shallow dell and disappeared from sight. Keshlik pointed to the head of yellow rocks about a mile away then urged Lashkat ahead.

Chuuri followed. The horses trotted forward, yellow prairie

grass swishing against the boots of the riders. The loudest sound was the buzzing of grasshoppers.

They crested the outcropping. The prairie opened before them as a sea of yellow and green, riven by streams. At the bottom of the depression below them glittered the river, and crossing it at that moment was a line of pale figures, moving in single file.

"Those are not deer," Keshlik said.

"No," Chuuri said flatly. There was fear hiding in the corners of his mouth, but his teeth were clenched as if to prevent his courage from escaping. "But are they Yakhat?"

"They have no horses," Keshlik said. "Have you ever known a Yakhat band to travel on foot?"

"No." His dismay was clearer this time.

"Light the signal."

Chuuri unwound the greased torch strapped to his shoulder. At the touch of an ember from his fire pouch, the torch leapt with flame, and a trickle of black smoke curled into the sky. The two nearest pairs of riders begin to move toward Keshlik, their horses cleaving the grass into feathery wakes. The line of pale Prasei reached the near shore and crept forward in the grass. "Do you think they've seen us?"

"If they have, they aren't showing it. Or they're so confident that they don't think they need to change course." His voice crackled with fear.

Keshlik searched for a cloud. Alas, the sky was a pale, flawless blue from horizon to horizon. None of Golgoyat's mounts would bolster their courage today. But he was not afraid. He and Bhaalit had drilled the men on how they could defeat the earth witch, and he felt as confident as he ever had that they would prevail.

The first pair of sentries reached them just before the second. "What have you spotted?" the eldest rider asked.

"A large band of Prasei," Keshlik said. "Moving toward our camp."

"Have you seen the witch among them?" one of the younger ones asked.

"Too far away," Keshlik said. "But we have to assume that she's there."

There was fear in their eyes, and he needed to cast it out now. "I hope she's there, so we can teach her the taste of her own blood." He glanced over them and picked out the youngest and most nervous fighter. "Dhalyat, you return to the camp. Rouse the rest of the warriors."

Dhalyat nodded and galloped away.

Keshlik turned to the others. "So are you ready to teach the earth bitch to fear the Yakhat?" He didn't wait for them to respond and give voice to their own uncertainty. "Ready your bows. Remember what Bhaalit and I taught you and that Golgoyat himself fights among us."

Their assent was not as fierce as Keshlik would have wanted, but it would do.

They walked their horses toward the advancing band. A line of little hills hid them from view, but when they crested the next ridge, they saw the band about a mile away, jogging through the grass at a surprising clip. The leader of their enemies stopped and pointed, and the line drew together.

Chuuri drew his breath in sharply and put his hand on his spear.

Keshlik reached and put his hand over the youth's to calm him. "Follow me."

The two groups slowly advanced toward each other. The other band formed into a vague ball, moving forward through the grass with an awkward, uncoordinated pace. No hardened warriors, then. And a circle was a formation to be used when protecting something—and of course they were. The witch. She was the only reason that the rabbits had ventured out of their holes in the first place.

They were just outside of arrow range now. Keshlik loosed his bow and nocked an arrow on the string, squeezing his horse with his knees to guide her to the left. "Run without fear," he shouted to his men. "Like the hawk against its prey."

The bows of the others rattled behind him.

Those on the edge of the Prasei circle bent away from his approach like mice. He knelt to the right and let his arrow fly into the middle of the circle. It hardly mattered if he hit anything, just that the enemy recoil and stop moving. By the time he straightened himself in the saddle, his horse had carried him out of arrow range again, and he slowed her down to a trot and watched those following him. The last man in his line was shooting into the circle, and the others already formed up behind him, slowing and preparing to turn back. The Prasei had fallen back and drawn together, and he saw a few arrows held crookedly against bows to threaten their next pass.

"Again!" He plucked another arrow from the quiver. This tactic to harry a slow-moving enemy was as old as the plains, and the Yakhat knew it like their skin. The challenge would come when the witch began to attack. A few Prasei arrows fell past him, harmless as leaves as he thundered by and sent his point singing into their midst. For the second time, the little group, unharmed, formed up again beyond the huddled knot of Prasei.

"This band of trembling mice meant to attack us?" Keshlik called out. "Five Yakhat warriors have them hemmed in! And where is this witch of theirs?"

"They'd be better off throwing sticks, for all the good their arrows do!" Chuuri echoed. "Shall we go again?"

"Again!" Keshlik shouted. He charged back at their cringing circle.

At first he thought that Lashkat had almost misstepped. Then she nearly fell, her legs suddenly akilter beneath her, and a deep, omnipresent moaning buffeted the air. The ground trembled. His mare regained her feet, and he dropped the arrow from his fingers.

He leapt from the saddle in midstride, and when his feet touched the ground, he slapped her flank. "Run!"

There was a thunderclap, then a hail of earth. Lashkat whinnied in terror. He glanced back: a fountain of earth gushed up from the place that he had just been, widening and tearing, vomiting up a geyser of stones and soil. The rain of stones battered his head and his mare's flank. Lashkat bolted away from him, and he sprinted after her. He hoped they might both escape the range of the earthen hail, but no—a dark shape passed overhead, and the world became a twisted blanket of color. The lurching earth hurled him to the ground, and stones beat against his chest.

The earth was shaking like a flag in a gale. Keshlik tried to stand, pitched forward, and got a mouthful of dirt where he fell. He crawled. Lashkat was gone, all the better for her. He could dig himself out of the ground, but the horse couldn't. The air was a soup of dust and falling stones, and the only sound was the earth's sorrowful roar. *Golgoyat's balls.* He had no idea if he was moving toward the fight or away from it, but he sure wasn't going to stand still. Forward, forward, on his belly, battered by the downpour of fist-sized stones.

The soil split open like a wound in front of him, grass parting to release smothering loam. He rolled to one side, pushed himself to his feet, and ran blindly to escape the brown, bloody tide.

Suddenly he was sliding down a short rocky slope, scraping his knees and shins against the exposed teeth of the hill. The force of his landing stole his breath.

Air returned to his lungs, and he realized it was clear. No stones fell here. He had escaped the range of the witch's wrath.

He crept to the top of the rise and peered at the course of the battle. The rest of his band had done exactly as trained. They scattered so that the witch couldn't take more than one in any one swipe, and they loosed arrows into the heart of the Prasei formation as fast as they could draw the strings. But the Prasei were returning fire as they advanced with raucous, discordant elation. Fools. Keeping order in a charge was at least as hard as keeping order in a retreat, and more important. But let them be fools.

The tiny outcrop of rock that Keshlik had slid down protected him from their eyes, if only he stayed low. Their front line sprinted out of the dust clouds the witch had stirred up, and behind them came the core, walking more slowly, and with a stately reserve.

He caught a glimpse of the witch in their midst. A woman with unruly gray hair sticking out around her head like wisps of clouds around the moon, hunched and pale. She was being carried by two men with interlocked arms, and Keshlik briefly thought she had fainted. But she moved, and her bearers moved where she pointed. They were following their front line to the Khaatat encampment to the east. And behind them came a few stragglers bearing more bows and stakes, shooting back at Chuuri on their rear.

Well. That gave him an idea.

His bow and his spear were with Lashkat, so the knife on his belt would have to be enough. He waited until the last of the Prasei were about a quarter-mile ahead of him, and he crouched and followed. He held his head just above the level of the grass, and he kept to the little hollows and dips of the plain whenever possible, to be sure that the enemy's rear guard wouldn't see him. But the enemy band was making a beeline for the encampment, and their guard, if it could even be called that, barely gave a glance at their flanks. If not for the witch in the midst of them, these people would be among the easiest targets he had ever taken.

Ahead, the peaks of the yurts rose from the grass. A few were stripped of their wrappings, and around their bases a horde of women moved like ants, trickling away to the south where their line disappeared. Between the attackers and the women stood a long line of horses with warriors on their backs. Spears and bows glittered in their hands. The knot of attackers drew itself together as it approached the Khaatat camp, but the Khaatat dispersed, assailing them with shouts and jeers. The warriors could certainly see the witch in the middle of the attackers, but they showed no signs of fear. Keshlik and Bhaalit's plan had been to scatter the warriors like gnats, giving the witch no neat lines or clusters of warriors to strike against, and then sting her to death while she swatted at them one by one. And they were doing it flawlessly.

"Golgoyat himself fights among us," he muttered. "Don't fear the witch." He touched the knife at his waist.

The Prasei force stopped. Keshlik dropped to a knee and watched them through the leaves of the grass. Like fools, they began to spread out, the rear guard splitting to both sides, the better to guard against the Khaatat swarm. The two men carrying the witch set her on her feet. She wobbled like a woman in her dotage, unsure of her step, then she reached for the ground.

The Khaatat did not wait to see what sorcery she would do. Shouts sounded from their lips, and they began to encircle the Prasei formation. A few brave men darted forward to spit arrows toward the witch, then retreated, weaving into the swarm.

The ground opened in front of the woman. A chasm spread, the earth splitting like a sheet beneath a knife, the soil in the wound churning like whitewater. The Khaatat fled from the line, but Keshlik saw a few who did not run in time and were swallowed by the earth. Cheers rose from the Prasei. The men in the rear line looked forward to watch the witch's magic. *Now.*

Keshlik drew his knife and sprinted.

The witch was kneeling, her hands sunk into the earth up to the elbows. Another heartbeat and he would be upon her—but one of the men guarding her glanced back. He moved to block. Keshlik crouched and hit him at a sprint.

His shoulder struck the other man's chest. The world spun. The ground smacked them both, but Keshlik kept his knife. He struck and met flesh. The other man's scream vibrated through the knife blade.

He rose and turned. The witch was in front of him. She turned those horrible white eyes toward him, and the certainty on her face shook him to his bones—her Power had confirmed his presence. The moment in which they regarded each other stretched out glittering like a flake of flint, all other movement of the battlefield sliding to the edges of his vision.

"Die." Keshlik sprang forward.

Before his blade could strike, one of the Prasei leapt onto his back and wrapped his arm around Keshlik's throat. Keshlik jerked his head back and crushed his attacker's nose. The man screamed and his grip loosened, but he maintained his hold. Keshlik charged forward, dragging the man behind him. He slashed at the witch. Missed. She was on her hands and knees, crawling backward, babbling in her serpentine tongue. The ground shook like a drumhead beneath them.

He lunged forward and slashed again. A corner of the woman's shawl tore away. The man clinging to Keshlik's back fell off. Keshlik leapt and stabbed. The tip of his knife pricked the witch's shoulder and knocked against her bone. A mist of blood followed his slash.

The witch slumped against the ground, forehead first, then screamed against the dirt.

A fist of earth struck Keshlik in the chest like a hammer, throwing him into the air. The world turned to noise. He landed with a hail of stones.

He lay on the ground, stunned. *Get up! Get up!* pounded inside his skull. His feet and hands found the ground, and he rose.

He fell immediately. The ground wriggled like a serpent beneath him. The turf tore itself free to batter at his head. He tore it apart in chunks. Clods of dirt swarmed up his chest and burrowed into his mouth. He spat and tore them away, then spat again. *No air.* The soil rose up to bury him. He clawed and dug. *No air.* His lungs ached. He would scream, but his mouth was packed with dirt, dirt that fought and sought his throat to clog his voice forever.

Then it ended.

The dirt slumped away from him. He rolled onto his side, vomited a black puddle onto the ground, then fell forward into it. Dirtied snot dribbled from his nose. He spat gravel. *Get up! Get up!* ran his thoughts again.

His legs refused him.

The ground thundered. The bitch was coming to finish him off. "No," he said. "No."

His right hand formed a fist. He pushed himself up to an elbow. There were voices and screams all around him. Another push, and he regained his knees. If he could only get to his feet, he would finish off the witch. He raised his head to find her in the forest of shapes that fought around him.

But these were not Prasei. He saw horses. Khaatat riders. One of them looked at him, then shouted with terrified joy. "Keshlik!"

The Prasei were running, sprinting at full speed back to the west in a scattered, defenseless line. One of them held the witch in his arms like a babe.

Keshlik took a wobbly step toward them and coughed. "Go after them!"

The cry was spreading among the Khaatat: *Keshlik lives! Keshlik lives!* The riders around him slowed and ran to his aid. Their charge dissipated.

Keshlik spat another mouthful of mud and shouted, "Go after them, you fools! Forget me! They escape!"

As he said it, he felt the earth shudder. The Prasei had reached the top of the nearest hill. The witch slipped from the grasp of the man carrying her and planted her hands and knees in the soil. The ground creaked and shook. Nearby horses started. The riders at the head of the charge clung desperately to their panicked mounts. Keshlik braced for another attack.

The ground between the Yakhat and the Prasei bent, bulged, and buckled. A spine of stone rent the prairie's skin, growing upward, shedding strips of sod and earthy clods as it grew. It

STORM BRIDE

widened faster than a horse could run. A mile, two miles—Keshlik lost sight of the end of it before the ridge ceased to grow.

The rumbling of the earth subsided. The stone ridge was twice as tall as a man, but it grew no taller. And the Prasei were hidden behind it.

Silence loomed over the prairie. Warriors stared in disbelief at the ridge of stone that had not existed seconds before. Keshlik took a few steps toward the vast, impossible wall. He dropped to a knee. "She got away." He couldn't imagine how the Yakhat would get a better strike at her than this, and *still* she got away.

Keshlik's chest grew hot with fury. He gathered his strength and strode into the midst of the riders. His voice rumbled over the plain like thunder. "Do you hear me, witch? If you're hoping to keep yourself safe from me, then this was not enough! The earthworks of Prasa did not keep me out. Neither will your stones."

That was the last of his power. He fell to a knee and collapsed to the ground. The hands of warriors closed over him and carried him back to the tents.

CHAPTER 16

UYA

THERE WAS SHOUTING OUTSIDE THE yurt, from the direction of the main encampment. Uya and Tuulo looked up at the same time, eyes darting to the door of the yurt, but Dhuja barked a short, sharp command at them. Tuulo folded back to the ground.

Uya dropped her head into her hands. "She always tells us to stay."

Tuulo looked at Uya with her big cow eyes and shrugged. She didn't understand a word Uya said, but at least she seemed to sympathize with being cooped up in this reeking yurt. And she was better than the old midwife.

Boredom. She would not have guessed that the biggest problem with being captured by savages from beyond the mountains would be *boredom*. At first Dhuja had tried to order her to churn butter and serve food to Tuulo, but Uya had sulked and dragged her feet until Dhuja gave up. Now she sat in the yurt every day, doing nothing, and wished they would try to order her around again. Tuulo at least sometimes made little weavings with her fingers, but no one would let Uya try. Not that she even wanted to learn their savage patterns anyway. And in the *enna* she had whittled, carved, and done book work. The *enna*...

Oh, now she was crying again, and Tuulo was watching her with fake concern. The woman reached out her brown hand, but Uya swatted it away and wiped her own tears on her sleeve. She felt her family's absence like a knife in her stomach. Sometimes, she went a whole day without thinking of them, but then Tuulo would say something, or Dhuja would look at her in a way that reminded her of Nei, and the knife twisted again. Most nights she cried herself silently to sleep.

If she did not have the promise of her baby, she thought, she would have died of despair weeks ago.

The earth quivered beneath the yurt. Tuulo shrieked and leapt to her feet. A stream of gibberish poured from her mouth.

"Calm down," Uya said. "That was nothing important."

Then she felt a beat in the ground, like the sound of a distant drum. Dhuja burst through the door of the yurt and shouted a command at Tuulo.

Immediately, both women flew into motion. Dhuja danced as nimbly as a deer fly, gathering up small things here and there throughout the yurt and packing them into a small box. Tuulo waddled, but she too picked up a handful of items and laid them in Dhuja's box. Uya stood there, dumb and useless. She lumbered over to the open box and peered in, but Dhuja slapped her hand. She pointed at the door and shouted a single word.

"Do you want me to leave?" Uya asked.

The word leapt three more times from Dhuja's mouth, and she pushed Uya to the door. Fine, she would leave. She had wanted to get outside from the moment the barbarians brought her there.

Outside, the air was parched and hot, and the sunlight, like a fist. Sweat beaded on her face. At the edge of the earthen circle, she precariously lowered herself into a squat, her belly hanging between her knees. The noise of some ruckus from the far side of the camp reached her, though she had no idea what it could be.

Dhuja and Tuulo appeared carrying the little chest between them. Dhuja grabbed a fistful of salt from the pouch that was always between her breasts and threw it onto the burnt circle, muttering a prayer so fast that Uya wasn't sure she actually used words. She stepped through, holding Tuulo's hand, then motioned for Uya to follow.

Uya hesitated, dumbstruck. She had figured out one thing in her time here, and that was that she was not supposed to cross the line of burnt earth. She had no idea *why* the savages kept this custom, but every time she got within two paces of the line Dhuja appeared from somewhere and, screaming, dragged her back into the yurt. And now they wanted her to cross.

She almost wanted to sit, just to be petulant. But Dhuja's face bore not her ordinary scowl, but terror. Tuulo's eyes were grim with worry. Maybe she should listen to what they suggested.

She crossed the bridge of salt that Dhuja had laid.

Reaching the other side of the burnt circle felt like liberation, as if the boundary of earth were a wall that kept her from breathing real air. She straightened a bit and felt the baby squirm in her belly.

Two horses approached them from the camp. The first rider took the chest that Dhuja and Tuulo had packed, strapped it to the horse's rump, then helped Tuulo onto the back of the horse, sitting with her legs on one side of the animal. The second rider extended his hand to Uya.

The rider and Dhuja helped her to ascend and settle onto the horse's back with her legs resting alongside the saddle. Then Dhuja got up with a surprisingly agile leap and settled herself beside Uya. The horses began to walk away from camp.

Away? Uya craned her head and took in the Khaatat encampment with a jolt of sudden realization. About a quarter of the yurts were in the middle of hasty deconstruction. Women and men scurried through the camp like squirrels. Many more little chests, leather pouches, and other things were being loaded onto the backs of horses.

And she finally realized what she was hearing further down,

beyond the far end of the camp circle. It was the violent crash of fighting. The Yakhat were under attack. And they were fleeing.

Joy fluttered up through her breast. Who would attack the Yakhat but the Prasei? Her people, the people of her city and her *enna*! And if the fighting were here, she just might reach them. They might drive off the Yakhat entirely. If only she could get there, they'd take her back with them, back to the city, after they had driven away the last of the savages. If only.

The women joined a thin line of people trickling away from the camp. Every step that the horse took was taking her further away from her people and closer to whatever retreat these Yakhat had prepared. If she were going to do it, she would have to do it now.

She jumped from the back of the horse.

The ground slapped the soles of her feet with unexpected violence, and she pitched forward to catch herself on her palms. The baby squirmed at the sudden movement, and her belly groaned in pain. She pushed herself to her feet. Running was bulky and awkward. Her knees pushed against her belly, and she cupped her hands about the extra weight to reduce the painful jostling. Her whole body seemed to sway with the bulk of her added girth. The grass prickled her swollen feet, her breasts bounced like dead fish, and her lungs heaved with exertion. But she ran.

Shouts followed her. Ahead, there was a tremendous roaring. The ground seemed to be shaking under her feet, but that had to be only the exertion of the pregnancy. Horses were flying about madly in front of her, mingled with—yes, it was, just as she had hoped. Prasei! Yellow-skinned, white-clad, unhorsed. Her own people. They had come for her. She was almost free. She began to smile.

Hooves pounded the earth behind her. She glanced back. One of the men who guarded the retreat was running after her.

"Not this time." Uya gulped a breath and willed her legs to
143

carry her forward faster, swallowing the pain of her breasts and stomach.

Not fast enough. The rider snagged her by the edge of her tunic. She squirmed, pulled away, and fell to a knee in the grass. She clutched at her wobbling stomach, then scrambled forward on her hands and knees. The earth *was* moving, she realized once all her limbs were on the ground. *Why?*

No time to think of that. Her pursuer turned back to her. She heaved herself to her feet and ran again. Only a hundred feet from the battle where her people could find her. She ran as fast as her legs and her swollen body could carry her. But the horse gained. Another breath, and he would be on her again.

The earth pitched. The shaking sent her sprawling forward. She glimpsed a horse above her, its frothy neck stretched out splitting the sky, its lips opened in panic. Hooves pounded the earth on either side of her. The ground lurched again. A geyser of stones erupted on every side, and the horse fell, screaming.

A hoof glanced off her face. Her vision splintered, and she tasted blood. The horse's flailing legs struck her chest, her belly, her thighs. Her whole body burst with pain.

She tried to breathe in but only choked. Her eyes opened, but everything she saw was haloed in hazy white. Beside her, the horse still thrashed, unable to regain its feet. Its rider was pinned beneath it, shouting madly and thrashing about on the ground. Pain was *everywhere*, pressing down on her like a pestle crushing corn. She gasped in a mouthful of air.

The rider appeared above her, shouting incoherently. It didn't matter. She couldn't do anything at all except wrench one breath at a time from her bruised lungs. Every time her chest filled, they pressed against her ribs like a knife. She sobbed once, but the sound sent splinters of pain through her body. She bit her lip to hold back any further sound.

The man went away. She worked on breathing.

Now Dhuja appeared above her. What a strange relief it was to see that horrible woman. There were others, too, shadows moving in her peripheral vision, but they were irrelevant to her goal of continuing to breathe despite the agony. Hands slipped under her arms and around her ankles. Dhuja gave a command, and they lifted her off the ground.

She screamed then bit her tongue against the pain. Blood filled her mouth. They carried her for a very, very long time. It felt as if they were taking her all the way back to Prasa. Finally, Dhuja gave another command, and they lowered her onto a blanket on the grass. The men disappeared. Dhuja stripped away Uya's torn and bloody tunic and began to prod at her abdomen with her bony fingers.

It was becoming easier to breathe. Dhuja's fingers found a place on Uya's belly that made her breaths into screams. She played her hands across the rest of Uya's body, finding the places that were tender, all the while muttering. Then she dipped her fingers in salt and began to touch it to Uya's wounds. Uya whimpered and winced back, but the sting of the salt was almost a gentle pain. She could handle it. She locked her teeth. Tears gushed silently from her eyes.

Dhuja barked an order at someone. Up came her shoulders, padded by a roll of blankets, and a leather canteen was thrust into her mouth. She swallowed two mouthfuls of water, then rested, gasping for breath. She opened her eyes and looked down her abdomen.

Bloody red gashes stretched from her sternum across her right breast. A thin cut oozed blood, but Dhuja pressed rags against it as she watched. A scrape scored the top of her belly. Everywhere there was blood smeared with dirt. Her back was a single blade of pain, beginning below her shoulders and stabbing down between her legs. She didn't think she could stand, let alone walk.

Dhuja wiped the blood from Uya's skin and took out a knife. Its tip found the edge of her skirt and cut down, splitting the winding fabric so that the old midwife could fold it aside.

That was when Uya saw that her thighs were greasy with blood that dripped out from between her legs and pooled on the ground.

A horror greater than pain bubbled up. "No," she whispered, "Please, no."

There was movement at her head, and she realized that Tuulo was kneeling there, holding Uya's head on the roll of blankets. Tuulo hushed her and placed her hand on Uya's cheek.

Dhuja used the torn skirt to mop up the blood gathered between Uya's legs. With quiet, steady movements Dhuja went again over Uya's nude, bloodied body, wiped away the blood, and pressed salt into every gash she found.

Uya closed her eyes. She was tired. So tired. Dhuja's treatments felt like caresses. Only once did she feel a prick that stirred her awake, and when she looked down, she saw that a thorn was sticking out of her skin, holding the widest of her wounds together.

Then her stomach tightened.

It was as if every muscle of her abdomen had drawn together at once over a thorn. She whimpered and clutched at Tuulo's hand on her cheek. It hurt, but she had felt nothing *but* pain for so long that it hardly made any difference.

It receded, and her breath came back to her at its regular pace.

But that sensation meant it was starting, really and truly starting. "Mother," she whimpered. "Mother, where are you? Saotse, Nei, Rada. Do I really have to do this without you? Please, can't you be here with me?" She began to weep.

Tuulo reached down and wiped the tears from Uya's cheeks. She muttered something in their barbarian tongue. Uya clutched at Tuulo's wrist and folded her hand inside Tuulo's. A savage's hand, a murderer's wife in place of her own *enna*.

Another tightness passed over her, stronger and more painful than the first. Then another, and another. They were coming fast, too fast. Uya had been there when Aunt Mariku gave birth to Chrasu, and her mother had prepared her in every way she could. So she knew that something was wrong, that a normal birth would not gallop forward at this rate. A glance at Dhuja's grim face confirmed it.

A pang of agony crushed her thought. Each pain came quicker, and each time it was sharper, brighter, longer. Teeth of hot bronze tore at her insides. The bones beneath her belly seemed to be breaking in half. The wounds on her breast and stomach no longer even registered. The valleys that came between the peaks of anguish gave her just enough time to breathe deep and pull together the tatters of her energy. There was no more time to think. There was rest, sweet rest, all too short, and then screaming.

Tuulo pushed a brine-soaked rag into her mouth. Uya ground the threads in her teeth when the pain came, and she sucked the brine when it passed. Dhuja poured hot water over her belly and thighs. It scalded, and the scalding was like a kiss.

She looked up, once, and saw that the sky was dark. It had been noon when they fled the yurt. Had so much time passed?

Why isn't it over yet?

Tuulo wrapped her arms around Uya's shoulders and pushed her upright, as if to make her stand. "No, no," Uya said. Her strength was gone, her energy wrung out by labor. "I can't stand. I have no strength." But Tuulo got her onto her knees, propping her up and holding her from behind. Dhuja crouched in front of them, one hand on the top of Uya's belly, the other between her legs seeking whatever clues the midwife knew to find.

The pain went on. The valleys and respites from the labor disappeared, smearing the thrashing of her womb together into an unending, unbearable agony.

It changed, becoming, if such a thing were possible, *worse*. The bones of her hips felt as if they were being torn apart, inch by inch, but they wouldn't just *break* and give her some relief. And in the middle of the torment came an urgency. A need to push. To expel. To *end* it.

She pushed. Dhuja and Tuulo were both murmuring at her, though she understood nothing that they said. Her teeth ground

147

together as she grunted and groaned. She had a few breaths' respite, then again. Then again. Then again.

Her strength was flagging. Tuulo was all that kept her upright, and when the next urge to push seized her, she pressed only a moment, then relented. "I can't," she said. "I can't. I'm done."

A vicious stream of language erupted from Dhuja's mouth. She stuck her fingers into the birth canal, then held up a single bloody finger, pointing at the highest knuckle. Uya understood: That was all the further she had left.

She pushed. She pushed again. On the third time she felt something slip. Dhuja was pulling. Tuulo was shouting. Then once more, and it was over.

She collapsed against Tuulo. She breathed, feeling the absence of pain as if it were the most blessed thing in the world.

Only after a moment of rest was she aware of the silence.

No.

She had known. She had known when the horse fell atop her, from the time she felt the blow to her belly, from Dhuja's face as the labor began too quickly. *But still, no, please, no. Not here. Not alone, not after this.* Not when everything else she loved had also died, too.

"Let me see!" She shook herself free of Tuulo's grasp. Tuulo tried to take hold of her again, but Dhuja reached out and stopped Tuulo's wrist. With her other hand she offered something tiny and blue to Uya.

It was a boy. He was beautiful.

He had been dead for hours.

She cupped her hands around her son, and she pressed his limp, motionless body against her breasts. Silently cooing, she rocked him back and forth, and she washed the blood off him with her tears.

CHAPTER 17

SAOTSE

NIGHT FELL, AND THE PARTY collapsed onto the ground as if they had been dropped. Saotse fell out of the Tagoa's arms onto all fours. Pain cascaded down her arm, and she cried and collapsed to the ground. The smell of grass and wet earth filled her mouth, and the mournful, vicious buzz of Sorrow welled up. She thrust it firmly aside. Another minute in the fullness of the Power, and she might die.

"Help her," Tagoa said. "Someone."

Hands and muttering voices descended over her and rolled her onto her back.

"I'm fine," she tried to say. "I'll be all right." But the words were feathery and choked with dust, and they knew better. And perhaps she wasn't fine. She felt her limbs shaking as she lay on the ground, and her heart warbled in her chest. The nearness of the earth made her breath unsteady. Sorrow rose up from the ground like water from a spring, and though Saotse pushed the Power away, it threatened to drown her.

Someone said, "It's still bleeding." Voices clattered together like rocks in the surf above her.

"Do we have any rags?"

"The wall that she raised..."

"No, we—"

"I don't care, tear your shirt."

"Oarsa help us, it terrifies me."

"... have to keep her alive."

She cleared her throat and gathered enough voice to say, "Lift me up."

"What was that?"

"Raise me up. Put something under me. Don't let me touch the ground."

So they did, and the sweet, smothering nimbus of the Power receded a little. Saotse's heart calmed, and she began to breathe air rather than earth.

"I'm sorry," she whispered so only Sorrow could hear. "This old mortal cannot hold so much of you."

She was aware, now, of the pain in her shoulder, like a hot, bright shard of pottery against the grinding ache in all her bones and muscles. They were dabbing her with water, cleaning the wound, binding it with rags.

"It's not bad," the voice nearest her said. "He only got the tip of his knife into your shoulder. You'll be fine, Grandmother."

The next voice was Tagoa's. "A little closer, a little further down, and she would be dead. And then we all would be dead."

Palam's voice broke the awkward silence. "So we would be. What's your point?"

"This was a bad idea."

"I don't see why you think that. I'd say that the attack was a great success. We killed a tremendous number of them, and we got all the way to their camp itself. And we escaped with our lives."

"Not all of us did," said someone else, whose name Saotse could not recall.

Palam grumbled. "No battle is without losses. Their totems will get the highest honor on your ancestor totem."

Tagoa raised his voice. "You'd care a little more if it had been you. And what would the *kenda* have said if we lost one of his *enna*?"

Another awkward silence followed.

"I'm sorry," Palam said. "I spoke rashly."

The man standing over Saotse finished dressing her wound. "There. You'll be good at least until we make it back to Ruhasu."

"Thank you," Saotse said. She lifted her voice just enough to make it heard by Tagoa and the messenger. "I agree with Palam. We brought the battle to the Yakhat and made them know fear. And we did this untrained and unprepared. If any of us knew much about the art of war, the man who came from behind would never have reached me."

"The fact that none of us know anything about war isn't a reason to consider this a victory," Tagoa said. "We should be mourning."

"The *kenda*'s forces know how to carry weapons," Palam said with a puff of pride. "When we add the Kept to their number, the Yakhat will be no match for us. Especially if you can repeat the miracle you performed today of raising a wall of stone behind us."

"Ah." In truth, she probably could not repeat a feat of that magnitude, at least not for a long time. That had been an act of desperation. She had not thought that the Powers could become tired, but when at last she and Sorrow had ceased to raise the wall, her weariness had reached beyond her own bones and into the roots of the earth, where for a little while, the stones stopped their creaking and the earthworms ceased to till, undone by the exhaustion of the Power that animated them. She had come closer to dying then than when the Yakhat warrior had come at her with a knife.

Bedrolls unfurled and weary bodies stretched out around them. Crickets sang in the grass. Tagoa sat on the grass next to Saotse, and Palam lay down a little further away.

"So what is our plan now?" Tagoa asked Palam. "Since your first plan was, in your eyes, a total success."

"I would ask the Kept what she wants," he said.

Saotse coughed and cleared her throat. "I want what we originally called for. To meet up with the *kenda* and his forces and go out against the Yakhat."

"So we return to Ruhasu, then cross in canoes to where the *kenda* and his forces are gathered," Tagoa said.

"Good," Palam said, his voice honeyed with pride. "I'll have to send word ahead of us so that the *kenda* knows who we're bringing."

"I wouldn't have it any other way," Saotse said quietly.

The conversation ebbed around them, and sleep swallowed her before she was aware of its coming.

CHAPTER 18

KESHLIK

"SHE'S ALIVE," TUULO SAID. "THAT'S about all that I can say. She has terrible bruises from her face down to her thighs. But losing the child... That wounded her worse than the horse's hooves."

The silence between Keshlik and Tuulo was as palpable as a skirt of grass. The circle of burnt earth, swept and re-blessed by Dhuja, once again separated them with an impenetrable barrier, and their words seemed to acquire the weight of the earth as they spoke, as if Khou herself opposed their passing. Keshlik felt a deep and unnameable unease. The ground seemed murky and insubstantial beneath his feet, even when the Prasei witch wasn't using it as a lash against his warriors.

"I don't like it," he said. "I brought her here to protect her from the depredations of the other Yakhat. I didn't bring her to be trampled by a horse and miscarry."

Tuulo sighed and rested her hand on her belly. She, too, seemed distracted, her face clouded by unvoiced thoughts.

"Are you worried about our child?" Keshlik asked.

"No," she said. "I mean, not any more than before. Dhuja brought Uya through labor as best as any midwife could. But still... It had been a long time since I was with a woman giving birth. Is it too girlish to say that I'm afraid?"

"I wouldn't know. What goes on in Khou's circle is beyond my ken."

"Khou's circle, feh. Dhuja says that the woman miscarried because she left Khou's circle and delivered outside of the blessing. I say that the woman miscarried because a horse tripped over her. Nonetheless, it's a bad sign. I don't like it."

"You'll give birth inside the circle."

"But its protection was broken. I went outside it. Whether Khou still protects me..."

He grumbled in frustration. "I can't tell you anything about that. Isn't Dhuja the one who knows how to invoke Khou's blessing?"

"I'm not asking you to *know* anything, Keshlik. I'm just—oh, never mind." Her mouth was twisted down into a half-hidden frown, and she looked away from him, toward the east. A blade of grass spun distractedly in her hand. "Juyut is coming," she said abruptly.

Keshlik glanced over. His brother hobbled toward them from the direction of the camp. His steps were cramped by pain, but he walked with his head high, biting his tongue to avoid giving any other hint of the depths of his injury.

"Well, well," Tuulo said, raising her voice. "Is that my brother-in-law risen from the dead, or is it another woman waddling with a baby?"

"Ah, sister-in-law," Juyut said. "When I was hurt, I had only Dhuja and the other old ladies to comfort me. Now I remember why I was so anxious to get back onto my feet. Otherwise, where would I hear such lovely greetings?"

"I'm pleased to offer any help I can to get you out from under Dhuja's care," Tuulo said.

Juyut grinned. "And I'd offer help of my own, but there's a matter of this blessed circle between us."

"Oh, so now you respect Khou? I don't recall Juyut being afraid of a little burnt earth before."

"Afraid? No. But if *you're* not afraid, you could come out here. I'll bring a horse to help—"

"Stop," Keshlik said.

Awkward silence. Juyut looked away, ashamed.

"That is not the thing to joke about," Keshlik said.

"I'm not hurt," Tuulo said in a low voice. "And Uya can't understand anyway."

"Well," Juyut said, "that's good."

It was as close as they were going to get to an apology. "Why are you here, Juyut?" Keshlik asked.

"Emissaries from the Chalayit are here. They bring urgent news from Prasa."

"Bring me to them." He stood and bowed to his wife. "I have to go, Tuulo."

She nodded at him and heaved herself to her feet. "Of course. Go. And don't forget that I'm still waiting for you to bring me the witch's eyes."

"I haven't forgotten. It's going to be harder than I thought, but I'll get them." He turned away and helped Juyut limp back to the center of the encampment.

The fire in the center of the encampment was lit, and the elders of the Khaatat were seated next to two young Chalayit warriors. They rose and saluted as Keshlik approached.

"Golgoyat is among us," he said as he took his seat. Juyut settled down next to him. "You have news from Prasa?"

"We do," the elder of the Chalayit said. "But dare I ask a question before we begin?"

"Ask."

"What happened here? We barely found the encampment, and when we entered, we found the yurts full of wounded Khaatat and broken spears."

"Oh, so you haven't heard?" He scowled. "Did you notice the new stone ridge that we put up?"

They stared at him nervously. "We don't understand, Keshlik."

He sighed. "The city-dwellers have a witch. We lost half of a raiding party when she struck us, making the ground split open and swallow our warriors." He omitted Juyut's part, and he felt his brother stiffen then relax at the silent omission. "She attacked our encampment this morning and was driven off only after a grievous fight. As she and her party retreated, they raised the stone spine that you see to the west to protect their escape."

The Chalayit went wide-eyed with shock. "The ridge of stone to your west is four miles long," the younger said. "The witch called that out of the earth?"

"It was complete in less time than it would take a hawk to fly its length. But don't fear. The witch will be slain. We've already shown that we can drive her off. When we finally get to her, I'll pluck her eyes out and give them to my wife, and she'll give them to our son as toys."

The elder Chalayit cleared his throat. "I hope you're right, Keshlik, because we bring more news to disturb you. An enormous army is coming up from the south. We left to tell you as soon as our scouts reached the city."

He clenched his fists and swallowed a curse. "How far out?"

"The scouts were eight days' ride from the city when they saw the army. We reached you two days after they brought word to Prasa."

"Ten days," Keshlik said. "Were the forces mounted?"

"The scouts saw ponies pulling carts and wheeled chariots, but not mounts. Like the ponies of Prasa, the ponies of the army are small and long-haired, suitable for pulling a load but not much use for riding."

So they would move slowly. He couldn't be sure, of course, but he doubted that they could move with even half of the speed of his mounts, which meant that he still had time. Fortunately, the tribes had not spread out much since the sack of Prasa, so they would be quick to gather. He would be leaving Tuulo, though. A hollow feeling of frustration and disappointment soured his gut. "Juyut," he said, "call together our fastest riders. Tell them that the warriors of all of the tribes are to gather in Prasa, just as when we took the city."

"Yes." Juyut rose and walked away with steps that nearly hid his limp.

Keshlik turned back to the Chalayit. "So tell me. How far have your scouts gone, and what have they seen?"

The younger looked to the elder, who answered somewhat reluctantly. "We have had scouts as many as ten days to the south of Prasa, exploring the hilly land and the farms there. But as you commanded, we have refrained from raiding south of the river and kept most of our warriors in Prasa to defend the city. We found no cities in this area, only a multitude of villages and hamlets surrounded by little fields of corn. But there is a wide road that goes south from Prasa beginning at the stone bridge, broad and hard. This is the road that the army approaches on."

"Is it open grassland like these plains? Or is it like the mossy forest surrounding Prasa?"

"More like the forest of Prasa, though much more of it has been cleared for fields."

"Will our riders be hemmed in by the trees, then?"

"Not if we make battle in an appropriate place."

He smiled at them. "I wasn't expecting such auspicious news."

"Auspicious?" Both of the Chalayit looked at him incredulously. "But an army of that size—"

"Is like a tree waiting to be felled by the Yakhat axe. We've taken on armies of city-dwellers before. This is not a new challenge for the Yakhat." *Unlike the earth witch.* "Listen, tonight you are our guests. But tomorrow, you'll ride like the wind back to Prasa, and bring this message to the commanders of the Chalayit warriors there: Keep only the smallest possible force in Prasa to prevent the city from being taken. With every other warrior, form a vanguard and delay the approach of the army from the south. When I arrive with the rest of the Yakhat forces, we'll discuss a plan for the actual battle."

The messengers nodded. "As you command, Keshlik."

He stood to his feet. "For tonight, I propose a feast. Are you tired? Are you hungry?"

They glanced at each other warily, as if afraid of a trick. "We've ridden hard to reach you," the younger one offered.

"Our Khaatat warriors also deserve a feast, after the shame of our first defeat and our success in driving off the witch. So tonight we'll slaughter two calves and gorge ourselves on fat and butter."

"As you command," the older one said, with more relish than before.

"Very good. One of our women will find you a place to rest until then. Tomorrow, after we've eaten and slept, you two can fly back to Prasa, and we will strike the camp. The Khaatat will be coming to Prasa."

If the city-dwellers were raising armies from the south, he needed his camp at the most defensible position behind the line of battle. And also—he realized this was the most important reason, though he would not say it to any of the others—he wanted Tuulo closer to him. They would fight just a short ride from where she waited. And he could return as soon as the word reached him that she had given birth.

Perhaps Dhuja would worry about leaving Khou's circle again. But then again, if the circle had already been breached once, then they might as well burn a new one.

CHAPTER 19

SAOTSE

THE WATER THAT THEY CROSSED was murky and cold with the trembling of the Powers. Oarsa stirred in the deeps, as if readying to breach Saotse's defenses like a whale breaking the surface of the waters. But not yet. He was still far off, and as for Saotse, the earth, the soil, and the ground were her comfort and her friend.

With great relief she heard the gravel biting at the belly of the canoe and the voices of the Ruhasei barking orders to leave the boats, come up on the shore, carry packs, move forward. A core of men remained to paddle the canoes back across the bay to Ruhasu, where they would take up the next wave of fighters and refugees answering the *kenda*'s call. Saotse, Tagoa, Palam, and the rest in their group did not wait for them. The *kenda* was waiting, and Palam was impatient.

They traveled for a day on foot. When the group moved slowly, Saotse walked, her feet in moccasins to shield her from Sorrow's touch, and when they hurried, she was carried. They passed through a land of fragrant spruces and ferns, the twin of the north shore of the bay, gradually rising from the salty mist of the seashore to the drier, sun-lapped inland. The land was sprinkled with the villages and fields of the southern Prasei. A crooked little deer trail through the woods was the closest thing to a road.

The people they passed called out to them, "Are you going to the *kenda*?"

"Yes," Palam called back, "and we're bringing one of the Kept."

Guffaws of disbelief followed them, but Saotse was content to remain silent. Let the peasants of the forest laugh. She was going to meet the *kenda*.

The first night, they stopped in a larger village and begged shelter, in the name of the *kenda* and the Kept. The poor villagers openly disbelieved the messenger's claims about Saotse, but they sheltered them anyway.

Saotse refused to do a demonstration. "I am tired," she said, "and Sorrow rests in preparation for the battle to come." She didn't add that she doubted she could perform any demonstration without damaging the village.

The second and third days were much the same, passing through the alternating coolness of tree shadows and warm, fragrant stretches of cornfields at the edge of villages. They passed an outpost of the *kenda*, from which Palam dispatched couriers telling of their approach. They met other refugees of Prasa along the road and shared terrible stories of the city's fall. The lodges of their hosts were awash in remembered blood. This shared remembrance, more than any of the promises of the *kenda*'s support, was what endeared them to their hosts.

Around noon of the fourth day, Tagoa stopped suddenly in the path. "What is *that*?"

Saotse heard only the grinding of wheels on the path approaching them, like the sound of a cart, but with the tinkling of bells. The footfalls of the group around her fell silent.

Palam laughed. "Have none of you ever seen a chariot before?"

A voice like an oak beam battered the air, speaking in heavily accented Praseo: "We come in the name of the *kenda* of Kendilar. Is the Kept of the unknown Power among you?"

Saotse crept forward a few steps with Tagoa guiding her elbow. "I am she."

Silence hung in the air. Perhaps he disbelieved her. Twice she heard Palam open his mouth as if to say something, but twice he shut it again.

"Is this your entire party?" the speaker asked.

"There are others from Ruhasu," Palam said, "but they lag us by half a day."

This seemed to satisfy the other. "Come then, Grandmother. The *kenda* has sent a chariot and spears to carry you in honor to his side."

Tagoa touched her shoulder. "A little bit ahead is the chariot," he whispered. "It's a wide chair mounted on wheels as if it were a cart, with two horses pulling it. I'll guide you into it."

He led her toward the sound of the bells and the smell of horses, up a precarious step, and onto a little bench, wide enough for her but no other. She felt no reins. Was she supposed to drive this device herself? All around her, the voices of the rest of the party moved forward, wondering and muttering at the strange device and the Yivrian soldiers. Tagoa let go of her hand.

"Where are you going?" she asked, frantic.

"I'm right here," he said, resting a hand on her shoulder.

The leader of the soldiers tutted, and the chariot lurched forward. Bells on the reins tinkled like rain on water. The chariot swayed slightly as they moved, lurching and bouncing over the ruts in the road. Once her nervousness subsided, Saotse began to enjoy the chariot. It was easier than walking and more dignified than being carried. The rocking of the wheels and the gentle swaying of the reins established a comfortable rhythm.

The chariot traveled with the group for the rest of the day, until they reached and relied upon another village's hospitality. The villagers greeted the growing party with weariness, and Saotse heard them muttering about having to house the *kenda*'s guard again. But based on what the *kenda*'s men said, tomorrow Saotse and her companions would reach the camp.

It was afternoon the next day when Tagoa said to Saotse, "I believe that we're coming close."

She heard murmuring among the *kenda*'s men. They halted in a place where the voices of soldiers were thick and stern, where a tense discussion in Yivrian passed between the chariot driver and the guards. Then they passed beyond the sentries, and Tagoa let out a gasp that carried even over the creaking of the chariot's wheels.

"What do you see?" she asked.

"An army... I've never seen anything like it. I see spears like the blades of grass in a field. The forces are camped in groups, with banners over the top of them painted with totems and names. There must be, oh, a hundred different banners, with a hundred men under every banner. Over there—is that it? What else could it be? I think I see the *kenda*'s pavilion."

The sound-stifling canopy of the forest fell away from them, and Saotse heard the murmur of people crowded together like nesting gulls. It was like the furor of the market, a froth of speech and smoke, but *bigger*, as if the market had gone mad and spilled itself over the entire breadth of the city. The encampment assaulted her nose: unwashed men crowded together like cornstalks, smoking campfires with fat sizzling in pans, the odor of horses and hay, grass and pine trampled underfoot, and open latrines putrefying in the sun.

Saotse's companions went mute while the hubbub of the encampment rose up around them. They were going down a narrow path, with the noise of the encampment stretching away on both sides.

"What do you see?" Saotse asked Tagoa. "You said something about the *kenda*'s pavilion."

"Ahead of us," Tagoa said, "there are great tents, as big as a lodge, of white fabric with silver flags flying from the poles. There is a sword painted on the sides of the tent, with nine stars around it. Is that the *kenda*'s insignia?"

"I don't know," Saotse said. Her ignorance shamed her. Did the *kenda* raise an ancestor totem over his lodge as in Prasa? Should she salute it? Should she address him as "Grandfather," as she would the Eldest of another *enna*, or did he possess a title of his own?

They stopped. Ahead of them, someone conversed with Palam in Yivrian. Palam said to them, "The rest of you from Ruhasu will be shown to your camp. The Kept, her aide, and those of the *kenda*'s *enna* will come with me."

Saotse took a moment to realize that "her aide" was Tagoa. He padded up next to the chariot and clutched her arm as if it were a stone in the sea. A tide of grumbling and barked orders washed away the rest of the party from Ruhasu, leaving only the three that the leader had mentioned.

"Finally," Palam muttered.

The chariot lurched forward. Dimness swallowed Saotse's head, and the muffled sounds of the camp dropped away. Voices speaking in clear, sharp Yivrian filled a narrow, roofed space. The pavilion quieted. A question shot like an arrow through the silence in a voice raspy with age.

Palam carried on a short conversation with him, then addressed Saotse with a fear-drenched voice, "Grandmother, Kept of the unknown Power, can you rise?"

She clenched the sides of the chariot and pushed herself to her feet. She sought the ground with her foot and stepped forward.

To her surprise, the elderly speaker spoke in lightly accented Praseo. "Grandmother, you are the Kept who makes the earth shake?"

"I am." Her words bunched up on her tongue. "Forgive me, Grandfather, for I can't see you. But I believe you are the *kenda*."

"How bold of you to assume that the first person to speak to you is the *kenda* himself."

163

"I do not mean to be bold."

"No? Do you mean to flatter me, then?"

"No. I only... I just want to know with whom I speak."

He laughed. "Well, then I won't deny that I am the *kenda*. And you are either a *very* bold liar or someone even more significant than myself."

"I am not a liar."

"I have heard some rather unlikely stories of your exploits. Perhaps you let others lie for you."

"I don't know what stories you've heard. But I am truly Kept by the Power that I named Sorrow. My companions may tell you stories. *True* stories."

"So then, Grandchild," the *kenda* said.

"Yes, Grandfather?" Palam replied.

"Is it true that this woman split the ground open and raised up a wall of stone to protect your retreat from the savages?"

Palam began to answer in Yivrian, but the *kenda* cut him off. "Speak so that the Kept may understand you."

"My apologies, Grandfather," he said in Praseo. "As I said, I saw it with my own eyes."

"And did she ruin an acre of forest by making the ground roil like water around the roots of the spruces?"

"I didn't see that, but I saw the result. It was... impressive. And terrifying."

"Terrifying, yes. Would it be too terrifying to ask the Kept for a demonstration, then? Or would I be too afraid?"

Saotse straightened. "I would, Grandfather. But I worry that no one in this pavilion would survive."

She felt the quivering of the Power at her feet, and with a thought she could have joined herself to Sorrow and torn the pavilion apart. The Power was furious with grief, and the thought of sliding into her and losing herself in Sorrow's grief and anger was a perpetual temptation. Once she had stirred Sorrow to move, she didn't know if she could stop before someone was injured. So she resisted.

The *kenda* suddenly switched into the rapid, tinkling-water tones of Hiksilipsi, and he was answered in kind by a female voice at the edge of the tent. The woman's answer seemed to satisfy him, for he said, without the flinty edge of mockery that had marked his earlier conversation, "Well answered. Tliqyali, the Hiksilipsi woman here, will help you. You may call upon Sorrow, and she will ensure that nothing goes awry."

A soft female hand closed around hers. Saotse almost pulled away in fright, but the woman squeezed her hand and whispered to her, "I won't hurt you. I will hold your hand and ensure that you don't lose yourself in the Power."

"Can you do that?" Saotse asked.

"I can. Don't be afraid."

Saotse nodded, then bowed toward the *kenda*'s voice. "As you wish. Forgive me if this doesn't go well." And she opened herself to Sorrow.

All around her were men with spears. She began to shake, reaching toward them with fists of stone, eager to lash out against her persecutors. *Peace,* Saotse thought, *these are our allies,* and the thought dissolved like dust in the pool of Sorrow. The stone fists collapsed, but her earthen shoulders shook. She would not strike, but she would weep, and her weeping made the soil of her fingers shudder and crumble. Her mouth opened, lips of sod tearing away from one another, and—

A hand, a human hand, closed around hers, and pulled her out. The Power receded, and Saotse was a woman again, kneeling on the ground.

The tent roared with confused babble. The smell of freshly turned soil and torn sod filled the air. Shouts thundered on every side, and feet stamped the ground. The sound was strangely disturbed, as if she were deafened on one side, and then she guessed that half of the pavilion had collapsed, and the sounds on that side were muffled and reflected strangely. Tliqyali still held her hand, and she whispered in Saotse's ear, "Hurry forward!"

She stumbled forward a few paces across uneven ground and heard the *kenda* call out to her, "Well, Grandmother, that was more than I expected!"

Saotse had expected him to be angry, but his voice was friendly and bemused. "I've ruined your pavilion."

"They'll raise it again. But be sure that no one will doubt the ferocity of Sorrow after this. Now, Tlaqyali would like to speak to you, and I would like to speak to my grandchild and your companions. Ruhasu is, from what I understand, the only village to have driven off an attack by the Yakhat, and you are certainly the only ones brave or foolish enough to attempt to attack them back. My generals and I would hear everything you know about them. Will you indulge us?"

She wanted to say that she was by no means in charge of Ruhasu and that he should ask their *akan*. But rather than contradict the *kenda*, she simply said, "Yes."

"Excellent. You may rest for a while if you'd like. Tents have been prepared for you and for the entire contingent from Ruhasu. Tlaqyali will wait on you, and take you to their gathering as soon as you're ready."

The woman's soft, long-fingered hands slipped into Saotse's palm again. "Come, Grandmother," her heavily-accented Hiksilipsi voice said. "We have a table where you may rest and speak."

Tlaqyali led her out of the *kenda*'s pavilion across a stretch of grass through the smoke-rancid air and into another, cooler tent that smelled of pine and cedar. "Here," she said. "There is a cushion that you may lie on."

With the woman holding her hand Saotse lowered herself to the ground and rested against a silk-covered cushion. She reached out and touched a table in front of her, then groped across it for food. The Hiksilipsi woman closed Saotse's hand around a metal cup.

"Wine." She took Saotse's other hand and briefly touched her fingers to cornbread, smoked fish, and apples that were laid out in clay bowls. "Eat all that you'd like. Do you mind if I ask you questions while you eat?"

"No," Saotse said. She raised the cup of wine to her lips. The taste was sweet, heady, and fragrant. In Prasa, the *enna* rarely drank wine, and this was of a higher grade than she had ever tasted. She took two greedy swallows before setting the cup down with a twinge of embarrassment. She must not be seen to gorge herself. She had to maintain even more dignity than usual.

Behind her, Tlaqyali withdrew a whispering sheet of birch-bark paper and cut the nib of a feather quill. She knelt on the grass a pace away from Saotse. "So you have communed with the Powers."

"Yes." Saotse nibbled at a flake of smoked fish.

"When did this begin?"

"When I was a young woman." Saotse recounted how Oarsa had called her across the ocean to Prasa, and then how she had felt the touch of Sorrow during the sack of Prasa. Tliqyali's pen scratched over the paper. When she explained why she had given the name Sorrow to the unknown Power, the woman stopped.

"So you're certain that the Power who Keeps you is a woman?"

"Of course I'm certain."

"How do you know?"

Saotse paused. It wasn't as if the Powers had bodies, yet she had never felt the slightest doubt that Sorrow was a woman. "I don't know that I can explain," she said quietly. "I know in the same way that I know that you are a woman. She has a woman's voice, I might say."

"So she speaks to you in a voice that you can hear."

Saotse shook her head. "No. There is no voice, not in that way. But she has a *presence*, and her presence is female. I have no doubt about it."

"Interesting." Tlaqyali wrote again on her page. "Among the

Yivri, the Kept are always of the opposite sex of the Power that Keeps them."

"I have heard something of the sort," Saotse said. *What did this woman mean to imply?*

"So I wonder why you appear to be an exception."

"Are you saying there is something wrong with me? With Sorrow?"

The woman hesitated. "I am merely asking questions."

"And why are you asking *these* questions?"

"Because I am Hiksilipsi. Knowing the names and the habits of the Powers is my duty. And that's why the *kenda* asked me to visit you."

"Perhaps the Powers from beyond the Gap follow different customs from your own," Saotse said, more acidly than she meant to, and regretted it.

But Tliqyali just laughed. "I suppose they might." The whisper of pages suggested that the woman had put away her writing. "There is a shaman in Vanavar that you should speak to. He is not Kept, but he's the nearest we had before you."

"After the battle." Saotse yawned, feeling sluggish with wine and food. "I came here to give the *kenda* victory over the Yakhat, not to debate the nature of the Powers." She paused, then added, "May I ask you a question, though?"

"Of course."

"How did you pluck me out of Sorrow's power? I didn't know that such a thing was possible."

Tliqyali's voice brightened, and she began to talk quickly. "It is very hard, especially with one of the Kept. But we Hiksilipsi are trained to sense and speak to the Powers from our mothers' breasts, and we learn how to touch them and to withdraw from their touch as needed. So when I saw that you were too deep to quickly emerge, and that you had amply answered the *kenda*'s question, I pulled you out."

"But you aren't Kept."

The woman laughed. "Nothing like it. You were born hearing the Powers, while the Hiksilipsi are trained into it. I will never do anything like what you do, but when what is needed is restraint, sometimes training is better than the gift. So I am happy to help you."

"Ah," Saotse said. She would have liked to speak more with the woman, but she was exhausted from travel and from Sorrow. "Maybe when this is done I'll come to Vanavar, like you said. But for now, I'd like to sleep."

"Of course," the woman said. "I'll take you back to your people. Rest well."

CHAPTER 20

UYA

THE NIGHT WAS HOT AND clear, and the interior of the yurt was muggy. Tuulo lay on her side near one of the walls, talking quietly with Dhuja in the light of a butter lamp. Uya sat near the door, alone. She didn't understand their conversation. She wouldn't have spoken with them anyway. There were no words left in her mouth, no hope left in her heart.

She rose to her feet, slowly, painfully. The rags between her legs still showed blood every morning. The bruises along her face and body had mellowed, fading from crow black to yellow, but the torn flesh still throbbed. She limped to the door of the yurt and pulled aside the flap.

Dhuja barked a command from the rear of the tent. Her glare forbade Uya to leave. But Tuulo said something in return and rested her hand on Dhuja's, then waved Uya out the door. Uya shook her head and ducked outside. She wouldn't have listened to them anyway. What more could they possibly do to her? She wanted to go outside. To see again the ruin they had returned to.

Prasa.

When she had first realized that they were returning to Prasa, dread began to grow on her like a mold. The emptiness and desolation of the city were evidence that the Yakhat had won and that she would never have a home again. Watching the Yakhat set up their camp in the ruins was the final proof of that. The city was as scarred and dead as her womb. The Yakhat trampled the ravaged city, leaking blood from their boots and leaving her alone with her ruined body.

Her breasts were hard with milk. The pain kept her awake at night. Dhuja offered her herbs to ease it, but she refused to take them.

At least she could leave the filthy yurt, reeking of milk and blood. Her whole body was bent with pain. It was a quiet echo of the agony of birth, but it endured. It lay down with her every night and lashed her with its thorns. Sometimes she welcomed it, since it took her mind off the emptiness where her son should be. Other times she just wanted it to stop.

She straightened and looked over the ghosts of the city. The Yakhat were encamped on the north side of the city, largely, with most of the warriors bunking in the plundered lodges, and only a few yurts set up here and there in the empty spaces. More and more Yakhat kept coming, far more than she had seen in the encampment where they originally held her. They were rallying for some purpose. She didn't much care.

She limped to the edge of the burnt circle and stepped over the line. At least she was no longer bound by *that* superstition. Was the circle supposed to protect her pregnancy? It had certainly failed at that. She started walking to the south.

White moonlight lit the city's bones. Toppled ancestor totems lay helter-skelter like driftwood logs next to the path. The lodges seemed grim and ghastly in the moonlight. Some of them glowed with fires lit inside them, where Yakhat warriors lodged like worms burrowing into a corpse. She soon reached the old market square before the Prasada's lodge. It was strewn with the wreckage of plundered casks and muddy with horse manure. A few warriors and young women gathered in groups around the edges of the square. No one even spared her a glance. Perhaps they couldn't

171

even see her. She was the ghost of the dead city, invisible to them, the living, the murderers.

She was close to the river, now, and the smell of reeds and water reached her on a breath of night air. It occurred to her that she could go visit the *enna's* lodge. It was not much further, just across the bridge and a little ways down the path. A throb of homesickness pierced her. The *enna*, her home. She thought of the little path from the door down to the shore, the canoes that the men used for fishing, the hammock on the moon face of the lodge where she slept. Longing to see her home overwhelmed her, even if it was empty now, even if the *enna* was dead. She laughed bitterly. *She* was the Eldest of the *enna* now, which meant that by Prasei law the lodge was hers. Now she just had to convince the Yakhat to give it to her.

At the bridge, however, she paused. There were sentries here, two at each end of the bridge, lazing against the posts with spears on their knees, spitting over the side into the water. She paused in the shadow of a cedar, gathering her courage. Then she walked to the bridge and, without hesitating, started across. "I'm going to my lodge," she said boldly.

They shouted at her in Yakhat, and the nearest one ran forward and grabbed her arm. Upon seeing her face, he started and backed away, as if he only now recognized that she was not Yakhat. She continued across the bridge. They followed a pace behind her, shouting, but they seemed reluctant to touch her. Maybe they thought she was one of the city's dead. Maybe they were afraid of ghosts.

The two at the far end of the bridge tried to bar her way with their spears. She swatted their weapons aside and limped past them. They did not try to stop her. This surprised her, but she didn't linger on the surprise. She considered it a blessing from the Powers.

She followed the path to the lodge as the moon rose into the heights of the spruces. Her eyes searched the moonlit night for the outline of the lodge's peak. She should have seen it by now.

With a gasp of horror, she stopped. She had found it.

All that remained were the charred corner posts, the ancestor totem, and a few cedar planks of the rear wall. The rest had been eaten by fire. She had forgotten the fire, somehow, had forgotten that the smell of smoke was what had driven them out of the lodge and to their doom. She had imagined that the lodge still stood, empty but whole. The charcoaled posts gleamed like the wings of beetles in the moonlight. She walked slowly up to the cinders of the lodge and placed her hand on one of the posts.

A hoot haunted the night air. Wings whispered from the shadows of the lodge to the peak of the ancestor totem. Wide white feathers beat the air, and an owl settled onto the moonlit pole.

"You're late," Uya whispered. Then, louder, "You've missed them, Father Owl."

The bird turned its head and looked at her. It adjusted its wings.

"Did you come to warn us of our deaths?" she said. "Too late. Or were you thinking of warning me before my baby was stillborn? Because you missed that, too. What kind of omen are you, if you only appear weeks after death has eaten its fill of us? Did you just come to remind me?"

The owl hooted again. Soundlessly he leapt from the totem, beating the air once, twice, and flew off to the north. He passed in front of the moon, and Uya lost him in the brightness. She watched the place where the bird had disappeared, but she saw no further sign of him. She sighed. Not even death's owl would stop for her.

She stepped over the threshold into the ruins of the lodge. Burnt scraps of wood crunched under her feet, perfuming her steps with the smell of old woodsmoke. She walked up to the base of the ancestor totem and laid a reverent hand on it. A burnt, broken board, the remnants of the Eldest's chair, rested against the lowest totem. It was a bear, placed in memory of an ancestor whose name she couldn't even remember. Nei had known. Nei's own totem was nine levels above it, a sea otter, still showing a little of its red and white paint between the scars of soot. Since Uya was now the Eldest, she would have to commission totems for Oire and herself, and place them atop the pole. Nei would uphold them in her death as she had in her life.

But it would never happen. Instead, the totems would fall, and all their names would be forgotten, and their memory would be snuffed out forever.

She rested her head against her ancestors' totem and began to cry.

She cried for several minutes, her sobs beating against the bruises on her ribs. She fell to a knee, then cried out at the sudden pain in her bruised legs. Slowly, she lowered herself to the sooty ground and laid her head on her arms.

She had never been a girl who spoke to spirits. Saotse heard the Powers, and Nei dealt with the Hiksilipsi. But now, in the ashes of her home, she mustered up the first prayer of her own that she had ever spoken.

"Oarsa," she said. "Why? Lord of the ocean, why did you forsake us? Did we anger you? Were our offerings insufficient? I'm sorry." She sniffed and wiped her tears on her sleeve. "I don't know why this has happened, but please... listen. Hear me now, if you've never heard me before. The Yakhat took my *enna* and took my child. All I want now is a chance to repay them in kind."

A chilly wind from the sea stirred the ashes of the lodge. Uya's resolve faltered, but she hardened herself and went on. "This is my oath: I swear that if you give me a chance, I will kill Tuulo's child. It will not erase the pain they've dealt to me, but it will be enough."

Then she added as an afterthought, "And Keshlik will kill me afterward. But to die is all I can hope for anyway."

Her words echoed off the scorched wood of the ancestor pole and dissipated into the night. If the Powers had heard her, they gave no sign. But in the end, it didn't matter. She had made her oath, and she would keep it.

She returned to the bridge. She was blackened with soot, now, and when the sentries saw her, they made signs over their eyes and looked away, clutching at fetishes on their necks. Perhaps they mistook her for a vengeful spirit. Perhaps they were right to do so. She walked through the city in silence, not even glancing aside at the few Yakhat she saw, until she paused outside the circle protecting the yurt. She heard another hoot.

In a pine above the yurt, the owl moved again. The same owl? She caught a glimpse of it in the branches. It took to the air as a flurry of gray feathers and silently passed over the yurt where Dhuja and Tuulo slept. Then it dove into the grasses beyond and was gone.

CHAPTER 21

KESHLIK

"Y ou *LET HER GO*?" Keshlik raged. "What sort of calf-brained, rabbit-hearted sentries are you?"

"We believed she was a spirit," the oldest of them said, cowering.

"A spirit! Khou's tits! And what if she hadn't come back?"

"Fortunately," Bhaalit offered from over Keshlik's shoulder, "she did come back. Maybe we should leave things at that."

"Not just at that," said Danyak, the speaker for the Chalayit. "I posted those sentries, and I brought them before you to report. If nothing else, I'll have them shamed in front of the rest of the Chalayit. No one, spirit or otherwise, should be passing over that bridge before tomorrow."

"Yes, do that." Keshlik thrust his spear into the ground. He glowered at the sniveling, idiotic sentries. "And be glad that I don't cut off your spear hands. Now go."

Danyak saluted Keshlik and led the sentries away.

"Unbelievable," Keshlik muttered.

"Even if she *had* run away," Bhaalit said, "she couldn't have gotten far. She's alone, and she's still limping. We would have found her."

"We probably would have," Keshlik said. "But that doesn't

mean I can coddle the Chalayit calves who were supposed to be watching the bridge."

"No it doesn't." Bhaalit rose from his place atop a bale of hay and stretched his legs. "Still, if anyone else bothers you today, try to refrain from cutting off their spear hands. We *do* need to ride out in force tomorrow."

"I know." He groaned and spat. The whole day would be eaten up by securing provisions, counting spears, meeting with the speakers of the tribes, and answering every request the Yakhat brought to him. He did not relish it. And tonight he would see Tuulo for the last time before battle.

It was evening before he came to the circle of burnt earth. Tuulo was already outside, lying on her side on a bed of moss cut from the surrounding hummock. She lifted her head when she saw him come, but no smile brightened her face.

"Is it true our warriors have encountered a vast host?" she asked.

He sat on the ground across from her. "It's true. The Tanoutut vanguard sent word. They met the forces from the south and stopped their march a day south of here."

"So you're going, then." She pushed herself up to her elbows, grunting with the effort. "I should be used to it by now."

"I'll be close by. That's why I moved you here."

"Close by. Yes, well, it's not as if you would be able to enter the circle anyway."

"And the garrison that's remaining will call for me when our son is born. I'll be here to bless him. And I'll have the witch's eyes for you as a gift."

"Ah, that." Finally she did smile. "Good enough."

"By the time you breach this circle, the campaign will be over.

177

We'll have taught the city-dwellers to fear us, and the autumn and the winter will be ours to enjoy."

"I know. Tell me about something else, now. The battle to come. How many of them are there?"

"Many. More than there are of us. But they're all on foot and move slowly."

"As when we attacked Kourak that drove us from the Bans."

"You remember that?"

"I was a girl at the time. Not even a cow-maiden. But I *do* remember something."

"I fought there. A young warrior, my father's lieutenant. Like Juyut."

"Just as headstrong as that?"

He laughed. "No, no. It's a good thing that you didn't know me then, or you would never have let me into your yurt. I was a timid thing, borrowing courage from my father. If he hadn't had the thunder of Golgoyat in him, I would never have had the guts to follow him into battle."

"But you won."

"Of course, we won. Not due to me, of course. I just did what my father told me to do, and when he opened his mouth and shouted Golgoyat's thunder against the gates of the city... If he were still here, I wouldn't be devising traps to destroy the Prasei witch."

"I don't remember that. We girls were kept too far from the battle." She closed her eyes. "But as for you, even though you lack the audible power of Golgoyat that your father had, you've led the Yakhat from victory to victory."

"I suppose, if you call the last two skirmishes we've had 'victory.'"

"I do. But—oh."

The captured woman had emerged from the yurt and stared at the two of them. Her jaw sagged, and her mouth was a heavy, unmoving line like a river under a winter sky. Her gaze rested

STORM BRIDE

on Keshlik, carrying hatred like a knife grown dull with age. She proceeded with wounded, mincing steps to the opposite side of the circle.

An awkward silence fell over them until she was out of view. Finally Tuulo asked, "When do you pack out?"

"Tomorrow. Though I'll be among the last to leave, as we're counting the spears again as they cross the bridge, then I'll ride at the rear to the site of the battle."

She sighed. "I hope that'll be long enough."

They sat together as the evening ripened. The day was hot, with a dense, suffocating humidity that seemed to bleach the colors from the air. Flies buzzed at the sweat on their foreheads. Across the circle, the captive woman stirred and came around toward them. With a final, baleful glance at Keshlik and Tuulo she tucked back into the yurt.

"I don't like that she's here," Keshlik said. "I took her out of the city to keep her safe, but that failed. There's an evil doom on her."

"A doom worse than what she's already suffered?"

Keshlik grunted. He watched the yurt flap behind which the woman had disappeared.

"I'll be happy if I just escape her fate," Tuulo said. "So long as you have a chance to hold your son in your hands."

"Thank you." He sighed and kneaded the earth beneath his fingers. "It would be good to find a land to call our own again."

"You mean one that we can share?" Tuulo gestured to the blessed earth between them.

"I mean all of the Yakhat. I'm getting tired, Tuulo, and I'd like to put down my spear at some point. It would be nice to find peace. So few of us even still remember it."

Tuulo was quiet, tapping her fingers on top of her belly, with her eyes half-closed as if she were lost in reminiscence. "My earliest memory is of a wet, cold lean-to where my mother fed me and my brother gruel. Before Golgoyat came to your father, but after we were driven from the Bans. Would you call that a time of peace?"

"A kind of peace. But not the kind that I want. I meant the Bans, the old homes. The way the yellow sun glowed in the mist at dawn, and the lowing of the zebu on the hummocks."

Tuulo shook her head. "I don't remember that at all."

"And that's the problem. Most people younger than you don't remember anything but the plains and the spear. How could I ever convince them to take up a life of peace?"

"Well, has the Sorrow of Khaat Ban been avenged?"

"How will I know when it has? What sign will appear to tell us?"

Tuulo shook her head. "When you see it, you will know, and you'll be able to convey it to the Yakhat. Your father gave us back our courage. Maybe your lot will be to give us back our peace."

They sat together, neither speaking nor touching, until the sun fell into the ocean.

The morning after Keshlik arrived at the camp, scouts of the Lougok tribe left at dawn to survey the Yivrian forces. At midmorning they returned with their report. The Yakhat were thirty hundreds in eleven tribes, strung across two hilltops at the narrow end of the broad, green valley. The Yivrian host was packed together at the far end of the valley in dense, orderly lines. The scouts estimated seventy to ninety hundreds in their number, outnumbering the Yakhat three to one.

Those weren't the worst odds that Keshlik had ever faced.

And there was good news. Thanks to the short stride of the Yivrian ponies, the scouts' mares easily outran the sallies of the defenders that saw them. The Yivriindi were armed with long, heavy bronze spears for the most part, interspersed with men bearing slings and bows. Based on what the scouts had seen, the men were none too accurate with them. Their *only* advantage was their numbers. And the witch, if she was hiding among them.

Juyut was on his right and Bhaalit on his left. Behind them were two score mounted warriors, their spears upright, with their blades glittering in the sunlight.

A delegation from the Yivrian forces was approaching with a force of similar size. In their center was a chariot roofed in white fabric, holding a tall, elderly man and pulled by a pair of sturdy ponies.

"Remember the face of the man in the chariot," Keshlik said to Juyut and Bhaalit. "If we kill him, we can split his forces."

Bhaalit just grunted. Juyut shifted in his saddle. He was still bruised, and he winced every time his spear found its mark in the warriors' games. But he could ride, and he insisted on going out to the battle. If it were anyone else, Keshlik wouldn't have let him. But it was Juyut. He was the best warrior of the Khaatat, perhaps the best of all of the Yakhat. Even wounded, he was a force on the battlefield, and the young warriors of his generation looked up to him as if he were their commander. Keshlik couldn't leave him back.

A messenger preceded the main body of the Yivrian party, shouting in Guza: "The king of the Yivriindi comes in peace! He seeks parlay according to the agreed terms! Accept him in peace!"

"In peace, in peace," Juyut muttered. "We heard you the first time."

The Yivrian envoy stopped a hundred feet from where the Yakhat were waiting. As had been agreed through the messengers sent between the armies last night, Keshlik trotted into the middle of the open space between them, accompanied only by Juyut and Bhaalit.

"Have you come unarmed?" the messenger asked.

"We have no spears and no bows, as agreed," Keshlik said.

The block of spears surrounding the tented chariot split. A tall, white-haired figure began to approach.

The herald closed his eyes. "Behold, the High King of Kendilar! Whose ancestors are written on a pillar of stone, whose ancestry is founded upon Vanasenar, beloved of Lunelori, who carries the star-bright sword..."

The introduction went on for some time as the *kenda* approached. Keshlik suppressed the urge to tell the herald to stop piling on the titles, as if the battle would be won by the length of the *kenda*'s names. The herald bowed and scurried away as soon as the white-haired man reached them.

Keshlik looked down at the *kenda* from atop his mare. The man was tall, thin, and uncowed, looking up at Keshlik with haughty confidence. He was dressed in light blue cloth edged with silver embroidery, which was matched by a set of fine silver chains draped around his neck. The circlet on his brow was pleated with feathers, forming a crown of egret white and jay blue atop his head. The sword that the herald had mentioned was clasped at his side, a blade of shining steel, the etchings on its blade glittering in the sunlight.

But none of these things would make any difference in the battle. So Keshlik raised his voice and said, "Are you the *kenda* that this herald has been prattling about? Did you expect me to fall to the ground trembling at the mention of your ancestors? I've never heard of any of them. If you wish to speak to me, speak to me like a man."

The *kenda* crossed his arms and examined Keshlik with cool indifference. "Should I answer you as if you are a man or a demon? Are you not the murderer who ravaged the city of Prasa and slew my ally, the Prasada?"

"I am. Did you come to hear my exploits? They're more impressive than the list of your ancestors."

The *kenda* scowled. "Damn your exploits. I offer you a chance to surrender before you're crushed."

"We fight with Golgoyat of the thundercloud. The Yakhat will never surrender."

"Your Golgoyat is as meaningless to me as my ancestors are to you. But if you're not a fool, you'll listen to my offer. We have you massively outnumbered."

"The warriors of the Yakhat make yours look like children. Why should we fear your legion of rabbits?"

"We also have a woman who is Kept of Sorrow."

Keshlik's heart skipped. The phrase "Kept of Sorrow" was meaningless to him, but it meant the witch *was* here. He had guarded the faint hope that she wouldn't come to this battle, but he buried his fear. "Now why should we fear a woman? Is her spear bigger than yours?"

Juyut and Bhaalit chuckled.

The *kenda* cut them off. "You've met her before. The ground itself obeys her and revolts the insults of your warriors' hooves."

"So her spear *is* bigger than yours," Juyut said in Yakhat. Bhaalit laughed.

The *kenda* raked Juyut with his sharpened gaze. "Does your friend have something to say to me, or is he going to continue whispering like an old woman?"

"You just told me to be afraid of your old woman," Keshlik said, "so maybe I'll allow that comparison. We have faced your witch before."

"Then you know you ought to be afraid."

"We're both alive. Does she think she's going to get us on her third try? Now you should ask her if she remembers the tip of the knife I got into her."

"You will never see her. The Kept is defended by the whole of the army now. So unless you think you can tear through the entirety of my forces without the ground swallowing you up, you should hear my offer."

"Tell me, then," Keshlik said.

"I am prepared to suffer your presence in my realm on three conditions. First, you withdraw from the field of battle and all lands south of the River Prasa. Second, withdraw from the city of Prasa itself and all of its environs, including all settlements of the Prasei on the north bank. Finally, allow the survivors of those settlements to return and live peacefully in perpetuity. Never again will you come out in force against the Prasei or the Yivriindi, or be found south of the river."

Keshlik snorted. "Golgoyat forsake us if we accept those terms."

"I told you, I care nothing for your Golgoyat."

"Then start learning his name now. The warrior of the thundercloud fights among us and has given us victory over every enemy so far. You will be no exception."

"Then what is your counteroffer?"

"Our counteroffer is for you to die." He looked at Juyut and Bhaalit and said in Yakhat, "Do we need to hear anything else here?"

The both shook their heads.

"Then let's go." He tapped his horse's flank and turned her to leave.

A murmur of consternation stirred in the Yivrian forces behind them. Keshlik smiled slyly at Juyut as they returned to their own guard. He looked up at the sun, then back at the Yivrian lines. "If they engage today, we'll hold them off and wait until tomorrow. Tomorrow we crush them."

CHAPTER 22

UYA

THE WARRIORS HAD LEFT THAT morning. Like ants scurrying away from a carcass, carrying the last of the city's food stores with them so they could go... do what? Uya didn't know.

She knelt outside the cocoon of the yurt and watched the moon. She couldn't sleep. She hadn't slept since returning to Prasa and its defiled lodges, and especially not since crossing to her old *enna* and making her vow. She needed to be vigilant.

Inside the tent, Tuulo whimpered in her sleep. Uya watched the cloud-scarred sky for any sign of the owl that she had seen, or any other omen of the Powers' presence. So far tonight, nothing. The sun had long since set, and the air was growing chilly and damp. Perhaps she should go inside and try to rest. It was better than waiting outside in the cold.

She ducked into the yurt. The smells of curdled milk, butter lamps, and blood washed over her. But there was another sweet, damp odor in the tent tonight. Curious, Uya stepped forward. Her foot touched a puddle of warm fluid. She gasped. Tuulo twitched awake with a cry.

Dhuja woke and jabbered at Tuulo, who responded with short, quiet sentences. A wooden box scraped open, and the midwife's face appeared briefly in the glow of an ember. A moment later, the whole yurt came awake in the soft light of the butter lamp. Tuulo was propped on an elbow, her skirt soaked from the waist down with the hot, sweet-smelling liquid slowly seeping into the ground below her. Dhuja crouched over her, continuing her stream of sharp, clipped commands.

Uya stepped back. A memory of panic and pain swallowed her. Her breath came quick. She groped for the door of the yurt behind her but found only the felt of the walls.

Dhuja looked up at her and barked a single word. Uya slid to the ground and began to weep.

Not again. Not—oh, it wasn't even *her* baby, but she felt it as if it were, as if right now the thorn was entering between her legs and splitting her in half. Again, the stench of blood and the feel of her bones being wrenched apart. Again, her baby's dead face staring up at her, stringy with shreds of afterbirth. No breath in the child she bore. No cries except her own.

A hand closed over hers. She looked up.

Tuulo was there. She smiled—she *smiled* somehow, holding the bottom of her belly with one hand and clasping Uya's fist in hers. How could she smile, how could she *move* in the middle of that pain?

Tuulo tugged at Uya's hand. Of course. Her water had just burst. The pain hadn't even started yet. So she could smile. She could look at Uya with that horrible face full of pity and sympathy.

Though... the pinched look in her eyes, the quivering of the hand that clutched her belly as if she thought it might drop off. They showed fear. She had seen Uya's travail and the dead thing that had come out in place of her living son. She, too, had grown slick with Uya's blood and sweat that night.

She was afraid, and she was asking for Uya's help, hoping that Uya might repay the help that she had received.

Repay? Uya's oath rose up inside her, grumbling like a thundercloud, burning her stomach with its lightning.

She took Tuulo's hand and led the woman back to the mat. Dhuja was pinning open the doors and opening the flue in the peak of the yurt, inviting the cool night air into the enclosure. Uya helped Tuulo lie on her side and straightened her coarse braid.

Then she leaned close and whispered into the woman's ear, "I'll help you, Tuulo. You helped me give birth, and I'll help you. But you'll never see your son alive. I'll give you back exactly what you and your warriors gave me. And maybe when you see your child's broken neck and your husband holds his cold, limp body, you'll know the smallest part of what you've done to me and my people."

Uya spent the first hours after midnight helping the other two women prepare for an imminent birth. Dhuja directed Uya with barks and gestures to build a fire outside the yurt, and a pair of Yakhat women rolled an enormous clay pot in from the camp and filled it with water. The midwife dressed Tuulo in a loose woven garment that barely reached to her thighs, then set her pacing the boundaries of the blessed circle. Tuulo padded repeatedly past Uya, grinning nervously every time. Sweat pooled on the tops of her ruddy cheeks, visible as greasy puddles even in the moonlight, but she seemed calm, even cheerful. Uya scowled and turned back to making the bed of coals for the water pot.

The moon crawled across the sky.

Every time Tuulo walked by, Uya expected to see her grimacing in pain, and every time, she was disappointed. A few times, Tuulo winced, as if she had stepped on a thorn. But where were the roaring pains that Uya had experienced?

As the night wore on, Dhuja kept grimacing and muttering in gravelly anger. Once Uya's bed of coals was white and hot, she called Tuulo over and made the woman squat by the water pot. Her hand disappeared briefly under Tuulo's skirt, and Tuulo clenched her teeth. Dhuja scowled.

She spat a word at Tuulo. Tuulo answered mildly. They seemed to argue for a few minutes, then Tuulo shrugged and returned to the yurt. At the entrance flap, she turned to Uya and said a Guza word.

"I don't understand you," Uya muttered.

Tuulo tried another word, then another. That third one, Uya recognized from the Guza trade manifests: "Blanket."

"Blanket? You want a blanket. Why are you bothering me about this?"

Tuulo closed her eyes and patted the back of her head. Then she pointed back into the yurt.

"Ah, *sleep*," Uya said. "You're going back to sleep." The labor was moving slowly—so slowly that Tuulo was going to return to her bed and *sleep*!

Dhuja made a sour-sounding comment, which Tuulo shushed. She disappeared into the yurt. Uya threw down the stick with which she had been stirring the coals. "Well, I'm certainly not going to stay here heating up water for a sleeping bitch. The moon's still up. I'm going to get some rest, too."

Dhuja looked back in incomprehension but made no effort to stop Uya as she limped back into the yurt.

The interior was lit in a soft orange glow of the lamp suspended from the ceiling. Tuulo opened her eyes and smiled at Uya when she came in. Uya found her own mat and lay down with her back turned to Tuulo.

Sleep washed over her like an ocean wave. A few times during the night, she awoke just enough to hear Tuulo murmuring and groaning in the pain, but she didn't stir from her bed. She hadn't forgotten that Tuulo was still her enemy.

The hours from midnight to dawn crawled by. She heard chickadees chirping at sunrise, but exhaustion tugged at her eyelids and pushed her back into restless slumber.

Finally, when the sun was a hand's height above the eastern horizon, Uya came fully awake.

Tuulo was gone. The reed mat had bunched up from Tuulo's shifting. Had something happened? Had the baby come? That couldn't be. They would have called her. They *needed* her.

She left the yurt and found Tuulo and Dhuja together, a little ways from the now-dormant fire. Dhuja seemed not to have slept, but she had changed clothes. She wore a loose black skirt that came only to her knees, exposing her bony, veined calves to the wind, and a simple cloth around her breasts and shoulders. Her waist and belly were bound with a broad red strip of fabric wrapped around her midsection.

Tuulo had her skirt hiked above her belly, and Dhuja was drawing lines on her with the burnt soil that bounded their yurt. A circle encompassed her belly, connected by waving lines to her thighs and breasts, with a double straight line descending directly downward. Dhuja gave Uya a dismissive glance, but Tuulo smiled at her and said something in greeting.

The last word of her greeting caught in her throat, and she winced, bending forward and grabbing Dhuja's hand. Dhuja squeezed the hand back. Tuulo stood there, face hammered down in pain, then let out her breath with a desperate, wheezing gasp.

So her pains had finally begun in earnest. It was about time. *May they be difficult and fruitless*, Uya prayed.

Dhuja grimaced at Uya, and a long string of gibberish poured from her mouth. She pointed to Uya and then gestured toward the city, across the blessed circle.

"What?" Uya said. "You want me to leave?"

"No," Tuulo said. Her voice was hoarse, and she pieced together the Guza words with slow, broken cadence. "Go. Go bring here... a man."

Dhuja was back at Tuulo's side. Uya rose, hesitant, but Dhuja barked at her again, and she sped out of the circle.

The sun had risen, and yellow dawn light lanced through the

city. Where was she supposed to go? To find someone. A man. Any man, or some particular man? But she couldn't possibly find anyone in particular, so she would have to take the first man she found and hope that Dhuja would take him. She ran toward the old market where the yurts had been pitched.

There were old Yakhat women crouched over crocks of milk at the edges of the market. Beyond the women were empty, blank buildings. She ran past them, past stalls of horses and burnt ancestor poles, and—there. A warrior sentry, alone, mounted. She ran to him and clasped his hand, shouting, "Tuulo! Tuulo!"

He cursed and kicked at her. She closed both her hands over his, repeating in Guza, "Dhuja! Tuulo! Come!" He scowled down at her with irritation but began to walk his horse forward at her insistence. She ran a few paces ahead, motioned for him to follow, and ran to the yurt with the warrior at her heels.

He waited at the boundary of the blessed circle while she ducked into the fetid yurt, where Dhuja and Tuulo had disappeared. On entering, she pointed back in the direction of the horseman, then knelt next to Tuulo. Dhuja shouted a command, then left with Tuulo kneeling next to Uya.

Tuulo wrapped her hands around Uya, then winced and leaned forward. Her breath stopped in her throat. Her fingers dug into Uya's back, and she ground her teeth.

"Quiet," Uya said in Praseo. She doubted Tuulo heard her words, anyway. "Quiet. It'll be all right. You'll make it."

Though your son won't. Even if you birth him alive, I'll make sure of that.

CHAPTER 23

SAOTSE

T HE HOOVES OF HORSES SOUNDED like raindrops hitting the head of a drum. Saotse pinched the grass between her toes, and brushed briefly against Sorrow. The Power shuddered and keened. Danger and woe clashed in her voice, wild and unbound. Saotse only suffered a touch before pulling away.

Soon. Soon, my mother. The Yakhat are near. Soon we'll meet them and crush our enemies.

It was morning. The meeting with the Yakhat commander had taken place the previous day, and she had gotten the full report of his threats against the Yivriindi, the Prasei, and against her personally. The report had not frightened her. The Yakhat remembered her, which meant they were afraid. *Good.*

She sat on the ground, though the *kenda* and most of his retinue were in chariots. She had insisted. If battle began in earnest, there would be no time to dismount from a chariot, and she needed to touch the earth to reach Sorrow. Tagoa had held her hand and led her through the line of chariots and spears to where she now sat.

The *kenda* himself sat in a chariot just beyond her reach. He whispered to his herald, and the herald repeated the command in a tremendous voice: "*Tokotya!*"

A drumbeat split the air. Three long, sonorous strikes beat

against the air—*gau gau gau*—then the drums settled into an even two-stroke rhythm of *thrim-throm, thrim-throm.* The army stuttered forward in time to the beat, the spears clattering like the roar of the sea. They moved slowly, well within what Saotse could manage. Sorrow followed their every step.

The next command came: "*Tonaltoya!*"

The drums quieted. The march sputtered out and stopped. Quiet roared over the valley, pregnant with the army's muttering, punctuated by the sound of distant hoofbeats.

"What do you see?" Saotse asked Tagoa.

"The *kenda*'s two lines of spears are set up in front of us," he said. "The Yakhat are in clusters a half-mile away. They watched us march forward, but they haven't moved to attack yet. Now the commanders are arranging the front line. They crouch. Their spears are planted in the dirt, pointed out in a line toward the horses, like a porcupine's tail."

The commands from the front line reached her as little scraps of Yivrian carried on the air. Spear shafts thudded against the ground. The wind rustled the clothes of the waiting soldiers.

Tagoa drew in his breath. "Now some of the Yakhat begin to move."

The rumble of horses sounded like far-off thunder, growing closer.

"Do nothing yet, Kept," the *kenda* said. "I will give the order."

"They're charging the line," Tagoa went on, half to Saotse, half as if in response to the *kenda*. "No, they're breaking away. Parallel to the line, now—look out!"

He grabbed Saotse's hand and pulled her to the ground. An arrow whistled through the air and pricked the ground beyond them. Sorrow felt it as if the arrow had torn open her flesh, gurgling up in a geyser of fury and boiling earth. Saotse wrestled against the urge to lash out. *Not yet.*

"They're shooting arrows into the front line," Tagoa said, "charging past and firing wantonly, just like they did when we

192

began our attack outside of the encampment. They move quickly, spread out, darting like bees."

The *kenda's* Yivrian commands rumbled out through his commanders. Arrows from their own side sang off bows. Howls of pain creaked up from their line, and on the far side, one or two injured horses wailed. The thunder of the hooves waned, then roared again. More arrows split the air.

The *kenda* shouted a new command in Yivrian, then repeated to Saotse and Tagoa, "Follow us! We move into battle!"

Tagoa pulled Saotse to her feet, and they bolted forward. There followed a confused time of shouting and running; of commands screamed in Yivrian, booming back and forth on every side; of pounding feet and clattering spears mixing on every side. Wild ululations from the Yakhat savages goaded them. Arrows buzzed through the air. Saotse ran, her hands clenching Tagoa's, trusting his direction to ensure they wouldn't fall prey to a stray spear or arrow. The creaking of the *kenda's* chariot followed them, and shields and spearpoints battered each other on every side. Tagoa panted. Saotse's knees burned.

They stopped. There was melee before them and to the right.

"What's happening?" Saotse cried.

"The front line charged!" Tagoa said. "We caught up with them! But I see Yakhat on both sides of us, though the line holds—for now. Down!"

He pulled her to the ground. Arrows buzzed through the air like flies. Shields clattered against each other to their right, and frantic voices, shrill with panic, cried out in Yivrian. Hooves pounded the earth like hailstones.

Above the din, the *kenda's* voice rolled across the battlefield like a wave crashing over the rocks—urging the Yivriindi to fight, to withstand, and to lash back—and a roar went up from the Yivrian host.

But thunder rumbled in the Yakhat hoofbeats. A black wind buffeted Saotse, meeting the courageous roaring where the *kenda* stood, and Saotse felt as if she were adrift at sea, being beaten by their vast forces. The Yivrian cry of hope turned to dismay. She heard screams to the right.

"The line is broken," Tagoa said. "The Yakhat charge through! Oarsa save us—"

The *kenda* roared, "Kept of Sorrow!"

She dropped to the ground and pressed her face into the dirt as if diving into the soil.

Sorrow and Saotse raged. At first she merely thrashed, sending cascades of dirt in every direction, insensitive to friend or foe. Men crawled over her like flies, and she swatted at them. But then, from the depths of the Power, Saotse remembered who she was. She mastered her fury and then directed it to where it needed to be.

Here her soil was pressed by unbound feet. She let these be. *Here* the points of hooves bruised her skin. She tore up the turf beneath them and buried them in a vomit of stone and soil. A line of horses charged. She opened her mouth, and they tumbled in to be chewed by her rocky teeth.

Spears crossed in battle a little ways away. She shook like a dog and threw them all to the ground, then spit up stones to fall on the horses and their riders. Their bones crunched beneath her missiles, and their blood watered her grasses.

Horses were retreating. She heard screams and felt injured men crawling across her like worms. A wave of rolling earth chased the fleeing line, pitching horses into the air, breaking their legs, throwing riders to the ground. The screams of men and horses sang. She crushed a man in her rocky fist.

A man's hand was on her shoulder. She was a woman again, though the raging Power below her begged her to return.

"Enough." It took her a moment to realize that it was the *kenda*, not Tagoa. "They're retreating from the center. Quickly now, to the flank!"

He picked her off the ground as if she were a child and set her onto the bench of his chariot. He barked a command to his driver. The chariot bolted away, and they fell together onto the bench. Saotse could hear no change in the sounds of battle—the same cacophony of spears and shouts and hoofbeats assaulted her from every side, built upon the urgent clatter of the chariot's wheels. But the *kenda* clearly saw something. Their harrowing ride lasted only a few seconds before the horses screamed and the chariot ground to a stop again. The *kenda* leapt down from the bench.

Saotse leaned forward and began to ask, "Where—"

She did not finish. As soon as her feet touched the ground, the Power took her.

Saotse roared; the earth screamed. She was its master, and as the weeping of Sorrow turned to rage against the forces that insulted her, she guided and damped them. The ground around her remained firm. Beyond the line of standing men, where the horses danced, she shook the earth with sobs. Horses stumbled, men fell, and she raised fists of earth to smash them like ants.

As before, the line of attackers fell back, and her fury ebbed out into weariness and loneliness. She hurled stones after those that retreated, chasing them with waves of earth, but soon they were beyond her reach. Her tormentors fled, and she was still alone, still...

With a tremendous exertion of will, Saotse separated herself from the embrace of the Power before the bottomlessness of Sorrow swallowed her. Dirt was wedged under her fingernails. She bent her arms and felt muddy earth flake away from her arms and shoulders. Her hair was sticking to her head as if it were plastered there with honey. She bent one knee and attempted to rise to her feet.

Her vigor drained like water from a broken pitcher. She wavered on one knee then collapsed onto the ground.

A muffled voice shouted above her. Two pairs of hands rolled her onto her back, and a waterskin touched her lips. She drank. The water on her tongue reminded her to be thirsty, and she sucked at the skin like a greedy infant until she had swallowed the last drops. Questions were muttered in Yivrian around her, then a voice she recognized.

"You will ride in my chariot," the *kenda* said. He repeated the order in Yivrian to the two that had tended to her. They picked her up by shoulders and ankles and arranged her on the bench.

The valley's sound had changed. The drumbeat had ceased. She heard only a few horse hooves pattering, very far away. The hubbub of the battle rippled around her; spears and shields knocked haphazardly against each other, without the intensity of battle. Men wept in pain or sorrow. Others laughed. Shouted commands leapt up and down the line, but they seemed impotent or redundant. The battle scene was like a drumhead that had become loose, and the strokes that beat against it were soft and noiseless.

She made out the *kenda*'s voice amid a pack of heavy footsteps. A hand closed over Saotse's bony, muddy fingers, and his lips kissed her palm.

"Grandmother Kept," he said. "How can I reward you? The battle was a heartbeat away from turning against us when you turned the savages away. We would not have prevailed without you."

She cleared her throat. Her voice came reluctantly, and it sounded scratchy and thin in her ears. "I need no reward. I only want to drive away the Yakhat forever."

"And so we will." He dropped her hand and began to address those gathered in Yivrian. His words, whatever they were, aroused a cheer, which quickly bound itself together into a chant of "Saotse! Saotse!"

The *kenda* seated himself on the bench next to her. They began to slowly roll away, the joyous shout of "Saotse! Saotse!" following them to the camp. She flushed with pride, but someone was missing. She listened for his voice and his gait, and when she didn't find them, she asked the *kenda*, "Grandfather, where is Tagoa?"

"You... you don't know." A pause. "He has perished in battle."

"A Yakhat arrow reached him?"

A longer pause. "Let us say he was killed defending against the savages."

She felt a pitch of vertigo, as if the chariot had been overturned. *It was me. Because Sorrow overwhelmed me at first.* The fear that had kept her from demonstrating Sorrow's power earlier had proved correct. She asked quietly, "Were many of our own killed by the earth's rages?"

"I would not burden you with that knowledge."

"Answer my question."

"Do you insist on knowing? It was some, but not too many. I'm sorry your friend was among them."

She probably would not have called Tagoa a friend. A benefactor, perhaps at the beginning. A guide and translator. But he was the nearest thing she had to an *enna*. "I should have restrained myself. I could have—"

"Cease," the *kenda* said. "This is a battle. Men die. If you had done differently, more would have died."

Saotse folded her hands in her lap and attempted to assume the tone of beneficient patience that Nei had once used. "I understand."

"You will remain in my retinue for the remainder of the day while we see if the Yakhat feel like testing us again. If they attack, do not hold back for even a heartbeat. Do not weep for those harmed in the blindness of the Power. Without you, we are surely lost."

CHAPTER 24

KESHLIK

DEAD HORSES AND DEAD MEN lay like debris on a riverbank after flood. Huge mounds of overturned earth ran parallel to the morning's battle lines, echoed on each side by newborn dunes of scarred, smoking earth. Stones pocked the grass. The valley looked as if it had been plowed by a demon.

Riders returned to the Yakhat encampment, fleeing from the chaos of the lines. Keshlik had given the order that they should regroup at the camp and tend the wounded. Danyak rode back and forth along the front edge of the Yakhat encampment, repeating the directive. Juyut was next to Keshlik—pensive, waiting.

"Begin a count of how many spears were broken," Keshlik commanded. "I want the number within an hour."

"Too many," Juyut said. "I'll begin with the Khaatat." He started his horse toward the tents.

Keshlik called after him, "And Juyut! Get me a true count. I don't want any idiots insisting that their brother must still be alive. Better to count more dead than fewer."

Riders continued to flee in from the battlefield. He named their tribal emblems as they passed. Lougok. Chalayit. Khaatat. Budhut. More Chalayit. Most who returned were whole and had blood on their spearheads. A few came bloodied and earth-stained, but only a few. Most of those that the witch hit were buried in the earth and wouldn't return at all.

The morning's battle had been much less effective than he had hoped. He had instructed the men to ride out in dispersed swarms, striking at the Yivrian lines with arrows, as they had done when the Prasei attacked the Khaatat encampment. If they could've drawn the Yivriindi from their armored lines into a disordered melee, then the battle would've been theirs, for the Yakhat were faster and more nimble, and any attack that the witch put up would harm her own people as much as theirs. But the *kenda*'s men were too well-trained. Their lines held, and they both charged and retreated as one. And though the riders had used Keshlik's tactics, the witch had still hurt them grievously.

If the Yivriindi had pressed their advantage, they might have chased the Yakhat all the way back into their yurts. But as it was, they held back their attack once the Yakhat quit the field, giving Keshlik and Bhaalit this chance to regroup. Keshlik grimaced and spat. He went to his own tent, dismounted, and waited. They would have to do something different this afternoon.

He chewed a scrap of dried fish for his lunch.

Juyut rode up as he finished. "Four hundred and thirty spears were broken in the morning's attack."

Keshlik spat. "Golgoyat's piss. How do the men feel?"

"Some of them seemed angry. Some of them were listless, drained of spirit. But not too many."

"They all have to fight anyway." He grabbed a stick of charcoal from the edge of the fire. "And you can tell them that this afternoon we'll slaughter the Yivrian army. And that's not just a boast."

"Yes," Juyut said.

"Now I'm going to go through the camp and select a small force. We'll be splitting the army."

"As you order, Keshlik."

The nearest yurt to theirs was Bhaalit's, then Chuuri's. Keshlik found Chuuri crouching next to the unlit remnants of last night's fire, holding his head in his hands. His shoulders were slumped, and his spear lay beside him. He was the perfect person to start Keshlik's band.

"Chuuri," he said, "why are you downcast?"

The youth looked up, startled, and winced in embarrassment. He grabbed his spear from the ground and straightened. "I was resting, Keshlik."

"Are you afraid?"

He swallowed and shook his head.

Keshlik stepped closer to Chuuri and put his hands on the other's shoulders. He leaned close until their faces almost touched. "Don't lie to me. I see your fear. Don't be ashamed of it."

Chuuri blinked and looked away. "How can we win? Keshlik, I trust you, but I don't see how—"

"Then come with me."

"What?"

"You're afraid? Good. The witch is a fearsome creature, and if you weren't afraid, you'd be a fool. I need men wise enough to be afraid to come with me."

"Come with you where?"

"We will form a separate cohort. You see as well as I do that we can't defeat the witch and her allies in open battle. But I have a plan. Come with me, and see how Golgoyat will give us victory again."

A dim light kindled in Chuuri's eyes. His hand clenched his spear, and he bowed his head to Keshlik. "I'll come, if you call me."

Keshlik nodded and mounted Lashkat again. "Come. Follow me as I gather the rest of our force."

He went from yurt to yurt, witnessing the truth of what Juyut had said. Many were afraid. Many were angry. Many of them stank of defeat. These last were the ones he selected. He stoked their pride with carefully chosen words. He was leading a strike force. They were chosen, honored, blessed. They would be the point of the spear driving into the heart of the Yivrian army. And when he spoke, he saw their fierceness rekindle. He didn't have the voice of Golgoyat as his father had, but Golgoyat still fought among them.

And when he was done, he had a quarter of the Yakhat army tagged for his purpose.

***

The sun had passed its zenith. The Yivrian forces still waited, holding a perimeter around their encampment. The Yakhat clumped together around their yurts at the opposite end of the valley.

Keshlik called the speakers of the tribes together. "Are you rested? Are you ready?"

Danyak spoke first for the Chalayit: "Yes."

The consent continued around the circle of clan speakers.

"Good. I give command of the main force to Juyut, with Bhaalit as his right hand. He will lead you down the valley, until you are parallel to the Yivrian army and may attack over open ground. I will take my force and retreat into the trees." He turned to the speaker of the Lougok. "Choudhap, how far out have your sentries held the perimeter?"

"A half a mile," he said. "Well into the forest."

"Have them extend to the west and the south, until they have the Yivrian cordon in sight. My force will come behind them, but I do not want the Yivrian sentries to see our approach until we are ready to strike. Let them only see your scouts and sentries."

"I will give the order," he said.

"Juyut, lead the force to the east mouth of the valley and wait there. When the Yivrian rabbits find their balls and attack you, make an orderly retreat, then hold the line. When they have engaged with your force, I will strike from the forest on the side of them, and they'll be crushed between our forces like a mouse in the talons of a hawk."

Juyut grinned. "That I can do."

"Don't head out until my men have all slipped away. And when you ride forth, be noisy. The bigger you sound, the more they will believe all of us are with you."

Agreement rumbled around the circle.

"Good." His next words were broken apart by a cry that flew through the eaves of the forest. "Keshlik! Keshlik!"

A lad in Lougok paint rode out from the shadows of the trees. His mare was foamy with sweat and nearly stumbled as she emerged into the light. With a *tut tut* the youth stopped the horse and slid from her back to the ground, running to Keshlik.

"Stop your yelling, child," Keshlik said. "What are you doing here?"

"I bring news from Prasa," he said, breathless as if he himself had run the six hours from the city.

"Well?"

"Dhuja says that Tuulo is ready to give birth, but she worries that the labor may be difficult. She thinks you should come."

"Trouble." Keshlik wiped the sweat from his eyes. On the other side of the valley, the Yivrian tents still stood, their flags limp and weak. *But still standing. Mockery.*

Yet Tuulo was in trouble. "How difficult is the labor? What is the problem?"

"Dhuja didn't tell me anything more." He suddenly seemed very young and abashed at his ignorance.

He glanced once at Juyut and again across the faces of his lieutenants.

Bhaalit said, "You could go to her. We understand your orders."

"No," he said. He drew a leaden breath. "Not while our enemies still stand. Tuulo is as strong as I am, and she can fight her own battle. I'll go to her when we both meet as victors."

"Whatever you want," Bhaalit said. "We're ready."

Keshlik looked at the boy. "Go get some water and grass for your horse. And stay out of the way. This is a battlefield, which means that you're now a warrior, and my order to you is to hide and don't let anyone see you." The boy bowed and ran back to his horse.

A wind brushed the tops of the pines. Keshlik spotted a line of black to the north of the valley. His heart leapt.

"Look," he said to those around him. "Look to the north and see the omen of our victory."

A line of clouds filled the sky at the very edge of the horizon, their crowns gleaming white in the light, their bottoms as black as anvils. The trees rustled in the wind. A fierce murmur rippled through the Yakhat ranks.

"The Power of the thunder is moving. Do you see it? The storm clouds are his mares, and the lightning is his spear. Remember this, warriors of the Yakhat! Before the storm breaks tonight, we will be victorious. Golgoyat himself fights among us!"

The Yakhat shouted the blessing back at him in assent.

Keshlik nodded to Juyut. "Fight well, brother. We'll meet over the witch's body."

CHAPTER 25

UYA

AFTER THE HORSEMAN LEFT BEARING Dhuja's message, Dhuja resumed drawing her lines on Tuulo's belly. After she finished, she and Uya helped Tuulo to her feet, and she resumed walking her circuit of the blessed circle. Dhuja tutted at Uya and pointed at the pot of water, now cold.

"I'll get it lit," Uya said. "Whatever you want." She lit up a bundle of tinder from the embers of the night before and soon had the fire built up to a steady flame, with the water pot steaming in the coals.

Tuulo's gait was notably more distressed than it had been the night before. She frequently stopped and bent over, eyes squeezed shut, fingernails digging into her kneecaps. A little whimper of pain escaped her now and then. But the pangs passed, and she straightened and continued to walk.

Dhuja watched her faithfully. Every few rounds, she called Tuulo over and reached her hand beneath the skirt, then said a few gravelly words in Yakhat. Uya could read the consternation hidden in her face. Whether Tuulo also saw it, Uya didn't know.

The day slithered by. The sun glowered, drawing sweat from Uya and Dhuja. The pains of labor had long since wrung streaks of sweat from the armpits and between the breasts of Tuulo's gown.

They ate strips of dried fish, plundered from the city. They drank boiled milk and chewed soft, sweet curds. They swallowed warm water from leather canteens. Noon turned to afternoon.

Dhuja grew progressively more alarmed as the hours crept by and the child did not seem imminent. She said nothing to Uya, of course, and only spoke to Tuulo in short commands. She called the mother over periodically to feel her belly and probe between her legs, feeling for whatever signs the midwife knew, then sent Tuulo circling the yurt again. But when Tuulo's back was turned, Uya saw anxiety in the old woman's stares, mutters, and knotting of her hands.

Tuulo's walk devolved to a crawl. She moaned periodically, her face twisted by waves of labor, and she tore tufts of grass from the earth when the pain shook her body. Once or twice Uya began to rise, thinking to help, but Dhuja gave her a knife-edged glare as soon as she stirred from her place near the pot of water.

The pot had been refilled once already as its contents boiled away. But Dhuja ensured that a stack of split wood stayed filled at Uya's right hand, replenished from time to time by the guardian warriors and old men who had stayed behind in Prasa. Uya wasn't sure what she was going to do with the water.

Tuulo limped feebly to Dhuja for another examination. An alarmed word dropped from the midwife's mouth. She pointed to the yurt and to Uya.

Tuulo reached a hand out to Uya and looked at her with expectant eyes. Uya glanced at Dhuja once, wondering if the midwife would scold her again. Instead, the woman shouted, ran over, and grabbed the stick for stirring the fire from Uya's hand, and pushed her toward Tuulo and the yurt.

Fine, then. She took Tuulo's hands, which were trembling and greasy with sweat. Tuulo leaned into Uya, nearly toppling her. Uya wrapped her arms around her and supported her as they hobbled into the yurt. The warm, musty darkness enveloped them.

"We need light," Uya said. "Can you stand?"

205

She tried to help her to the ground, but Tuulo cried out and clutched Uya's arms. Her lips moved with plaintive whispers, too quiet for Uya to hear.

"Let me help you down." She had seen Dhuja prepare a birthing stool earlier, during a pause in Tuulo's labor, but Uya couldn't find it in the darkness. Carefully, arduously, she helped the whimpering woman to her knees.

Tuulo cried out, pitched forward onto her hands and knees, and let out a piercing sob. Uya waited with her hands on the woman's waist, feeling her muscles tighten and spasm.

It passed. Tuulo breathed more easily.

Dhuja entered, letting in a narrow sliver of sunlight. Uya heard her muttering and scraping around the edges of the yurt, then the scrape of the ember box and hiss of a newly lit butter lamp. The soft light showed Tuulo on the ground, sweat-soaked gown hanging off her, and Dhuja cradling her head and muttering instructions. At the entrance to the yurt, she had left the pot of water, still steaming, and a lacquered tray filled with hot stones taken from the fire pit. Dhuja's hands stroked Tuulo's head, and she slowly lifted the flimsy gown up Tuulo's back and over her shoulders. Dhuja snapped at Uya and gestured that they were to help the unclothed Tuulo onto the birthing stool.

The stool was a simple reed platform braced a few feet off the floor, covered with a red-dyed blanket. One end was built up and padded with a horsehair cushion to support the mother's back. Uya put her shoulder under Tuulo's arm, clasping her sweat-slicked wrist, and with Dhuja's help, lifted the woman. Tuulo collapsed back against the cushion. Dhuja spread her legs and arranged them on either side of the seat.

Tuulo lay there a minute, head thrown back. Her breasts and belly heaved. Sweat glistened in lamplight. The lines that Dhuja had drawn that morning were smeared and streaked from perspiration. Yet she lifted her head and briefly smiled at Uya and Dhuja.

She moaned again, bending forward and squeezing the sides of the seat. The moan became a growl, then a swallowed scream. Dhuja was at her side, holding her hand, wiping away the sweat and tears that streamed down her face. Glaring at Uya, she shouted a brief command.

Uya winced and backed against the wall of the yurt. "I'm sorry. I don't understand."

Dhuja spat a single word that could only be a curse. Tuulo's scream petered out into a whimper, and she straightened back again into the cushions, her hands falling limp at her sides. Dhuja scuttled away, pulled a bundle of loose white woolen cloth from one of her packs at the edge of the yurt, and plunged it into the pot of hot water. Then, with impatient jabbers and much pointing, she indicated to Uya that they should each take one end of the cloth.

The cloth scalded Uya's hands when she touched it. She almost dropped it. Dhuja glared contemptuously then pointed her to Tuulo. They took the hot, heavy, waterlogged cloth over, then wound it tightly around her belly. Uya winced at the thought of the scalding fabric binding her skin, but Tuulo seemed not even to notice, as another labor pang had taken her, and she seized Uya's hand. She gritted her teeth and let out a tiny groan, squeezing until Uya wanted to cry out in pain.

It passed. Dhuja waved Uya back to the water pot and handed her a ladle. She pantomimed dipping the ladle into the water and pouring it out.

"You want me to pour out the water?" Uya asked. "I'm sorry—"

Dhuja grabbed the ladle from her hand, filled it from the pot, and poured it gently over the tray of hot stones. A cloud of steam hissed up into the yurt. She threw the ladle back to Uya and returned to Tuulo's side.

Uya waited for the stones to stop popping and hissing then poured another ladle of water across them. The yurt began to fill with steam. When the stones were wet and cold, she left the yurt to refill the tray from the fire. She took the stones from the hottest part of the fire, where the embers were white and shuddering with rosy heat, and laid a few new branches across the coals so the fire would be replenished by the time she returned again.

She returned to the yurt and resumed ladling water across the stones. The yurt became a muggy, smoky pit. The heat and the steam clung to Uya's flesh, running rivulets down her back. Blood and mucus trickled out of Tuulo to the ever-present accompaniment of her moans. Dhuja called Uya over, and they helped Tuulo to stand, holding her up between them while she shook like a speared fish. They helped her from position to position as the hours passed. Her cries never stopped now. Her howls rose and fell in intensity and pitch, like a coyote's keening. And whenever Dhuja did not need Uya, she returned to stir the fire and steam the yurt.

Dhuja re-wet the fabric around Tuulo's belly, and Uya went out again for more stones. The first breath of the air outside felt cold and dry as winter. To her shock, she saw the sun slipping behind the mountains. In the east, the horizon was black. Had the day already passed?

When she returned to the yurt, she saw it as if for the first time. Tuulo sobbed, leaning into Dhuja's shoulder. Her hands were limp with exhaustion. Dhuja cradled her and massaged her lower back. Tuulo gasped and doubled forward, her knees came up, and her fingers bit into Dhuja's flesh. Her whole body tensed. She *pushed*.

Her breath ebbed away, and she fell back again into Dhuja's arms.

Dhuja reached up between Tuulo's thighs. Her hand emerged bloody, and she wiped it clean on the blanket without making any indication to Tuulo or Uya what she had found. But she grimaced.

Uya steamed the room, then put the ladle down and came to Tuulo's side. Dhuja didn't scold her, so perhaps she had done well. She held Tuulo's hand when the next push came, though Tuulo's grip seemed ready to break Uya's fingers. When it had passed, she wiped the sweat-matted hair of out Tuulo's eyes.

For a moment, she let herself feel the warmth of pity for Tuulo. A long, difficult labor had been her own dread, back when—but that was why she had killed her compassion. In the pain of Tuulo's struggle, she had almost forgotten.

Tuulo rested her head against Uya's shoulder, and Uya patted her cheek. *A little while longer, and we'll all share the same pain.*

CHAPTER 26

SAOTSE

T LIQYALI WIPED SAOTSE'S FOREHEAD WITH a rag dipped in cool water. "Is Sorrow still near to you?"

Saotse's feet rested on a woven mat, and beneath the crackling reeds, the earth trembled. "Yes. Why do you ask?"

Tliqyali hesitated. "Because something may be different."

After the battle had dispersed around noon, Saotse had rested with the *kenda*'s entourage, and she listened to Sorrow in the soil and attempted to feel the movements of the Yakhat in her skin. But to her surprise, Tliqyali was right. Saotse wasn't sure what the Hiksilipsi woman could sense, but something *had* changed. Sorrow was present, but she was not wholly with Saotse. Her attention was divided. "How do you know?"

"I don't have any direct touch with Sorrow, if that's what you're wondering," Tliqyali said, amusement edging her voice. "But I can touch you, and your spirit has changed its tone. Your heart is beating differently. Something has shifted."

Saotse held her tongue for a while. This Hiksilipsi woman was the best aid she was likely to get, but would she immediately go tell the *kenda* if she admitted her uncertainty? But did she have a choice? If she were to charge into battle and find that Sorrow no longer answered...

Saotse swallowed her pride. "I don't know what's happening. Something else, or someone else, has begged for Sorrow's presence. She is here, but she's not *all* here. Do you understand what I mean?"

"A little," Tliqyali said.

"Do you know why? Does your training give you a way to ask Sorrow what has happened?"

Tliqyali laughed. "You should know better than me that the Powers don't speak as we do. Their language is the twisting of the wind, the color of leaves, and the pattern of lichen on a rock. You can ask them a question, but rarely will you get an answer expressible in words."

"But I've communed with Sorrow so many times. If she shared this—whatever it is—with me, then I could speak the words."

"Have you tried to commune with her now?"

Saotse paused. She hadn't, mostly because it would require her to go deeper into the Power than was safe when she was alone and with friends.

But she wasn't alone. She clenched Tliqyali's hand. "If I immerse myself in Sorrow now, it would be like when I knocked down the *kenda*'s pavilion. But worse. I'm not sure that this is wise." *I already lost one friend today to Sorrow's recklessness.*

"I'll help you," Tliqyali said. "Give me a moment to prepare."

The woman began to sing in Hiksilipsi, a light, pattering rhythm like rain falling on still water. Saotse heard her move around the little tent, open satchels, and scrape something into a bowl. The smell of burning sage suffused the tent. A bell rang nine times, then the rustling of her skirt settled in front of Saotse. She folded the mat back with a crunch of bending reeds then took both of Saotse's hands.

"I haven't done this before with one of the Kept," she said with a nervous laugh. "But the principles are the same. When you're ready, step off the mat and onto the bare earth."

Saotse's heart pounded with anxiety. "What am I supposed to do?"

"You are the Kept. Do what comes naturally, what you've done before. You were born hearing the language of the Powers, so speak it now with the Power that Keeps you. I will be your guardian and your guide. If you go too deep, I'll pull you out."

Saotse nodded. She stepped onto the ground and fell into Sorrow.

At first, she knew only the vastness of Sorrow's pain, and the ground began to shudder with her sobs. But Tliqyali's palms, pressed against hers, provided a slender reminder that she was a woman, and she was among friends. Saotse stilled her weeping. Sorrow was not consoled, but she quieted. And in their wordless union, Saotse asked, *Who else is here?*

The answer: A black stormcloud thundered from horizon to horizon. Rain sliced through the sky, lightning pounded the earth, hail bruised the trees, and wind screamed. Sorrow had sadness mingled with rage, but the stormcloud had only hatred: hot, black, and boiling with cruelty. Saotse shrank back in terror, but Sorrow dissolved it. She remembered that the storm was not wicked. Once the wind had been a dance and not a fist, and the rain had been a kiss instead of a slap. Once, and maybe again.

The earth swelled to touch the sky, soil bulging beneath sod and creaking its stony bones—and fell back again with a shudder of frustration. The pain was too great, and the labor of reunion was unfinished.

But realization thundered through Saotse: *Sorrow does not labor alone.*

It wasn't just the storm that split Sorrow's attention, but another person, whose struggle rippled through Sorrow like the splashing of a child in shallow water. The woman contracted; the earth contracted. The woman screamed; the stones screamed.

And Tliqyali pulled Saotse from the depths of the Power and dropped her, sweating and quivering, onto the reed mat.

The cool rag dabbed her forehead again, and Tliqyali pressed a skin of water to her lips. Shaking, Saotse spilled the water all down her shirt. Tliqyali caught her head, laid her gently out on the mat, then covered her quickly with a blanket.

Saotse grabbed the woman's hand. "What did I do? What happened when I was with Sorrow?"

"Very little," Tliqyali said. "There was some shaking, and you screamed. And the earth shouted. It was *very* loud."

"What did I say?"

"Nothing I could understand. Do you not remember?"

Saotse waited for the trembling to cease. "I remember. But I don't understand. Someone else is in Sorrow."

"Someone other than you was communing with Sorrow?"

"Yes. Another Kept?"

Tliqyali tucked the blanket around her. "I doubt it was another Kept."

"Then who?"

"It could be anyone. All flesh influences the Powers, just as the Powers speak to all flesh. Do you not know this?"

"No. The Hiksilipsi were seldom in Prasa to teach." And she hadn't wanted to go to them when they were present. Admitting to anyone that Oarsa had ceased to speak to her was more pain than she had wanted to bear.

"It's unfortunate that you couldn't learn more from us," Tliqyali said. "As Kept of Sorrow, you are gifted to perceive the Powers directly, and for this reason when Sorrow joins herself to you, you can invoke and direct her power. But the Powers may join themselves to anyone. This other person, if she isn't Kept, cannot command the earth as you can, and she may not even know what is happening. But Sorrow may bind to her nonetheless."

"But why would Sorrow do that?"

"I don't know. You'll have to ask her."

Saotse groaned in frustration. Sorrow had shown her sadness, separation, and struggle. The other woman was somehow bound up in it. But the explanation that Saotse wanted was not something Sorrow could give.

There was a noise at the entrance of the tent, and a rough male voice called out to Tliqyali in Yivrian. Tliqyali answered, then said to Saotse, "The *kenda* wants to see you. Can you walk?"

"Help me to my feet," Saotse said.

Tliqyali took her by the hand and helped her up, and Saotse stood for a moment to see if she had the strength. She did. She shuffled forward, leaning on Tliqyali's arm.

The *kenda*'s pavilion was open on every side to let in a cool breeze, and Saotse could hear the *kenda* pacing. "Saotse," he said when she was still several paces away. "What was the tremor and the great noise we all heard a little while ago?"

"I was speaking to Sorrow," Saotse said. "We screamed. That's all."

"Is there something wrong?"

Saotse hesitated. But no, Sorrow's *presence* was as strong as ever, even if the Power's *attention* was split. "Nothing is wrong. Tliqyali was guiding me to understand the Powers better."

"Very well," the *kenda* said, in a tone that made it very clear he didn't want to hear any more about what Saotse and Tliqyali had done. "The Yakhat are forming up again on the far side of the valley. I think they mean to make a second battle this afternoon. And we'll meet them with spears forward, as many times as they want, until they either scatter or surrender. Are you prepared to join us?"

"I am prepared." She suffered a pang of doubt as to whether Sorrow would still respond to her and allow her to call up the soil as she had before. She reached out to the Power and felt the strong, bitter embrace of Sorrow, which assuaged her fears. Whatever the other influence of the powers, Sorrow would still come to Saotse. She could still bring them victory.

"Very well," the *kenda* said. "We'll ride out within an hour, possibly sooner if the Yakhat move quickly. Tliqyali will accompany you in place of Tagoa. Prepare however you need to, but I expect to see you here and ready before we ride."

CHAPTER 27

KESHLIK

THE AFTERNOON SUN BLAZING ON the valley floor was a dim glow seen through the trunks of the trees. The fern-choked forest ran down a short, gentle grade to where the spruces guarded the edges of the field, and there, just inside the shadows afforded by a moss-swaddled log, crouched the scout. The fist behind his back signalled Keshlik's force to stay put.

Keshlik heard, very far off, the feathery beat of hooves and the raindrop sound of spear meeting spear. Juyut had met the Yivriindi in battle. The scout's signal would not continue much longer. Behind Keshlik, his men held their spears at the ready, their faces showing their eagerness to redeem themselves from the morning's shame. *Good.* He needed every drop of ferocity he could get from them.

The scout ducked and ran over to Keshlik in a crouch. Once he was in the shadow of Lashkat, he stood. "The battle is joined. The Yivrian line has their back to us. They're at the far end of the valley, with their tents between us and them, but they've left a minimal reserve at the perimeter."

"And their chief?" Keshlik asked. "Has he remained in the camp or joined the battle?"

"The chariot with the blue banners followed the Yivrian force out. He remains behind the front line. A white-haired woman accompanied him."

"Are they in the last line? Is there a force behind them?"

The scout nodded. "He's in the middle. There is a shorter line of spearmen that guards his rear."

Keshlik nodded. He turned to the men nearest him. "We ride out like the storm wind. Do not attack their encampment or engage with their perimeter. Fly past it and charge the rear guard that protects the witch and the chief. The battle will be over once we have crushed the Yivrian center and met up with our brothers on the other side."

The warriors murmured assent, and the order was repeated through the ranks. Keshlik rode cautiously to the edge of the forest. Ahead, in the open valley, he saw the Yivrian encampment, the battle line, and the flags of the Yivrian chief as the scout had described them. He tutted to Lashkat, and she began to run through the open. The rest of his force poured out behind him.

They charged into the open field to the west of the Yivrian encampment, shouts in their throats and spears in their hands. The encampment sentries called out warnings and prepared for the attack, but the Yakhat rode by them like a river around a stone. The grass flew beneath Lashkat's feet. To his left lay the furrows of the witch's rage. The Yivrian line approached.

Behind them, drums began to sound in the Yivrian camp, warning of Keshlik's approach. His warriors passed through the narrow throat formed between the camp and the result of the morning's battle and began to spread, matching the width of the rear line.

The rear guard of Yivriindi had seen them. Their bronze spearpoints glittered as they turned. The Yivrian soldiers lowered the shafts of their spears into the soil. But the line was loose, ragged, panicked. The witch in the *kenda*'s chariot hadn't yet disturbed the soil.

Keshlik rebalanced his spear in his hand, leaned to the left, and prepared to meet the Yivrian line. His mark was an adobe-skinned man with eyes wide and teeth clenched in fear. When Keshlik was a heartbeat away from riding into the man's spear, he threw his own, forcing the man to dodge aside. Keshlik flashed past him and through the gap.

He rode to his spear and plucked it from the ground and turned Lashkat. The man he had just leapt past had found his feet and struggled to bring his spearhead around, but not quickly enough. Keshlik planted the point of his spear in the man's throat.

A quick glance around showed that the Yakhat had broken through the rear line in several places and were engaged in melee with the rear defenders. The front line, where Juyut attacked, had begun to buckle. Cries of dismay rang from both fronts.

Keshlik shouted, "To the chief!" He charged toward the silver chariot and its shell of guards.

He was unsurprised to hear the earth rumble angrily once again. But anything she did now would harm her own as much as it did the Yakhat.

Far ahead of him, on the front line, the turf warped and belched. The Yakhat were already pressing through, and the soil buried the Yivrian foot soldiers as rapidly as it did the Yakhat horsemen. More horses poured through.

The earth rumbled behind Keshlik, and a rift split the ground, cutting off any escape back to the forest. But he had no intention of retreating: the *kenda*'s guard was before him, and he was two breaths away from celebrating his enemy's death.

He turned Lashkat and charged into the gap between two men. They brought their spears together. Wood crunched. His horse screamed, and Keshlik pitched forward over her head.

The world spun. He landed on his back with a grunt. Behind him, Lashkat battered the defenders with her hooves, half a spear sticking out of her chest. More defenders were rushing at him. His own spear was still in his hand.

Keshlik roared and leapt to his feet. He parried an incoming blow and planted the head of his spear in someone's gut. Horses screamed and ran past him. Yakhat and Yivrian men traded spear thrusts.

The chief's chariot was pulling away. Keshlik shoved two of the panting rabbits aside and made chase.

The chariot's ponies reared, and a Yakhat horse appeared on the other side. The horse's rider carried a spearhead dripping with blood. One of the ponies collapsed, the other bolted, and the imbalance caused the chariot to rise up on one wheel.

Keshlik threw himself against the high side of the chariot. The wheel broke. The chariot collapsed onto its side.

The earth around them moaned and shuddered. Keshlik leapt atop the chariot and blindly thrust his spear downward. A flash of metal deflected his spearhead. The *kenda* tumbled out of the wrecked chariot, his ancient sword flashing in his hand. He stepped back and raised his sword to parry Keshlik's strike.

A spear took the *kenda* in the back.

Blood gushed from his mouth. He fell to the ground atop his precious blade, revealing Juyut standing triumphantly behind him. Juyut screamed in celebration and leapt off his mount to plant his feet on the dead man's back, then raised his spear in salute. "Yakhat, the victory is ours! The *kenda* is dead! Golgoyat fights among us!"

Keshlik raised his spear to match, even as the ground coughed and buckled again. The shout of victory leapt from mouth to mouth among the Yakhat, while a wail of dismay arose from the Yivriindi. Their defensive lines started to buckle and flee even where they had still been strong. It was turning into a rout.

After a final violent heave, the ground stilled and did not move again.

Keshlik glanced around. "Where is the witch?"

"I haven't seen her," Juyut said.

The *kenda*'s guard was strewn in bloody heaps on the ground around them, but he saw no sign of a small old woman among them. But neither did he see any sign of her bringing up her Power. Perhaps she had been taken by a stray arrow. It would be irony for her to fall so accidentally—but he would take her death any way he could get it.

He considered staying to direct the battle until the witch's body was found and he could bring her eyes back to Tuulo. But his heart betrayed him. "Juyut, I need to return to Prasa. But Lashkat is fallen."

Dismay flashed across Juyut's face. "Lashkat? I'll ensure that she is burned with a warrior's honor. Take mine, and fly to your wife."

Keshlik nodded. He swept aside the pang of sorrow at the loss of his mare. "Lead the battle to its conclusion. The victory is yours."

Juyut reddened with pride. "Send my greetings to my sister-in-law and my nephew." He saluted Keshlik with his spear and slid off his mare.

Keshlik leapt atop Juyut's mare, and they sped off the battlefield toward Prasa, toward Tuulo, and toward his son.

CHAPTER 28

UYA

TUULO LEANED INTO UYA'S CHEST. Her arms wrapped around Uya's shoulders, and her head lay pressed against her cheek. Sweat and water dripped down both of their faces. Her breath came hot and fast, and then with a gasp, she squeezed Uya's shoulders and clenched her teeth on a scream.

Beside them, Dhuja muttered a chant, resting her palm in the small of Tuulo's back. Between verses of the chant, she whispered to the mother. Tuulo's grip relaxed, and she let out an exhausted sigh. Dhuja asked something, and Tuulo merely nodded, her hair tickling Uya's cheek.

Tuulo had barely caught her breath when she crushed Uya's hand again. Uya listened to the grinding of her teeth and the gasping of her breath.

Time seemed to both leap and crawl, the waves of Tuulo's labor galloping one after another, but the pain of delivery stretched before and after them as endless as the plains.

After a long, immeasurable time, a new urgency seized Tuulo's face, and Dhuja, seeing the change, began to jabber. She gestured impatiently at Uya with her knobby fingers.

"What?" Uya asked.

Dhuja waved with her palms and scolded, sounding frustrated.

Uya moved to the position that Dhuja indicated with her gestures, supporting Tuulo from behind with her legs alongside her on the seat, and she let the midwife take her seat in front. Just as Uya sat down, Tuulo dug her fingers into Uya's thighs and let out a throaty groan.

Dhuja put her hand on Tuulo's stomach and felt for the baby's head. She muttered something to Tuulo, who seemed not even to notice. Tuulo pushed. Uya lost track of how many times.

Tuulo's breath grew shallow, as if her strength waned, but then her teeth would clench and her muscles would tighten, and with a ferocious grunt, she would drive the child further.

Dhuja checked the child's position again, and her expression darkened. She did not show Tuulo how far she had yet to go.

Did the child face the wrong way? Was there another obstruction? Uya didn't know how to ask.

Tuulo braced herself against Uya for another push. But her groan ended with a scream, and she spasmed in Uya's arms. Dhuja shouted in alarm.

Tuulo was bleeding. Not the little trickle of blood that had leaked from her since the beginning, but a gush of hot red blood pouring out like water from a broken pot.

She screamed again, from terror or pain, and shook in Uya's grip, her hands scrabbling over Uya's legs. Dhuja began to babble, pressing her hand against Tuulo's belly and searching in the torrent for some clue as to what had given way.

Tuulo fought in Uya's grip. Her shouting might have been words, but Uya couldn't understand a bit of it. Dhuja attempted to calm the mother, then she drew herself to her feet and looked down at Tuulo and Uya with an expression of dreadful pity. She ducked outside the yurt.

"Wait!" Uya shouted. "Where are you going? Are you *leaving* me here?"

Tuulo twisted to the side and fell from the seat, her hands grabbing at her belly. Blood drenched her hips to her ankles.

Uya bent and attempted to get her arms under Tuulo's armpits to lift her back into the chair, but Tuulo twisted and swatted Uya's away hands. Sobbing, she looked into Uya's eyes. Her face seemed sad, haggard, wearied, as if she had aged two centuries in the last minutes. A tiny, barely audible whimper slipped between her lips.

"I don't think I can help you," Uya said. "I'm sorry."

The pity she had been beating back rose in her chest again. *No.* She gritted her teeth and repeated her oath.

The door of the yurt rustled, and Dhuja reappeared. Uya stepped back in surprise. Dhuja had blackened her face with dirt from the sacred circle, and she had stripped down to nothing but the red sash around her waist. She knelt next to Tuulo and put her hand on Tuulo's cheek. Tuulo had gone pale, and her eyes were closed. At Dhuja's touch, they fluttered open, but her eyes darted back and forth, without comprehension. She whispered a word that Uya could not understand.

Dhuja nodded. She crouched between Tuulo's ankles, her hands kneading the mother's thighs. She let out a low, mournful cry and began to unwind the sash at her waist. When the last fold of red cloth dropped into the pool of Tuulo's blood, a knife with a bone handle dropped with it. Dhuja bent and picked up the knife.

"No," Uya said. "Dhuja, what are you doing?"

Dhuja looked at Uya and shook her head. She kissed the blade of the knife, then leant forward and kissed Tuulo's belly.

Uya bolted for the door to escape the horror. Her heart battered against her ribs, and bile threatened to erupt from her mouth. As she passed through the slit of the yurt's entrance her feet betrayed her, and she fell into the yellow grass. The weight of her oath fought with the pity in her throat as the muggy, blood-scented air of the yurt leached away from her. The ground smelled of crushed grass and prairie mint and earthworms. Wind stirred the grasses and hushed her in the heads of the wildflowers.

Tuulo was going to die.

But Uya had sworn an oath. Why should she pity the savage woman?

She struggled to her feet. A stiff breeze blew out of the east, and on the horizon, she saw a line of boiling white clouds, with darkness at their feet. The sun was falling into the west, and it lit the crowns of the thunderheads with luminescent gold.

"Chaoare," Uya asked, "is this how you answer me? You steal the breath from my enemy?"

The wind hissed through the empty houses of Prasa. To her left and right were broken shells of lodges where *ennas* had dwelt. Their ancestor poles were broken, their totems defaced. Grass had grown up around them, and it bowed and fled from the coming storm.

Uya remembered Nei. Her mother. Saotse. Rada. Her dead son, whom the Yakhat monsters had cast away on the plain.

Tuulo had cradled her head and sopped up her tears then, just as Uya had held Tuulo's hands now.

But—no. Tuulo could not pay for all the murders of her people with a few hours of kindness and a few hours of pain.

"I remember my oath," she whispered.

A cry escaped from the yurt. It was soaked in weariness, wrung out with pain. It ended almost as soon as it started.

The only sound was the rustle of grasses in the wind.

And then a baby cried.

Uya returned to the yurt in a heartbeat. For a moment, she saw only darkness and smelled blood and death. Her eyes began to readjust to the dim lamplight, and she made out the outline of the mother's ruined body, slashed open in a final desperate effort to save the child. No, she would not look. Dhuja was kneeling, holding the knife that had opened Tuulo to find the child. And beside her—a boy, lain on a bolt of new white wool, screaming and shaking tiny fists.

He was wet with blood and mucus. The cord distending from his purple belly was uncut. He howled, mouth open like a frog's, eyes clenched shut. Dhuja looked up at Uya. Her face was wet with tears, but she shouted at Uya and pointed at the baby.

Uya picked him up. He weighed less than a quail hen. Dhuja severed the cord with her knife and pinched the end shut with a strip of leather. She muttered another incomprehensible command at Uya.

Tuulo's son. A boy, like her own child. Like her own dead son.

And like a cloud rising up from the sea, the darkness rose from her memory. Tuulo's son was Keshlik's son. The murderer's son. The monster's son. A boy sure to grow into another murderer.

Her heart blackened and hardened. She did not forget her oath.

She clutched the child to her chest and walked out of yurt.

Dhuja's shouts followed her. She willed herself not to hear, not to think. She began to run.

The ruins of Prasa flew by her. Her feet found familiar paths, old paths, routes she had walked in the city back when it was alive. The ways wound down to the sea. A few Yakhat women saw her and shouted after her. She ignored them. There was nothing left in her, nothing but the beating of her own heart and the squirming and yelling of the infant pressed against her breast.

Down, down, down to the seaside. Through the wall of grasses at the edge. Over the pebbled beach. The storm wind was at her back, pushing her, lashing her hair forward toward the sea. She ran into the gentle surf and stopped where the water reached her knees.

The boy screamed in the blanket. She raised it above her head. The wind howled around her.

"Oarsa!" she screamed. "Chaoare! I did not forget my oath!"

She threw him into the surf.

The body hit the water and disappeared.

The quiet accused her where the baby's cry should have been. The waves drew back, declaring her guilt.

Black horror chilled her. Uya whispered, "Great Oarsa, what have I done?"

She lunged forward into the surf. He was tiny. He had just barely gone under. Would he float? A wave surged forward and gave her a mouthful of saltwater. She spat and stood, frantically scanning the water.

"No, no, no! No. Oarsa, hear me." She dove headfirst into the next wave, searching the surf with her arms. Her knees beat against the stones of the sea floor.

A wave cast her back against the shore. "Help me," she sobbed. "Powers of the ocean, help me. Oarsa, forgive me."

A new wave battered her thighs.

"Help me. Forgive me." She regained her feet.

And in the next wave, she saw a bolt of white cloth.

She bloodied her toes against the stones, but in three strides she reached it. The waterlogged blanket pressed against her chest. The water drained out of it, leaving nothing. *It's empty.*

She unwrapped it and saw the blue body.

It was too late. The boy was cold, his fragile limbs the temperature of the seawater. She pressed the body between her breasts. It was like holding a fish—tiny, cold, and motionless.

"I'm sorry." Tears mingled with the seawater running down her face. "I'm sorry. I'm sorry."

The sea foam swirled around her knees. The storm wind beat at her back, colder than the merciless water. She began to shiver.

She set the infant against her shoulder and began to tap his back as if he had just nursed. "I'm sorry, little one. Forgive me."

The body spasmed.

The boy vomited seawater down her back. His limbs squirmed. He spit again and shivered. And his tiny mouth opened and let out a quavery cry.

Uya began to shake with relief, and her anger and hatred drifted away like feathers from a molting bird. She gently wrapped her arms around him and rocked, holding him as tightly as she dared against the warmth of her stomach. She cast the soaked blankets away.

Fumbling with one hand, she tore open the front of the Yakhat blouse and found her breast, still bursting with unused milk. Her nipple was rough and dry, but the boy found it and greedily closed his mouth over it. His gums pulled, and she winced in pain.

He suckled like a colt. As he ate, his squirming stilled, and his color warmed from blue to summery red. Uya waded out of the water, climbed up the shore, and set herself down in the grass. The northern horizon pulsed with lightning. Thunder split the air. The earth seemed to shake in response, but the rumble passed away.

Uya cooed at the child and sang a lullaby, and drew it to her chest to keep it warm against the storm.

CHAPTER 29

SAOTSE

S HE WAS ALIVE.

The air smelled like wet earth, and a weight pinned her legs to the ground. Her hands were full of mud, and her face was pressed into soft, sandy soil. Her breath echoed in a small, enclosed space. The feet of men and horses beat against the ground somewhere nearby, though none seemed to find her. Blood and earth mingled in her nostrils.

She lifted her head and gasped for air. The footsteps were far from her—she was feeling the thunder of their movements through the ground.

Something heavy pinned her legs, and another weight pressed against her shoulders. She pushed herself up to her elbows and felt the weight above her buckle and loosen. Loose dirt trickled down her arms and legs, and the smell of bruised grass filled the air. She kicked her legs free of the soil and shook dirt from her shoulders, and she realized with a late-blooming horror that she had been *buried*.

Heavy, wet earth fell away on either side of her. She was covered up to her neck with soil.

Had Sorrow engulfed her? She fought to remember. She had touched the Power briefly, then the *kenda* had seized her and taken her back into the chariot. The Yakhat were attacking from the rear, and they needed to find a safe place where she could touch the soil and call up Sorrow. She had heard horses, shouting, the chariot had tipped, and Sorrow had swallowed her up with just enough air to keep her alive.

She pulled herself forward like a worm emerging from the ground. Her hands were grimy with clay, and her hair was matted down with earth. Something heavy pinned her ankles to the ground. She wrenched herself forward another inch and twisted her legs out from beneath it. Metal and wood creaked, and with a gasp, she wrangled free.

She stopped to massage her feet and felt to see what had lain atop her. Her hands confirmed that it was the *kenda*'s chariot. The chariot's cover and the soil's embrace were what had saved her from the Yakhat spears. *Is the battle over?* She heard nothing nearby, but further up the valley, horses and men still moved. *Yivriindi or Yakhat?* She couldn't tell.

She crawled forward on her belly. Her hands found a dead human face.

She swallowed a scream and shoved it away. She scrambled back a pace, heart beating wildly, bile rising in her throat. Her hands were sticky with blood.

She had to wait, to *think*. She had felt silk and silver beneath her hands when she scrambled away from the body. Cautiously she crept forward and felt again, finding the edges of the dead man's garment, the fine stitching on the edges, the silver chains around his cold neck. The circlet and the sword had been looted, but she was sure.

The *kenda*.

She lay her head against the ground and shivered. They had lost. They were doomed.

How much time had passed? Enough for the *kenda*'s body to grow cold. The battle had moved on. Far away, the last shouts of fighting still sounded, but she lay in a glade of silence. The day's heat clung to the ground, but a chilly wind stirred the grass. Evening approached.

She would have to crawl to safety—if there were such thing as safety for her. The Yakhat would kill her as soon as they saw her, and now she was uncovered to any passing eye. She needed to hide.

She wiped the blood off her hands in the grass and began to inch forward, away from the sounds of men. As her fingers dug in the soil, she realized the echoing absence of what she did *not* feel.

Sorrow was gone.

At the start of the battle, she could barely touch the ground, lest the Power swallow her immediately. Now she pressed her hands and knees into the grass and felt nothing, not the yawning loneliness of Sorrow, nor her fury or vengeance.

Saotse opened herself, broad and yearning, and listened for any whisper of the Power. Nothing.

"Sorrow," she said. "Sorrow, my mother, my sister. Where are you?"

She scrambled forward, searching for a plot of bare earth. Crisp yellow grass crackled beneath her hands. Sorrow had to be here. Saotse couldn't be left alone again.

"Don't leave me. My sister, don't leave me! I need you now, more than ever."

Just like Oarsa had left her. To be alone, a burden, a fool who had trusted one of the Powers and been abandoned. Not *again*. Not scrambling blind and alone across a field littered with the dead, with the Power that she had served silent and far away.

"My enemies—*our* enemies—will overrun us. Sorrow, can you hear me?"

Her hands found the corpses of men bent over broken spears, and the bodies of horses slick with sweat and blood. She pushed her fists into the soil and pressed her cheek against the ground.

"Answer me," she whispered.

There was *someone*, but it was not Sorrow. Other Powers

babbled in the wind. Putting aside the danger, she rose slowly to her feet. Her bones creaked in protest, but she swallowed their pain.

The storm wind buffeted her, icy with anger and whistling with revenge. This was not Sorrow—this was the storm cloud, and he was not her friend. She dropped back to her knees. She feared the attention of this Power more than she did the Yakhat warriors.

But the stormy Power was not all she felt. Another Power moved at the edges of the battlefield. Someone familiar. She would find him.

She crawled forward with renewed purpose, parting the grasses before her like a snake. Bodies were everywhere. Yivrian soldiers with shirts of linen and cloaks of rough canvas. The Yakhat, clad in leather, their faces greasy with paint. And horses, legs bent and broken, sides scored by spears. She crept over and around them, dirtying her hands with mud and blood.

The bodies grew fewer as she fled the sounds of fighting and the epicenter of the battle. She clambered up a short, rocky rise where the grass did not grow and emerged into the exhalations of the stormy Power. Rain stung her face. Thunder growled in the distant north. The cloud lanced her with sleet.

Onward. The ground tumbled downward after the rise, turning into gravel and scrub. The rain thickened into a downpour, and the ground turned muddy. A loose rock sent her sliding and scrabbling down the muddy slope, until the mudslide cast her into a patch of ferns.

She stopped. There were trees above her. The rain struck their branches like beads in a rattle. There was a stream nearby, too, just audible above the rain, and its gurgle was rising into a roar. Thunder cracked the sky.

She rose to her feet, stumbled forward, and fell into the trunk of a moss-covered pine. Her fingers bloodied against the bark, but her pain didn't matter: the Power was here. It was calling to her. It was waiting for her. She slogged forward through the mud, soggy ferns swiping at her waist, until she reached the riverbank.

She stopped where she felt the grasses give way and heard the rush of water by her feet. She was at the very lip of the riverbank. Windbeaten grasses lashed her legs. Rain pelted her. Thunder boomed.

The Power greeted her. It was a little thing, the Power of the stream, drinking rainwater off the hills and running full of song down to River Prasa, which received its blessings and carried them out to the sea. Saotse would not have noticed it at all, except that it was awake and alert and shouting her name in the wordless tongue of the Powers.

"What do you want?" Rain poured down her face. "Why did you call me here?"

The answer was a burst of joy, mingled with expectation. Warning. Terror. Desire.

Someone was coming.

She didn't care whom the little river Power expected. "Where is Sorrow? Where is the Power who Kept me?"

Coming. He is coming.

But Sorrow was not—

He came. She fell to her knees.

The sandy-bottomed stream seemed to deepen and widen to hold the enormity of the Power that strode in its water. A cataract of ancient waters surged up the channel, which bowed to receive him, trembling with pleasure and torment.

He was vast. He was bottomless. His heartbeat was the pounding of waves against the shore. Mussels and anemones encrusted his hands, numberless salmon swarmed in his eyes, and the great whales sang in his wake.

"Oarsa." Saotse had never felt him this close, not even when he had first beckoned to her from the sea. Opening her mouth felt like swallowing the tide. She struggled to breathe. "Why are you here? *Now* you come to me? You left me for fifty years. When every ally I had has been slaughtered on the battlefield, you come?"

The storm wind slapped her hair against her face. The icy sting of the rain spurred her anger. "Where were you when Prasa fell? Where were you when the *kenda* died? Now that everything is lost, *now* you come to me?"

Come to me, the waters said.

And the Power withdrew.

Thunder shattered the air. The roar of the flood grew more insistent, and the mud began to crumble away beneath her feet. She scrabbled at the grasses, but they were sliding and falling with her.

The river water swallowed her. She thrashed and got a breath half of air and half of water. The torrent tumbled her. She flailed for the surface but could not find it. There was only water and formless mud. Her nose and mouth filled.

She sank.

She descended in the muddy water. Down, down, down.

Little minnows swarmed like sparks. They spoke with voices like crickets, so she asked them, "Where is the Power of the great waters?"

"Further down and further out," they answered, then they scattered with the sound of laughter into the arms of the little river Power who was their shepherd.

She kept descending, and the current carried her to the bay where the water grew colder and wilder. She reached the place where the orcas played. They greeted her as a long-lost sister, pressing their noses to her face and clicking their tongues in greeting, and they thrashed the great flukes of their tails.

But she could not join them in their celebration. "Where is the Power of the great waters?"

"Further down and further out." They touched her with their fins and swam toward the surface, trilling and singing.

So she continued downward to the place where the water was cold and still and there was no sound.

The great whale, the steed of the Power, approached her. She felt the pressure of his gaze. He allowed her hands to brush against his old and knobby skin, scarred and rehealed countless times by his battles with the kraken in the darkness. The stroke of his tail was a whirlwind, but he made no other sound.

She asked him, "Where is the Power of the great waters?"

"Near." His voice was barely a whisper in the deep, but it made Saotse shiver. "Why will you go to him?"

"Because he brought me across the sea then left me. Because he was cruel. Because I want to accuse him."

"Then you are the one," the whale replied. "Come with me."

She put a hand on his battle-scarred fin, and they descended into the deepest place of the ocean, where there was silence and stillness. And out of the stillness the waters stirred, and a voice that had no sound spoke.

Accuse me now, my precious daughter. For did you think that I forgot, when once I sang to you upon the ocean shore—you, whose name I blessed, who rode on whaleback across my foamy skin?

"Yes, I accuse you," she said. "Because you carried me across the sea, and left me among strangers, and did not hear my prayers."

Do not believe your weeping went unseen. As raindrops beat the weary earth, the tears of mortals run like torrents to the sea. My silence was neither careless nor forgetful, but I am thrice constrained—for in the deeps, I wage a war. The kraken stirs, and on your shores, old horrors would arise if ever I forsook my watch. Brief leave I took to kiss your feet, to carry you to where your gifts were sought; and having laid you at the foreign shore, I fled. Little time had I, and little now I have to speak before my battle resumes. Forgive me.

She raised her voice, but the sound seemed to dissolve in the deep darkness, and she heard herself whisper. "Why? Why now?"

The water stirred. *Ponder, daughter, distant marshy banks where first was born the cold divorce 'twixt earthy bride and thundering, wrathful son. The wedding broke, and strife poured out from wounds unkindly torn. Already then I plotted peace to make for fragile human hearts, but I was stopped by distance, and by the stony ears of men—which seldom hear what we, the ageless phantoms, say. For we are bound by deeds of flesh, we bodiless Powers, unchanging save when men our names invoke, while we in turn bestir with soundless whispers mortal hands to move. I sought to cut the chain of wrath, to salve the wounds the earthy bride had borne, so she might bless again the sacred circle, which when forgotten cursed her daughters with unfruitful birth. But flesh is healed by flesh, and only mortal hands can mortal wounds repair.*

So thrice did I rejoice when first your feet were touched by surf— for you, bright daughter, are of the few who hear what Powers beg, and having borne you to this shore, I watched your years. Your cries I could not answer, for in the deeps, the war does not abate; but never did my care forget you, that when the sire of storms and grief-rent mother came, your tongue might be the bridge of peace.

But not alone. For blessed by sorrow is the breast which suckles peace and purges war. Behold, had not the laboring womb been split, had not the war-wracked mother dared forgive and take to breast her captor's child, the earthy bride would not be healed. Behold! The curse is broken, and peace is born from sorrow; now let it perish not. Yours is the tongue and hers is the breast, and only the hand remains.

A torrent of water churned through her, and the flood was a revelation. She knew at once why Sorrow had left her, and to whom Sorrow had returned. A memory or a prophecy—she couldn't tell which one—bloomed in her mind: her hands were waves and lifted up a newborn child to the hands of flesh which had cast him in. A captive Praseo woman, bereaved by the death of her own child, but with enough pity to save her captor's son. Saotse sank deeper into the water, as if weighed down by knowledge, and she said, "Sorrow and mercy. I understand. But who is the hand, and what am I to say to him?"

You must go to meet him. The cloud-lord must forget his boiling rage, put aside his spears, consent again to wed. His bride has cast away her mourning shroud and readies for the dawn; yet even now the groom may falter, and peace betray. The mortal son of thunder, tasting sorrow, might turn again to wrath, but let him not. Go now. I bless your tongue with salt, to speak in unknown tongues, to fight the kraken beneath the skies, as I do in the deeps. Take courage, Daughter. Arise.

CHAPTER 30

KESHLIK

GOLGOYAT ROARED IN THE SKY as Keshlik pounded across the bridge into Prasa. Raindrops stung Keshlik's face, hurled by the wind. The sky was striped with lines of tattered gray cloud. To the east and north, the clouds were a roiling black, lit from within by pink-tinted lightning. The horizon was tinted a sickly green.

If he had waited any longer to leave the battle, he would have been caught in the heart of the storm. Not even for Tuulo would he have risked riding into the very center of Golgoyat's wrath.

The mare he had borrowed from Juyut whinnied and whined, shaking her mane against the rain and flicking her ears. The sentries at the bridge were huddled under lashed-together spruce branches, and they merely saluted him as he passed. Ferocious wind whistled and howled around the ruined buildings. The driven rain formed a gray mist on the cedar roofs, haloing the tops of the ancestor totems in ash. There was no one in the streets. He rode, prodding and kicking his recalcitrant mare, until they reached the central square.

He drove her to the door of the warehouse where the horses were stabled and beat against the wooden frame. A startled old woman peered at him out of the gloom.

"Get my mare into shelter!" He dismounted and hurried through the door, casting aside the soggy leather cloak that he had carried over his shoulders. "I'm going to Tuulo."

"Wait!" the woman said, putting her hand on his arm. "You shouldn't. Not yet."

He shook her off. "I'm going."

Keshlik took off running through the streets. The rain had thickened into a downpour. The routes between the lodges were muddy sloughs, their puddles dancing with the rain. The thrum of rain beat the ground, and the lodges waxed and waned with the gusts of the gale. Mud pulled at his feet. The beach thundered with wind-lashed waves. The sky overhead pulsed with lightning.

He came to the little clearing on the north side of the city, which had a circle of burnt earth in its center. The rain had turned the blessed ring to mud.

He paused at the edge of the circle. If the child had been born, he was allowed to enter. Khou's blessing would have been given, and the sacred circle used up. But he hesitated, nonetheless, to cross the line that had split him from his wife for so long. Breaching it now felt like sacrilege.

"Tuulo!" he shouted. "Tuulo! Come and show me my son!"

The slit of the yurt door widened, and a woman emerged. Dhuja, not Tuulo. She looked at Keshlik with her face gnarled and hard, like an old, wind-bent tree.

"You've come," she said. "It's probably for the best that you came no sooner."

"What are you talking about? Where's my wife?"

She did not answer. Her face was blackened, and the rain ran in dark rivulets off her chin. The color stirred dread in Keshlik's chest. The last time he had seen a midwife so darkened...

"Come into the yurt. You'll see." She ducked through the door.

Keshlik drew a heavy breath, stepped across the line of sacred earth, and followed her in.

A single butter lamp burned inside the yurt, giving off a dim,

237

soft-edged light. On the bed in the center of the yurt lay Tuulo, unmoving, her eyes closed as if sleeping.

A red cloth was wound around her middle, covering her from her knees to her belly. The cloth was mottled with dark brown stains. She had no other covering. Her legs were bare below the knees, dark and stout. Her heavy mother's breasts rested against her belly, round, black-nippled, beautiful. Her hands lay palms-up on the ground.

She hadn't flinched or twitched when Keshlik entered the yurt.

"Tuulo," he said quietly. "Tuulo!"

Her chest was motionless and empty of breath.

His legs grew weak. Horror curdled in his belly. "Dhuja. Tell me what happened here."

The old midwife's voice rattled like blades of dry grass in the wind. "She brought the boy near to birth, but at the threshold of delivery, her womb was torn. She bled too much and too fast."

"What is... What did you do to her?" He sank to the ground.

"I waited until every drop of strength had been wrung from her, Keshlik. When I unwound the red sash, she had already sunk two-thirds of the way into death."

He briefly touched Tuulo's hand. It was cold. "You killed her."

"I did what every midwife must sometimes do. We do not bind the knife against our bellies unless we're prepared to use it."

"What are you talking about? I don't care about your midwife's traditions. Why did you kill her?"

"To save the child."

"But you failed at that, too!"

"What makes you think I failed?"

He stopped. "What? I don't see any child here."

Dhuja pointed into the shadow at the edge of the yurt. Something moved. In the darkness, a shape that he had taken for a mound of cloth looked up. The captive woman.

"Come here." Dhuja beckoned the woman.

The captive shook her head and pushed herself deeper into the darkness. She looked at Keshlik with terror and said something in her incomprehensible tongue. Dhuja sighed and walked over. She gave the woman a half-hearted scold and scooped something out of her arms.

The swaddled bundle in Dhuja's arms gave a brief squeal of protest. The midwife rocked him gently and brought him to Keshlik. "Your son."

A gift of impossible lightness was placed into Keshlik's hands. He weighed no more than a falcon in the hand. His squeal was like a mouse's. His hand formed a fist and beat at the air, then he tucked it into his chest to punctuate a tiny, quavering cry. Wisps of black hair stuck to his forehead. His beautiful brown lips parted to reveal a bright red mouth like a sparrow chick's.

Keshlik began to quake. Horror and wonder mixed in his chest, blocking out thought. Adrenaline and weariness mixed in his veins. He might crush the boy in his hands on accident in this state. "Take him," he barked at Dhuja. "Take him!" He held out the babe at arm's length.

Dhuja took the child back from Keshlik and laid him in the nurse-mother's arms. Keshlik turned away from them and buried his face in his arms. The baby's wails punctuated Keshlik's voiceless sobs. He heard the captive woman shush the child.

He gathered enough composure to speak. "How did the captive woman come to take him to breast?"

"I don't know. I cut him free from the womb, and the woman took him and fled. We found her on the seashore, drenched with water, nursing the child. No one saw what happened." Dhuja hesitated. "It is fortunate that she was here. Otherwise there would have been no one to nurse him."

"Fortunate," Keshlik muttered. He looked at Tuulo, wrapped in the midwife's death girdle, the yellow lamplight staining her brown, beautiful face. Fierce, kind Tuulo, the only woman he had ever knelt to. Strong enough to rebuke him, gentle enough to shame him. "Fortunate."

239

A gust of wind burst the door of the yurt and filled the space with chill air and the echo of rain. Dhuja pinched the flap shut.

"If I had come more quickly…"

"What would you have done?" Dhuja asked. "You couldn't have entered Khou's circle anyway."

"No, but…" A surge of anger passed through him. "Khou's blessing did nothing to save my wife."

Dhuja was silent.

He began to quake again. "I can't stay here." He pushed through the yurt door and into the storm. Rain blinded him as soon as he stepped outside. He slipped in the mud and fell. A curse burst from his lips. He rubbed the icy water from his eyes and struggled to his knees.

The sun was dying beyond the clouds in the west, and the storm whirled and crashed around him. Lightning flashed. Keshlik glimpsed towers of boiling clouds lancing the earth with rain, trees bent over and thrashing in the wind. Another spearpoint of lightning flashed on the horizon, again lighting up the storm-battered landscape in splinters of white.

"Golgoyat," he whispered. He rose to his feet. "Golgoyat! Do you hear me? Speak to me now, as you spoke to my father!"

Thunder shook the sky. Keshlik's cloak thrashed like a banner in the wind. "You gave us victory on the battlefield, but there was no blessing for my wife? Have I carried your spear across the mountains so that my son could be nursed by a slave woman? Has your power dried up? Has Khou's?"

His breath ran out, and he fell to a knee, gasping. "Help me, lord of sky and storm. Help me. Show me where to go."

Again thunder rumbled, rolling across the sky from the east to the west. Keshlik looked up into the darkness of the storm.

Lightning smote the shore. Thunder crashed. Through the trees between the yurt and the sea, he glimpsed the waves lifted like shields against the fury of the wind, and just above them was a shelf of rock that stood above the sea. Lightning flashed again, touching the stone, then struck the place a third time. The thunder sounded constantly, like the oncoming gallop of horses.

Keshlik stared out toward the sea, though the landscape had faded into blackness. He rose to his feet. "I see your sign, Golgoyat, my lord."

He didn't know what paths, if any, led from his position down to the sea, and he couldn't see them in the dark. He charged under the spruces anyway. The trees bent and groaned, and water sprayed from their branches. The muddy ground was treacherous. His hands were soon bloody from the stones and stumps that stopped his falls, and he himself was slick with mud up to his waist. Lightning flashed shards of white light through the wind-whipped spruces.

Keshlik stumbled out onto a grassy hillock above the beach. Lightning arced across the sky again, turning the sea a glaring white. The stone was a few hundred paces ahead on the beach.

He slid down the rain-slicked slope that descended from the pines to the beach. His feet crunched in the pebbles. "Golgoyat, I'm coming. I'm coming."

He cast aside his waterlogged riding cloak and ran up the beach. The surf roared next to him. He fell headfirst into a storm-swollen brook that cut through the sands, kicked, and emerged spitting mud from his mouth.

The rhythm of the storm drove him onward. The wind seemed to be his heartbeat. The thunder was his breath. When next a bolt painted the sky white, he saw the stone ahead of him, standing above the surf in defiance of the storm.

The stone formed a little table, twenty paces wide, and rose just above the surf. The tide was in and had left a strip of seawater frothing between the beach and his goal.

Keshlik hesitated. He did not fear lightning, but he couldn't swim. "Golgoyat save me," he muttered. He stripped off his pants and shirt and plunged into the water.

The shock of cold water rushed over his legs. He pushed

forward. The water rose to his knees, to his waist, to his belly, even as the rain pelted his back. Waves pulled at his feet, battered his chest, and splashed salt into his eyes.

The water reached his shoulders. Just a little farther to the stone. A wave roared over his head, filling his mouth and eyes with sea foam, lifting his feet from the rocky sea floor. He thrashed in panic until his toes found the ground again.

He spit the seawater from his mouth and lunged to the stone, digging his fingers into the slime-covered rock just in time to weather another wave.

The rock cut into his fingers. He found toeholds and heaved himself up onto his belly. He kicked and scrabbled madly, pulling himself forward inch by inch, until he rested atop the stone.

He waited there with his cheek against the rock, breathing heavily. His fingers, toes, and stomach bled.

The sounds of the storm began to abate. *No more time to rest.* He gathered his strength and heaved himself to his feet. The clouds had begun to break apart to the east, and brilliant moonlight leaked through.

He took a few steps forward. The moon lit something ahead of him, a dark shape rising out of the stone. He approached it, crushing shells under his bare feet.

Three yards from the shape, he stopped.

It was an old woman, silver-haired, wrapped in a white sheet. He bent and picked up a sharp stone—it was only an old woman, but he could not be too cautious—and crept forward.

"Who are you?" He raised the stone to strike.

She lifted her head, and he saw her face and her milk-colored eyes. He nearly dropped the stone.

The witch.

"Son of Golgoyat. You came." She spoke Yakhat. Her voice creaked and groaned.

He gripped the stone tighter and took a step closer. "What are you doing here? How did you get here?"

"I should ask you the same thing. Do you often plunge into the ocean at night during a storm?"

"Golgoyat called me here. Perhaps he called me to kill you."

"Perhaps he did." She remained seated, as if waiting for him to act. Her eyes did not follow him. The moonlight reflected off the milky cataracts in their center.

He stepped closer, cautious. She might split open the stone beneath him and swallow him up. But a quick blow to the head would bring her down, and he could crush her throat with a second blow. "Tell me why I shouldn't kill you."

She cocked her head, as if listening to a voice he couldn't perceive. "Because I am here. Because they were not human hands that pulled me from the water and clothed me in white."

"What do you mean? And where did you learn to speak our language?"

"The answer to your questions are one and the same: Oarsa, of the deepness of the sea."

"I have never heard that name."

"But he knows you, and he knows the patrons of your people, Golgoyat of the storm cloud and... and Khou." She paused, fingering the edge of the white cloth that swaddled her. "Yes, her name is Khou. I called her Sorrow before."

Keshlik clenched the rock in his hand. Whether she knew the names of Golgoyat and Khou through spies or sorcery, she was here and in his power. In a moment, he could avenge the deaths of the Yakhat the witch had killed, and his people could be free of the only thing that could hold them back from final victory. He bolted forward, stone raised to strike.

"Stop."

She had not moved, but her word struck him like an arrow.

"Son of Golgoyat, remember your wife," she said. "If you kill me here, war will not leave your people for the rest of your life."

"Why should I care whether war leaves my people? We've lived with war for more than a hundred years."

243

"Because war has already claimed your wife. It nearly claimed your child. It may soon claim your brother. Make peace quickly, lest you lose twice more than what you've lost already."

"My wife was not claimed by war," he said. The stone dug into the flesh of his fingers. But the sign he had demanded from Golgoyat had pointed here, and he would listen. For a while. "What do you know about my wife?"

"Khou left her. I know this, because Khou was with me, making war against the Yakhat warriors by burying them in the earth. Don't wonder that Khou sided with your enemies, son of Golgoyat. It was but a small step from the broken wedding to outright enmity between Golgoyat and Khou. And I called up the earth mother with memories of the homes which your warriors despoiled, just as the city-dwellers first despoiled the Bans. You have become the image of your enemies. It wasn't hard to bring Khou to my side."

She was quiet for a moment. "But do not fear. Khou has made peace and returned to her sacred circle. No stones will crush you now."

"But Tuulo..."

"Tuulo wasn't crushed by stones, but by a child who could not be born without Khou's blessing. It is good for you to weep for her. It's good for you to know a portion of the sorrow you've spread everywhere your spear has pointed."

The stone lay limply in his hand. He hurled it into the sea. "*I* have to know the sorrow I've spread? We Yakhat have known sorrow. Golgoyat urged the Yakhat to bring the Sorrow of Khaat Ban to everyone we touched. Making others know our sorrow was our calling."

"And, as was inevitable, that sorrow has returned to you again. Now if you insist, you can renew your campaign and pile weeping upon weeping, never resting from war. Every sorrow that you plant will eventually return to your own breast. But there is another way."

"There is no other way. The Sorrow of Khaat Ban—"

"Is your sorrow. Is my sorrow. It's the wounds suffered by the captive woman you gave to Tuulo. It's the sorrow of the stillborn child she held in her hands. Did you realize that she made the same oath that your people made so long ago, at the boundaries of the Bans?"

Keshlik spat. "What do you mean?"

"I mean that she swore to repay the sorrow she had been dealt and punish those who had wounded her. But though she had sworn to smother your son when he was born, and though she cast him into the water, she relented. She begged him back from the sea and put him to her breast."

The words struck him like a blow. *Tuulo is dead, and I can barely continue to live. If I had lost my son as well...* He gasped for words. He owed his son to the captive woman. She had sworn an oath—he would have done the same—but she had turned back.

"Now you, too, must put aside your wrathful oath, Golgoyat. Return to Khou your bride. Let her make her home here, in a land hallowed by blood and milk, and marry."

"I don't understand."

"Reconcile the Powers and put an end to this war." The woman paused. "Marry the woman who nurses your son."

A growl of rage erupted from his throat, and he stepped toward the witch to throw her into the sea for her grotesque suggestion. She did not flinch, and the serenity of her milk-white eyes made his fury falter. *Golgoyat brought me here. I will listen.* "How dare you suggest such a thing? I do not want another. I want Tuulo. Your promises of peace will not bring her back."

The witch answered quietly, "But peace may save your son."

"How will it save my son?"

"Without Uya, your child has no mother and will probably die. Even if you find a Yakhat nurse in time, you child will grow into war. Khou will leave your people, and she will not return. The sorrow you know today will be reaped by all the Yakhat—including your son, when his time comes."

"But the Sorrow is not avenged."

"It can never be avenged. Sorrow is not repaid with vengeance.

But perhaps it can be healed, and the wedding broken at Khaat Ban be restored."

Keshlik trembled. "I cannot."

"You can."

He sank to his knees. "I would betray Tuulo and my people."

"No. You would save them."

He covered his eyes and began to weep. *Tuulo, Tuulo. I cannot wed another. How could I set aside my spear?*

Yet the Praseo woman suffered my son to live, recanted her oath of vengeance. I cannot continue to make war against her people. "The Yakhat warriors will despise me."

He felt the witch's hand on his shoulder. "Be not afraid. Your people are more ready for peace than you think. You must have the courage to first say the word."

"Peace."

"For the sake of your child."

"But the Yakhat do not want peace. *I* do not want peace." The words tasted false. Perhaps he didn't want peace, but he had lost his hunger for war.

The witch's silence accused him.

Finally he asked, "Is there no other way?"

She shook her head. "Only the captive woman could heal the tears of Khou. And only you, son of Golgoyat, can quell the thunder's wrath."

He wanted to object, but every word that came to his tongue dissolved like salt in the rain. Tuulo was gone. The Sorrow of Khaat Ban, the rage of the Yakhat, the honor of the warriors— none of these mattered. What mattered was a newborn in a yurt, and the woman who had preserved the child for him.

"I will do it," he said.

The witch raised her head. "You will restore the marriage of the Powers?"

"Whatever is required. Let my son be the firstborn child of peace."

CHAPTER 31

UYA

THE BABY WAS CRYING AGAIN. Uya opened her eyes and saw daylight creeping through the door of the yurt. Morning. She had been up throughout the night nursing, after the sleepless night of attending Tuulo's labor. Her limbs cried out for sleep.

But the baby was crying again.

She rolled over, unwound the boy's swaddling, and cupped his warm, tiny body against her belly. He begged for her nipple, letting out a mousy squawk when she didn't comply quickly enough.

"I'm coming. I'm coming," she whispered. "Just a minute."

She arranged herself against the straw-filled cushions that Dhuja had brought her. The baby squealed until she tucked him into the crook of her elbow and pulled him up to her breast. He bit down. She whispered a grunt of pain. He suckled greedily, and the pain passed as her breast let down the milk. It dribbled from the corner of the boy's mouth and down Uya's stomach.

Dhuja was gone, and there was no sign of Tuulo's body. Finally. Uya had been none too happy about nursing with a dead body in the yurt, but after wrapping Tuulo in the red sash, Dhuja had seemed in no hurry to remove the dead mother. Plus, there had been the awful storm. A person would've had to be mad to go out in the storm.

Mad as the baby's monstrous father had been, charging in and out at the beginning of the evening. She held that word—*monstrous*—in her mind for a moment, but it had lost its teeth. Her hatred dissolved with the flow of her milk.

There was silence in the yurt, except for the tiny movements of the nursing child. Outside, birds warbled in the dawn. Uya switched the child to the other breast, then rested her head against the cushions and dozed. The baby nursed in silence.

When he was done, she bound him again in the white cloth and lay him to sleep. She curled herself around him and closed her eyes.

The sound of startled voices outside the yurt woke her. One voice belonged to Dhuja, and the other to a man. The third voice sounded familiar. She straightened. The baby, too, was awake, observing her quietly with his narrow brown eyes.

"They're making an awful lot of noise," Uya said. "They really ought to let us sleep."

The boy gurgled.

She picked him up and tucked him against her belly and began to rock. She was hungry. But she had no idea how to tell Dhuja, so she would have to wait for the midwife to think to bring her some food. Hopefully it wouldn't be too long.

Dhuja ducked through the door of the yurt. Looking panicked, the midwife took Uya's hand, pointing and jabbering and otherwise making it clear that she was supposed to come out.

Uya batted her hand away. She had been cowering before the old woman for weeks, and now she was done being so timid. "I'll come, but you'd better get me something to eat. Do you understand me?"

Dhuja disappeared back through the door without giving any indication that she had heard Uya's demand for food. Perhaps whoever was waiting outside would be more cooperative. Surely *someone* understood that a nursing woman needed to eat. Uya rose unsteadily to her feet and ducked through the door after the midwife, then blinked away the sudden morning brightness. Keshlik was there in mud-slathered clothes. Next to him stood an old woman, wrapped in a white sheet.

The woman seemed familiar. Uya looked at her more closely, and her heart stuttered.

"Saotse," she said. "Saotse!"

The old woman turned her head. "Uya?"

"Saotse! It *is* you!" Uya ran forward and threw her free arm around Saotse, pulled her into her chest, and covered her cheek with kisses. Then she began to cry.

Saotse brushed her hands against Uya's face, wiping away tears and running her fingers over Uya's features like water. A strange smile appeared on her face.

"Oh, Saotse. I thought you were dead! How did you get here?"

"Oarsa—no, there's too much to tell. You wouldn't believe me."

"I don't care. You're here, and I never thought I would see any of my *enna* again."

"Nor I. Nor I." Saotse wept then. She buried her face in Uya's shoulder, kissed her neck, and kneaded Uya's cheeks as if to make sure she was really there.

Uya pinned her sister to her breast and watched her blind eyes blink in wonder. "It's like you came back from the dead."

Saotse laughed. "Perhaps I did. I have to tell you." One hand rested lightly on the tiny, warm bundle that had been pressed between them during their embrace. "You have the child."

Uya blushed. The child had fallen asleep in the crook of her arm, undisturbed by their bustling. Saotse couldn't see the hue of his skin, so she wouldn't know. She felt a touch of shame mingled with sadness. "He's not mine. This is hard to explain."

"Sorry? Why should you be sorry? Most blessed, most sorrowful mother, without you— No, don't explain anything! I already know, and I have more to explain to you."

Dhuja broke in with a burst of Yakhat gibberish. Saotse responded with a matching hail of syllables.

"What?" Uya asked, shocked. "What is this? How—when did you learn their language?"

"Oarsa gave it to me," Saotse said. "I told you, I have much to explain."

Keshlik and Dhuja began to pepper Saotse with questions. Uya watched, astounded, as Saotse answered, the gravelly foreign sounds flying off her tongue as if she had been born to them.

"Tell me what they're saying. Please, Saotse, I've been living here for weeks with no one to talk to, doing my best with my tiny fragments of Guza and no real translator."

Saotse rested a comforting hand on her arm. "I told them you're my sister and that we're almost the same age. They nearly didn't believe me. Keshlik didn't realize until now that I'm one of the swift people, and that led to more questions—"

Keshlik interrupted Saotse with another demand. Saotse responded briefly, then said to Uya, "They want to know what we're saying. I told them that there's too much to explain right now, and I asked to speak with you alone for a while. Now, are you hungry?"

"Merciful Chaoare, yes. Can you ask them for food?"

Saotse relayed the request to Dhuja. "Dhuja says they'll bring us food in the yurt. Let's go in. Oh, Uya. We have so much to talk about."

———— ·❖· ————

"What? He wants to *marry* me?"

"A certain kind of marriage," Saotse said. "You won't be expected to lie with him, for one thing. But you'll be the mother of his child. You are already the child's foster mother, his nurse-mother, and by becoming Keshlik's wife, you will get recognition for this fact."

"But still…" Uya leaned her head on the cushions beside her. The bones of the fish on which she had gorged herself lay on the ground, but she picked one of them up to see if a scrap of flesh still clung to it. Her mind felt as if it had been filled with stones and shaken. The day had turned bright after the storm, and the yurt was becoming hot and stuffy. "Can you open the yurt door? Or maybe we can go outside."

Saotse shook her head. "You need to be in the yurt when Keshlik comes. He's going to formally petition you after he gets permission from the Khaatat elders."

"He's coming *now*? Oh sweet Chaoare, I can't deal with this."

"Not right now, but soon. Today."

"Today," Uya repeated, hoping that the word would become something else. "Today. You can't expect me to do anything today, Saotse! I've hardly slept in two days. My nipples are raw, I have to nurse every three hours, and it's not even my baby. Just yesterday, I was wishing death on all of them, including the boy—Oarsa forgive me for thinking it. The fact that I took his son to my breast doesn't mean that I'm ready to *marry* the man."

Saotse sat impassively in Dhuja's usual spot, eyes looking blankly ahead, her head cocked to catch all of Uya's words. She even looked like Dhuja in that position, and it didn't dispose Uya to think kindly of her. "I know, but—"

"Did you forget?" Uya spat. "I watched him butcher Nei and kill my mother. Am I supposed to just let that go? To become his wife?"

"He wants to make peace. He will make restitution, both to you and to the remnants of Prasa."

"And? Does that wash the blood of our *enna* from his hands? The blood of every other *enna* in Prasa?"

Saotse was quiet for a while. "No, it doesn't. And he has more

251

deaths on his hands than you imagine, Uya. He can't repay them all. He can't repay even one. He can only hope to be forgiven."

Uya folded her arms under her breasts. She couldn't do it. She might be willing to let Keshlik live. But she would never be his wife.

"You know," Saotse said after Uya's long silence, "they were my *enna*, too."

"It's not the same," Uya said. "They weren't your blood. And you had the Powers."

"I did not have them. I merely heard them, yet they would never answer me. Little comfort. And is blood the only thing that matters? Think of Tuulo's child, now. Your child."

"That's not the same thing."

"Isn't it?"

The baby began to cry. He had soiled his rags, and they spent several minutes finding the pot of water and extra rags to clean and change him. Then he wanted to nurse, and when at last the child was quietly suckling, Uya had forgotten what she was going to say. She closed her eyes. She needed to sleep, not to fend off proposals of marriage.

There were footsteps outside the yurt. Saotse slipped out into the brightness, and spent a few minutes speaking to someone. She heard several male voices, one of them Keshlik's. The sound of Saotse's voice speaking in Yakhat was still shocking and somewhat upsetting to her.

Saotse reentered the yurt. "Keshlik is here. He will be petitioning you to be his wife."

"Already? You said not right away."

"All I know is that he's here."

"Tell him I'm still nursing." She wiped the trickle of milk from the bottom of her left breast and moved the boy to the right. He gurgled and latched on.

"Will you come when you're done?"

"Do I have a choice?"

"You can refuse to meet him. But please, Uya. At least come out to hear his petition."

"When the baby is done nursing."

Nursing was finished more quickly than she wanted, and the boy fell asleep as soon as Uya finished swaddling him. All she wanted to do was sleep, too. Not to talk to Keshlik, or Dhuja, or even Saotse. She groaned and straightened. Saotse reached for her hand and followed her through the door of the yurt.

The sunlight blinded her for a moment. There was a small crowd of men in front of her yurt, some old men and a handful of warriors. One of them barked an order when Uya emerged, and all the men drew away except one. The sunlight softened, and she made out his face. Keshlik.

He held a spear in front of him in both of his hands, the point just in front of his mouth. He bowed to her, then began to speak rapidly in a sort of chant for a minute, then he struck the butt of his spear against the ground and knelt. He bowed his head and extended the spear to her in his open palms.

"Saotse," Uya said, "what's going on here?"

"He is offering to take you as his wife. And he makes a very generous offer."

"Is that all? He seemed to speak for a long time."

Saotse chuckled. She said something in Yakhat to Keshlik, who responded in a surprised tone. She relayed to Uya, "I'll repeat the terms to you."

Keshlik began to repeat the chant, more slowly.

Saotse translated, "First, Keshlik asks your leave to bury his wife Tuulo and to mourn her until the new moon."

"Yes, of course—"

"Don't interrupt. I have to keep translating."

Keshlik hadn't broken stride in his chant.

Saotse hurried to catch up. "He will make peace with your people at whatever price they demand, and he will bind the Yakhat to peace forever. And to you personally he offers his treasures in turquoise, gold and silver coins, cedar chests, mother-of-pearl, blankets, and... well, there's more, but I won't name all of it. They have quite a bit of plunder from all their fighting."

Keshlik finished. He bowed his head again and offered the spear to Uya.

"If you'll take his offer, receive his spear as a seal," Saotse said. "He will reclaim it when it's time for the wedding."

Uya looked at Keshlik, then at Saotse. The rest of the men who had accompanied Keshlik had withdrawn to the edges of the old sacred circle and watched them with apparent indifference.

"If I take his spear," Uya said, "would I have to stay here? With the Yakhat?"

Saotse repeated the question to Keshlik then translated his answer. "If you wanted to. But if not, he is willing to negotiate another agreement."

"But..." Uya felt her face growing hot, and her words got away from her. It wasn't just the thought of living perpetually with the Yakhat that disturbed her. It was everything. Even though she nursed a Yakhat boy, she wasn't ready to marry one of them. Even if it was a false marriage, a half-marriage.

She looked at Keshlik's face. He seemed older than she remembered, and his face was softened, scrubbed clean of the fury that had darkened it before, and haunted now by sadness. She remembered the way that he looked when he had captured her in Prasa, splattered with blood, red with fury and murder. She remembered, too, her hatred, but only as a memory. The deluge that had washed away her hatred had cleansed Keshlik, as well.

But still. It didn't mean she was ready to marry him.

"I'm sorry," she said. "Saotse, I can't. Not right now. No, I can't."

Saotse was quiet. "Are you sure?"

"As sure as I can be."

Saotse cleared her throat and said something long and drawn-out to Keshlik, much more than Uya had originally said. He answered in kind, and they conversed for a few minutes. Then Saotse said again to Uya, "He goes to offer peace to your people regardless, as soon as Tuulo is buried. Will you come with him?"

"Why?"

"Because he wants to show you to the representatives of the Yivriindi. Your presence with his child will demonstrate his desire for peace, even if you are not betrothed. And he wants to be near his son."

Uya sighed. More movement, more discomfort. But perhaps this was almost the end. "Yes, I'll go."

Saotse translated. Keshlik nodded and slowly rose to his feet, dropping the proffered spear back to his side with an awkward, self-conscious movement. He bowed to Uya, then repeated something to Saotse.

"Keshlik thanks you," Saotse said. "We're leaving in two days."

The men left. Saotse put her hand into Uya's.

Uya hugged the boy to her chest and closed her eyes. "Are you upset with me?"

Saotse was quiet for a while. "I understand your reasons," she said at last. "You should go inside and rest."

CHAPTER 32

KESHLIK

WARRIORS SINGING SONGS OF VICTORY met Keshlik's party when they reached the fringes of the camp in the woods. Late afternoon sunlight spilled like gold between the spruces, and the air was heavy with the scent of spruce and horses. Keshlik's party rode with cheers and ululations following them through the woods and onto the fields where the battle had taken place, where most of the camp had moved, spreading out over the grass and the streams in careless disregard for defensibility or perimeter. They were clearly not worried about a counterattack.

In the center of the expanded camp, Keshlik saw a tight ring of tents, with the Khaatat sign emblazoned on one of them. Just outside the ring was a careworn encampment of white Yivrian tents, with Yakhat warriors posted in a loose circle around it.

The Yivrian representatives, whomever they were, were in Juyut's power.

By the time they reached the center where Juyut's yurts lay, a train of shouting and crowing warriors had formed behind them and crowded in on both sides, forming an aisle. While Keshlik was still thirty yards away, Juyut emerged from his tent. He folded his arms and spread his legs wide, grinning like a coyote, and waited for Keshlik and the chieftains to come.

From the corner of his eye, Keshlik glimpsed the cart carrying Uya and Saotse fall back, and he drew his horse to a halt, stopping the entire procession. Uya was hunched over, as if trying to hide from the ruckus of the warriors, and Saotse had her arm around her. The baby seemed to be crying. He motioned for the warriors to quiet. At first, his movements prompted them only to shout louder, but gradually his scowl and his continued insistence calmed them.

"Is the child okay?" he asked Saotse.

"He stirred," she said, "but Uya calmed him. Don't worry."

Keshlik nodded to Saotse then dismounted. Juyut maintained his pose for just a moment after his feet touched the ground, then he ran forward and crushed Keshlik in his embrace.

"Golgoyat himself fought among us, brother!" He lifted his arms exultantly.

The warriors shook the ground with another shout.

"Quiet!" Keshlik barked, slapping his brother's arms to the ground. The baby's tremulous cry made itself heard in the silence.

"The baby," Juyut said, still grinning. "You brought Tuulo? Is it a son or a daughter?"

"A son. But Tuulo isn't here."

Juyut fell back a step. His smile faltered. "Where is she?"

Keshlik looked to the ground. He closed his eyes and put his hand across his brow. "Khou's bosom."

Juyut dropped his hand and retreated another pace. They stood an awkward distance apart. Then Juyut wrapped his brother in his arms and kissed him on the cheek. He pressed his cheek against Keshlik's.

"But the boy?" Juyut said at last. "Your son? He is well?"

"Yes."

"And have you named him?"

"Yes. His name is Tuulik."

"Tuulik! After his mother. And who is nursing him?"

"Uya." Seeing Juyut's confusion, he added, "The captive woman. The one that I gave to Tuulo as a slave."

"Ah. Then she's proved her worth." Juyut looked back at the cart, where the women waited. With a gasp of recognition, he reached for his knife. "The witch!"

Keshlik put his hand over Juyut's. "Yes. Her name is Saotse. She, too, is in our power now."

"But she lives!"

"The Power has left her. She cannot harm us. And she is under my care."

Juyut narrowed his eyes and squeezed his knife hilt. "Why have you kept her alive?"

"She will help us speak to the Yivrian envoys. She must live. I will explain soon."

Juyut grimaced, baring his teeth at the woman. "But I have good news. The rest of the Yivrian force, we routed after you left, driving them from the field. We pillaged their encampment and crushed their reserves. Most of them dispersed into woods and villages, but those who pulled together did send us an embassy under a flag of peace. I've kept them here as captives under guard, expecting that you'd want to speak to them. We have their precious relic sword, too, which we're keeping for ransom."

"Good," Keshlik said. "I have to speak to them—now, if possible. I have only a little time. Tuulo will be buried the day after tomorrow, and I have to return by then."

"Of course, of course. Is that why you brought the chiefs of the tribes?" Juyut glanced at the old men standing mixed in with the warriors.

"Yes." It had only been two days, yet Keshlik felt as though an absence of decades had fallen between them. He had changed. Juyut had not. They had much to speak about—and soon—but Keshlik had even more pressing matters to deal with first.

The Yivrian embassy joined Keshlik, Juyut, Bhaalit, and the rest of the Yakhat elders at the fire when evening fell. Juyut had them escorted by a squadron of mounted Yakhat warriors, as the captives that Juyut considered them to be. But Keshlik did not view them that way.

The Yivrian party was a worn-down, dishonored band. Most of them were dressed in white and blue linens that had been fine once, but which had come to bear the stains of rapid flight and blood. They stood in a little cluster in the gap between the chieftains, glancing across the weathered Yakhat faces in incomprehension. The movements of Yakhat warriors made them flinch.

"Is this all of them?" Keshlik asked.

"All of them," Juyut said. "But only two of them speak Guza, and not very well."

Keshlik waved that difficulty aside. "We have a translator. Saotse, will you greet them?"

Saotse bowed and presented her hands palm-up to the envoys. She said something in wispy, insubstantial Praseo. Murmurs of surprise sounded from the Yivriindi, and one of them responded in turn. A few rapid exchanges followed. A narrow-faced young man stepped forward and said something with a little more confidence than the rest of the group had shown. Saotse bowed and showed her palms again.

"This is Narista, the son of the *kenda*," she said to Juyut and Keshlik. "With the death of his father, he expects to soon take up the title of *kenda* himself, but he has to first return to Kendilar to—"

The man cut Saotse off, a storm of angry syllables pouring from his mouth. Saotse nodded rapidly and attempted to calm him enough to translate his words.

"He is disappointed. He says that he rallied the remainder of the Yivrian forces, and he came here under the color of peace so that he could speak to the Yakhat as civilized people, but he is not sure you qualify as civilized."

Keshlik frowned. "We're here because we, too, want to speak. Tell him that."

She did so, and Narista responded with a curt gesture that invited Keshlik to do just that.

Keshlik stepped forward and bowed to the young man. The other did not bow in turn. The insult burned, and Keshlik fought the urge to unsheathe his knife and strike the proud fool down where he stood. But that would be an inauspicious beginning for a truce.

"I've come to offer peace," he said.

"What?" Juyut said from the edge of the circle of elders. Mutters spread out through the gathered warriors.

Keshlik silenced them with a glare. "Listen to our offer." Saotse nodded at him to continue. "First, we will return the city of Prasa to the Prasei. All those who were cast out of it will be allowed to return. Furthermore, the Yakhat will provide to the city cattle in the number of four thousand cows giving milk and calving, one thousand gelding calves, and one hundred untouched bulls. We will also give horses from our own stocks in the number of eight hundred fertile mares, four hundred gelding colts, and fifty untouched stallions suitable for stud."

As he spoke, the mutter of the surrounding Yakhat warriors turned from a whisper to a growl. Juyut stared across the fire at Keshlik with fury and incomprehension. The chieftains attempted to calm the warriors around them, though even they looked uncomfortable and sour as Keshlik recited the numbers. They had all agreed on them and recited them the night before, but it was still a bitter root to chew.

Only the envoy seemed pleased as he listened to Saotse's translation, though confusion clouded his expression. He spoke to Saotse.

Saotse translated. "He says that this must be some kind of trick. What do you want in return?"

"In return, the Yakhat request the following: We ask for freedom to travel with our herds on the plains north of the River Prasa, from the mountains of the White Teeth, to Azatsi's Fingers and the Gap where the Guza once lived. We ask that we be allowed to trade in the city of Prasa, and that we may replace the Guza at the trading posts of the Gap where formerly the caravans from your cities met. And we ask that the Prasei and the Yivriindi enter with the Yakhat into a covenant of perpetual peace."

The envoy studied Keshlik intently while Saotse translated. The murmur of the Yakhat warriors around them had subsided, though Keshlik still saw them muttering and staring at him in shock and betrayal.

When Saotse had finished, the envoy responded in cold, bitter tones. She looked pained by the words but softly translated, "If those are your demands, was it necessary for you to sack Prasa, to plunder the farms and villages of the whole region, and to kill the *kenda* in a pitched battle?"

It was not necessary. But Keshlik didn't know how much he could, or should, explain himself to the boy. "No."

Judging by the murmuring and scowls on every side, neither the Yakhat nor the Yivriindi were pleased by his response.

With a sour grimace on his face, Narista replied, "Then why, after you've destroyed so many of our people, do you come to us suddenly seeking peace? Since we were injured, let us make our own demands."

"And what are your demands?" Keshlik asked.

Narista responded, and Saotse translated with an expression of surprise. "That you submit yourselves to the suzerainty of the *kenda* and pay perpetual tax in the form of gold or silver coin to the *kenda*, at the rate which he should establish."

Those terms were impossible. Keshlik had barely wrung the initial concessions from the chiefs, and if the condition of peace were submission to the *kenda*, then there would be no peace. The hard fact of any parlay was that the stronger party made the demands. He would have to be strong.

"You step beyond your place," he said. "We still hold you under our power. Where is your military might, that you make demands of us? I am making you a peace offering. The only other offer is war."

Saotse translated, and Narista flinched a little. He answered with less pride, and Saotse repeated, "Then why do you offer us peace now?"

He would have to explain. There was no way around it. And it would be better, for the Yakhat and for the Yivriindi, if everyone knew. "Because I have laid aside my spear forever, and I will hear no more of war."

And he told the envoy and all the gathered Yakhat what he had found when he returned to see his newborn son, how Golgoyat had answered him in the storm, and how he found the witch wrapped in a white sheet at the place that Golgoyat had shown him. He asked Saotse to repeat what the sea had told her. Then he reminded the warriors that the captive woman had given up her oath in order to save his son, and he repeated his plea for peace.

After he finished, there was a long silence.

The envoy said something quietly. Saotse laughed. "He says, 'Strange are the ways of the Powers.' I can only agree with that."

"Ask him if he believes me."

She asked. "He does," she translated. "My presence here, speaking Yakhat, is proof enough for him."

"Then ask him if he will make the pact of peace with us."

"He will."

"Wait," Juyut shouted from across the circle. "I don't agree to any such pact."

Bhaalit said, "You have no standing to speak here, Juyut."

"I led the Yakhat horde while we routed the enemy. The warriors followed *me*. And do any of them still follow me?"

He pounded the butt of his spear on the ground and jabbed the point into the air. Rumbles of agreement thundered through the warriors. Several of the chiefs looked upset, and some of them began to mutter among themselves.

Juyut folded his arms, his expression pleased. "I say that I have standing here."

"Then what do you suggest?" Keshlik spat the words like stones. He had known that he would face opposition, but he hadn't expected to fight his *brother*.

Juyut looked back at him, eyes burning with fury and betrayal. "I'm ashamed of what I've heard tonight. You've led the Yakhat horde through uncountable battles. I've never seen a warrior more courageous and more fierce than you. And yet you've been bewitched now by a woman telling lies? Golgoyat has fought among us since you were a child, and he rumbles still in the storm clouds. He has no need to lay aside his spear and marry. And the Yakhat have no need to lay aside their war and make peace with a nation of city-dwellers. You shame us with the stench of defeat when we should be exulting in victory."

Shouts and ululations of agreement sounded throughout the Yakhat horde. Juyut spoke more strongly, striking his spear repeatedly against the ground. The warriors were with him, Keshlik noted grimly.

"I say, let us press our victory to the end. When the voice of Golgoyat came to our father, he did not tell us when we should cease to war. And while Golgoyat fights, so do the Yakhat! We are warriors. We don't listen to witches weaving tales."

"But Tuulo," Keshlik said quietly.

"What about Tuulo?" Juyut's voice dropped, and he leaned closer to the fire to look Keshlik in the face, wearing an expression of pleading. "Brother, I weep with you for her death. But one man's dead wife does not mean that the Yakhat have to turn back from battle like rabbits."

"One man's wife might not mean that." Keshlik raised his

voice. Golgoyat help him, but he would have to convince them now if he had any hope of bringing the Yakhat horde to the peace table with him. "But most of you warriors here have wives, no? Will you give them up so that you can continue war? Will you drive a spear through their bellies when they ask you to come home to them and live peaceably?"

There was silence.

"Good," Keshlik continued. "Listen, men of the Yakhat, children of Golgoyat: Tuulo's death was a sign. She was the victim of war as surely as are the men being devoured by worms on the fields behind us. And this is the meaning of the sign: the spear that we have carried against our enemies since the Sorrow of Khaat Ban is thrust into our own hearts. If we continue in this manner, we create only sorrow after sorrow, and our wounds are neither healed nor repaid. The only way to win the battle is to cease from it. Let Golgoyat return to his bride. Let Khou bless this place as her home."

"No," Juyut said. "No. This is the witch's lie. Golgoyat is a warrior. The Yakhat are warriors. If we cease to fight, we die. The way you're offering us is the way of death."

"So what do you want then, Juyut?" Keshlik said. "Are you going to take your warriors and fight? Without the elders, without your clans, without your women, without the herds and the yurts and all the rest of the Yakhat?"

Juyut stiffened and raised his chin. He regarded Keshlik with a tempestuous glare. "I'll lead the Yakhat horde. If you're offering to lead the Yakhat into surrender, then I'll lead them into victory."

"What?" Keshlik's words thundered out of his mouth in equal parts fury and dismay. "Are you challenging my command?"

He briefly seemed to waver, his spear quivering in his hands. "Yes," he said at last. "If the chiefs will follow me."

Argument broke out at once all around the circle. Bhaalit shouted over the bickering of the elders, trying to restore order.

Keshlik stood silently, watching his brother. Juyut's eyes met his, his gaze as hard as a spearpoint.

Bhaalit's voice boomed across the council. "Let us not bicker like children! We can discuss this like free men. First, let every tribe declare who it stands with. Since Keshlik speaks here as leader of the war band and the chosen of Golgoyat, I will speak for the Khaatat in his place. And I declare the Khaatat for Keshlik."

The census went around the circle. Six tribes were with Keshlik. Five were with Juyut. Many of the chiefs added arguments of their own, pointing out Keshlik's century of leadership and his support by Saotse, or countering that Juyut was also a son of Keishul and an accomplished warrior. Few minds were changed.

Keshlik awaited the words Bhaalit would have to say next with dread.

Bhaalit shot Keshlik a heavy glance, his mouth pulled down into a sorrowful frown. He raised his palm and addressed the chiefs. "Since we are divided, shall we allow Juyut to challenge Keshlik?"

The chiefs assented.

"And will every one of us recognize and submit our warriors to the victor?"

Again, assent came from all around the circle.

Bhaalit sighed deeply and turned slowly to Keshlik. He lowered his voice, as if speaking to Keshlik alone. "And do you accept the challenge, Keshlik?"

Keshlik's mouth was dry. Dread of this very outcome had grown from the moment that Juyut had opposed him. If he wished to lay aside his spear, he would have to take it up one last time. He scraped his tongue against the roof of his mouth and said, "I do."

"And Juyut, you will abide by it?"

Juyut nodded.

"Then we have agreed," Bhaalit said, disappointment shadowing his face. He looked from Keshlik to Juyut and back in bewilderment. "If Juyut does not back down. We meet at dawn."

Saotse spoke up from where she had retreated to the fringes of the circle when he wasn't watching. "What shall I tell the envoy?"

The Yivrian prince still waited in the same spot, regarding the arguing warriors with wide eyes and a nervous posture.

Keshlik shook his head. "Tell him that his fate, like all of ours, will be decided tomorrow."

———◦⊰⊱◦———

Keshlik sat at a fire, across from Bhaalit. The logs crackled, and the sparks ascended to Golgoyat in the windless night. Somewhere nearby, the witch and the mother were sleeping in a tent, together with Keshlik's son. He had almost gone to wake them, to see the child one last time, but he restrained himself. Such a visit would only make the night more difficult, and he needed to keep his composure. If he did not let himself dwell on farewells, then there was a chance that the farewells would not be final.

A twig snapped at the edge of the fire's light. Bhaalit immediately leaned forward and had his hand on his spear.

Juyut appeared, his hands empty. "I've come alone. I want to talk to my brother."

Keshlik started to get up to meet Juyut alone, but Bhaalit waved him down.

"No," Bhaalit said. "I'll go. Juyut, take my place." He rose and disappeared into the dark, leaving Keshlik and Juyut alone.

Neither of them said anything for a while.

"I don't want to fight you," Juyut said.

"Then don't. Take back your challenge."

"It's too late for that. I cannot take it back without shame."

Keshlik murmured, "Are you still young enough to care about shame? I have more important cares." He gestured toward the tent where his son slept.

"Of course I care." Juyut seemed wounded. He searched out Keshlik's expression, his own reflecting dismay and distress. "It seems that you don't care. You care neither for your own honor nor for that of the Yakhat."

Keshlik threw a stone into the fire. "Honor will not save my child or bring back my wife. I desire peace. The Powers desire peace."

"The Powers." Juyut spat. "That is witch's speech. Golgoyat is the only Power that the Yakhat have ever needed."

Keshlik studied Juyut. "You actually believe that. That is the root of all our trouble. Those of you who do not remember the Bans have no memory of the marriage of Golgoyat and Khou. You have no knowledge of what it would mean, for them to wed again."

"That time is past. The Yakhat are warriors now. We cannot go back to what we were."

"We'll find that out, soon enough."

Juyut circled the fire and came to sit next to Keshlik. "I came to urge you to reconsider. The Yakhat should not be divided."

"And if I said those same words to you, would they change your mind?" Keshlik plucked a blade of grass from the ground and threw it into the fire, watching it bloom in flame, then fade into a writhing black line, then disappear. "You can no more change my mind than save the grass from the fire, Juyut. Even if I cannot make peace, I will not ride into battle again. Of all of the plunder of a thousand raids, Tuulo was the only prize I truly wanted. You know that when I first brought my spear to her yurt, she made me wait outside for three days before letting me in?"

Juyut chuckled. "You've told me the story."

"Then maybe you'll understand why I have no more desire to fight." He hung his head. He swallowed a sob, but he could not restrain the tears which leaked from his eyes.

Juyut reached over and brushed the tears from his cheeks. "Brother. Why are we suddenly on opposite sides, when we have fought so long as one?"

I wish we did not have to be. He could not say it, though.

Instead he swatted Juyut's hand away. "Leave me alone. If you cannot rescind your challenge to me, then don't make this harder than it must be."

Juyut reluctantly rose to his feet. He crossed to the far side of the fire, hesitated, then turned back to Keshlik. "I love you, Brother."

Keshlik covered his eyes. "Just go, Juyut."

He left.

Keshlik was alone with the fire and the darkness. He looked toward the tent where Tuulik slept, then to the place where Juyut had been. "I love you, Brother," he whispered.

CHAPTER 33

UYA

S AOTSE WOKE UYA FROM HER sleep. Uya would sleep the whole day if she could, if Saotse weren't shaking her shoulder and repeating her name insistently.

"Wake up, Uya. Please, Uya. It's important."

Of course it was important. Uya had experienced nothing but important events lately. And perhaps—probably—this important thing was more important than claiming a precious hour of rest while the baby slept. "What do you want, Saotse?"

She opened her eyes. The light of dawn poured in the door of her tent.

"Come to the battleground. And bring the child. In case... Just bring the child."

"Why?"

"Keshlik and Juyut are going to duel."

Uya blinked and allowed her eyes to take in the light while her ears absorbed Saotse's words. "Who is Juyut?"

"Keshlik's brother."

"Oh, him. Why would they duel?"

Saotse voice was heavy and scored as if by gravel. "Because Juyut will not consent to peace." She explained to Uya what had transpired while Uya and Tuulik slept.

Saotse's story jarred Uya into alertness, and she rose to her feet. Tuulik was tightly swaddled and lying on a blanket on the ground.

Uya touched his nose and brushed her finger against his cheek. "So you want me to come to the duel. What am I supposed to do?"

"Just be there. Keshlik will want to see his son. And if it comes to that, perhaps Juyut will pity us if he sees you carrying the child."

"Pity us? You mean..."

"If Juyut wins, I don't expect either of us will see tomorrow."

Uya looked down at Tuulik again then reached for the leather thongs that would bind him safely to her back—a gift from Dhuja. *I should be afraid*, she thought as she bound the lowermost straps above her hips. But she seemed to have run out of fear. *Too many days in the wolf's mouth, too much death all around me. I want to sleep, and I want to stay with the baby.* Everything else was a matter too distant and unimportant for her to waste her thoughts on.

"I'm coming," she said. "Just give me a moment."

<hr />

Dawn spilled like yellow wine across the battlefield. The grass was bent with dew that soaked Uya's and Saotse's leggings as they strode to the place of the duel. They were among the last to arrive. The Yakhat had already formed a ring around the designated place, though they parted to let Saotse and Uya through, tongues clicking with gossip when they saw the Yakhat child bound to Uya's back.

They emerged into the inside ring where Keshlik and the chiefs of his party were waiting. At the opposite end of the ring, Juyut crouched, five chiefs standing near him. The warriors who fenced the bounds of the arena with their spears were subdued and somber.

Keshlik greeted Saotse with a few words, and he bowed briefly to Uya. She nodded in response. He said something to Saotse.

She turned to Uya. "He asks if you are well, and he thanks you for coming."

Uya nodded. "I am well." What else could she say? Nothing seemed to fit the weight of the morning.

Juyut stripped to the waist and took a few strides toward the center of the ring. He carried a bronze spear in his right hand and an obsidian knife on his belt. A moment later, Keshlik took off his tunic and moved forward, similarly armed. He called out to the chiefs across the field from him in a long, sonorous speech.

"He asks whether they'll abide by the terms of the duel and follow whoever wins, whether to peace or to war," Saotse translated. She paused to listen. "They agree. Now he repeats the question to the rest of the Yakhat warriors."

A dreary thunder of agreement sounded from all around them. Tuulik began to cry.

Clucking her tongue, Uya released the child from his binding, unlaced her blouse, and tucked him close to nurse.

"The battle is starting," Saotse said.

Uya looked up. Keshlik was watching Tuulik nurse, and she caught his gaze. His face was stricken and bereaved, like a man who knew he was about to die. For a moment, Uya pitied him.

He looked away from her. He raised his spear to the ready, and advanced toward his brother. Uya turned her back to the duel and cast her gaze down at the nursing child.

"Won't you watch the battle?" Saotse asked.

"No," Uya answered. "This is more important."

Behind her, wood met wood. Bronze tore flesh. The watching warriors gasped and flinched. The sounds of fighting went on. But in front of her, lovely Tuulik suckled happily at her breast, his eyes closed. A drop of milk glistened on his cheek like a pearl. Uya wiped the milk away, then brushed the tips of her fingers through his wispy hair, as fine and gauzy as a spiderweb.

"Don't be afraid, little one," she whispered. "Your father is fighting for you."

But why would he be afraid? He knew nothing other than his mother's voice and the taste of her breast. She cooed and rocked him gently, and he continued to nurse.

She looked over her shoulder. If Tuulik was not afraid, she had no reason to be, either.

The two men still stood in the center of the arena. Both were bloodied. One of them—at first glance, she couldn't tell which it was—had suffered a major gash along his thigh, and his blood ran down his leg and soaked the ground. She had to look twice to recognize Keshlik. Both of their expressions were twisted by pain, and their faces were marred by sweat and blood.

Keshlik was limping, his movements with the injured leg hesitant and feeble, while Juyut danced outside of his reach. Keshlik prodded forward with the point of his spear, but Juyut darted aside. Juyut circled, looking for the place to strike.

She switched Tuulik to her other breast.

A gasp and a roar passed through the Yakhat horde.

Uya looked up. Keshlik was on his back, with Juyut sprawled atop him. Juyut's hand was curled around the haft of his knife, and the tip of the blade had entered Keshlik's side. Neither of them moved.

Perhaps she was going to die today, after all. She hoped that Tuulik got enough to nurse, first.

One of the warriors stirred. At first it seemed to be Juyut, rising from atop his elder brother. But then Keshlik's arm flexed. He put his hand over Juyut's on the haft of the knife. An agonized groan rent the silence as Keshlik pulled the knife from his side. Only a finger's width of the blade had entered, Uya saw with relief. He cast the knife aside and clapped his hand over the trickle of blood from his side.

Then he pushed Juyut from atop him, and Uya could see at last how the warriors had fallen: Juyut had leapt forward to plant his knife, but he had fallen onto the point of Keshlik's spear. The spear was broken in two, the spearhead buried in Juyut's ribs. The beam of the spear was still in Keshlik's hand.

Keshlik rose to his knees, visibly shaking with the effort. He looked down at his brother, then at the broken spear in his hand. He hurled the haft aside with a throat-rending curse. Then he lay his head on Juyut's chest and wept.

The Yakhat were silent.

"That's enough death." Uya tucked Tuulik into the crook of her arm and strode into the arena.

"What are you doing?" Saotse cried after her.

Uya ignored it. She found the beam of Keshlik's spear in the grass, picked it up, and walked over to him.

She touched his shoulder. He looked up, startled. His face was a ruin, splattered with blood and marred by tears, his eyes bloodshot with grief. She showed him the portion of the broken spear that she had taken, then touched the splinters bound to the bronze spearhead in Juyut's chest.

"I'm taking these," she said. "As you offered them to me."

He showed no sign of comprehension.

"Do you understand? I am taking your spear. We will marry, and our people will be at peace."

A moment passed in silence. Then he nodded.

Saotse appeared at her shoulder, then the Yakhat chiefs came, speaking to Keshlik. Tuulik began to fuss, and Uya opened her blouse again and gave him her nipple.

Exhaustion and relief flooded though her, and she knelt on the grass, cradling Tuulik against her belly. She would let the rest of them worry about terms and truces. She had done her part, and now she would rest.

A wind came out of the east, blowing gently toward where the dead rested. "Chaoare, carry my words to my mother and Nei and the rest of my *enna*," she prayed. "Tell them that I am a mother now, though not to the child they expected. Tell them that I miss them, but that I am not alone. I helped make peace. And when it's time, I'll repair the totems of our *enna* and raise them for their memory again."

CHAPTER 34

SAOTSE

THE YAKHAT WOMEN WERE DRIVING cattle toward Prasa and singing the wedding hymns of Khou. Their songs were slow, majestic things, redolent with the rejoicing of the blackbirds on the marsh and the bloom of wildflowers over the prairie. Chaoare danced above them, lifting their music to the summer-bright clouds, eager to bless the union of her air-bound brother and earthbound sister.

Saotse still could not make out the words of Chaoare's dancing, but she didn't mind. Dancing didn't need words. And Khou was coming. She now did not swallow Saotse with a barrage of grief, but touched her lightly and joyfully as she prepared to rejoin her husband.

Uya stood beside her, humming along with the passing women and gently rocking Tuulik. "I feel odd," she said. "I shouldn't be getting married while I'm still nursing a newborn."

"It is an unusual marriage," Saotse said.

Uya was dressed in a Yakhat bridal gown. She had described it to Saotse as a red wide-sleeved blouse and skirt that billowed behind her, and what seemed to be a thousand strands of gold, turquoise, and mother-of-pearl hung around her neck. They waited at the outskirts of the city while the Yakhat women brought in the yaks that Keshlik had promised, presented now as Uya's bride-price. A gaggle of young Yakhat women waited around them, Uya's attendants, treating the strange foreign woman with deferential shyness and curiosity.

The last of the cattle lowed as they plodded down the path, and the bridal procession prepared to follow them. Saotse quickly translated the last of the inevitable questions between Uya and her attendants, then they set off toward the city.

As they approached, Saotse heard the men singing, low sonorous chants that rumbled alongside the road like peals of thunder. They lined the path from the hill where the procession began, guarding the route through Prasa and to the river, ending finally at the place along the shore where the wedding was to take place. Through Khou, Saotse felt their spears tapping the ground, and as Uya passed them, they laid their weapons on the ground. Khou shivered with delight, and Saotse laughed.

The city smelled of cows and horses, of fresh-cut spruces and seawater. Behind the droning of the Yakhat warriors, Saotse picked out the chatter of Prasei and Yivrian voices, those scattered by the sacking of the city who had returned, and those who had come with the *kenda*'s forces and remained. Ravens cawed from the peaks of lodges.

"Oh!" Uya said brightly. "They've begun repairs on the Prasada's lodge. And that's not the only one." She squeezed Saotse's hand.

They neared the shore. Oarsa's crashing bellow pulsed in Saotse's chest, and she suppressed the urge to run to meet the sea. At the edge of the water, his feet moistened by Oarsa's foam, stood the storm Power. He was a maelstrom barely restrained, a gale rejoicing, thrumming with thunder and smelling of spring rain on dry leaves.

"Do you hear it?" Saotse asked. "Do you hear him? The air crackles with lightning—"

Uya laughed. "Lightning? The sky is clear. It's just Keshlik and the shrieking of gulls."

The ground underfoot changed from dirt to wave-worn pebbles. They stopped about halfway down the shore. Uya's attendants ceased singing, and the chanting warriors quieted. Saotse heard Keshlik's footsteps booming with thunder as he approached them from up the shore. He stopped just in front of them.

The gravel crunched before them. Through Khou, Saotse felt Keshlik's knees press the earth, and she felt him present the halves of his broken spear to Uya. As instructed, Uya took the spear and thrust the point of the spearhead into the ground with a solid grunt.

"Blessed be the lord of thunder, who rains and makes fertile the earth," Saotse intoned, first in Yakhat, then in Praseo.

Saotse heard Uya fumbling for the pouch of salt held around her neck and presenting it to Keshlik. As expected, Saotse heard him take a little salt from the pouch and sprinkle it over the spear, then touch some to his own lips and to Uya's lips.

"Blessed be the mother of the people, whose breasts delight her children," Saotse said.

Then Keshlik and Saotse together took the pouch of salt and hurled it into the sea. That action was not traditionally included in the ritual, but both Saotse and the Yakhat elders had agreed that it was needed.

"Blessed be the father of the waters," Saotse said, "whose tides wash away our tears."

Uya and Keshlik turned to face each other.

"Keshlik, son of Golgoyat, do you give your spear to this woman for marriage?" Saotse asked.

"Yes," he thundered.

She said the next line in Praseo. "Uya, daughter of Khou, do you take this man's spear for marriage?"

"Yes," she said, and the earth quivered and went silent.

"Then let the wedding begin."

Casks of wine filled the central square of Prasa. They were shared alongside bowls of kumis and sweet fresh curds. The smells of smoked salmon and roast veal perfumed the whole city, which spurred the Yakhat, Yivrian, and Prasei leaders to quickly formalize the final conditions of the truce, so they could get to the eating. The Prasei beat drums and the Yakhat sang, and gifts of turquoise and rubies changed hands. There was still distrust—Saotse could hear it in many voices, and a few drunk men had to be kept from fighting as the afternoon wore on. But those were the exceptions.

When the sun fell into the west, the feast was unabated. A dance began in the square, the Yakhat cow-maidens teaching the young women of Prasa a salacious dance that prompted guffaws and whistles from the watching Yakhat and Prasei alike. Saotse found a moment when no one was asking her to eat or translate, and she slipped quietly away.

Her feet found again the paths that ran down to the sea. The ways through the city had not changed much, and though most of the lodges were still empty, she remembered the crossings and wound her way down toward the pebbly beach. The grass rustled against her skirt as she wound down the paths, until the chanting of the waves and the grumble of stones on the shore met her ears.

The air was full of the sound of gulls. A rich, salted breeze blew in off the sea. She stepped onto the gravel of the shore, feeling the smooth pebbles beneath her feet, and walked until the cold water rushed up over her toes. The foam of the waves kissed her ankles, and she felt the old, familiar call of the ocean.

She stopped when the waves reached her calves. Oarsa was present in the current swirling around her, and his joy and gratitude churned around her. She heard the singing of the orcas waiting beneath the waves, eager to bear her on their backs once more.

The churning of the waves contained an offer, rising up like an ancient current from the depths of the sea. There were no words, but the intent was clear. She considered it.

"No," she said at last. "My home is here now. And I don't know if this old body would even survive the journey back across the sea."

The waves kissed her again.

She was suddenly exhausted. "It may be a while before I return to the sea. Uya needs me, and Keshlik, and probably the new Prasada and the *kenda*, eventually. And after all, I'm an old woman, and I shouldn't spend my time chilling my ankles in the seawater. I would like to rest."

Still, she waited a few more minutes while the sea rushed around her feet. Then she turned with a sigh, walked up the shore, and rejoined the celebration.

ABOUT THE AUTHOR

J.S Bangs lives in the American Midwest with his family of four. When not writing, he works as a computer programmer, and he can occasionally be found gardening, biking, or playing Magic: the Gathering.

His short fiction has appeared in Daily Science Fiction, Beneath Ceaseless Skies, Orson Scott Card's Intergalactic Medicine Show, Heroic Fantasy Quarterly, and other venues.

18978467R00169

Made in the USA
Middletown, DE
29 March 2015